A SIREN'S RETREAT NOVELLA DUET

A TRYST BY THE SEA & A SPINSTER BY THE SEA

GRACE BURROWES

GRACE BURROWES PUBLISHING

A Siren's Retreat Novella Duet

A TRYST BY THE SEA

To those who fear the flame has died

The Siren's Retreat Novella Quartet

A Tryst by the Sea—Grace Burrowes
An Affair by the Sea—Erica Ridley
A Spinster by the Sea—Grace Burrowes
Love Letters by the Sea—Erica Ridley

CHAPTER ONE

Vergilius George Santander Zeus Summers, Viscount Summerton, rose at dawn two weeks before the hated date. He dressed with his usual care—and without the aid of a valet—and made his way to the breakfast parlor.

He'd observed the same ritual every morning for most of the past nine years, and when spring perennially trudged into view, he told himself, *This year will be different*. Earlier in the marriage, his litany had been: *Today will be different.*

By the third year of wedded torment, he'd taken to assuring himself, *Next month will be different.* In the subsequent seasons as husband to his viscountess, Gill had learned patience, self-restraint, steadfastness, and a half dozen other manly virtues—belatedly, he admitted—but he had not yet learned to stop hoping.

He strode into the breakfast parlor, doing his best to exude purpose and confidence. Her ladyship, exuding gracious indifference to her spouse, sat at the far end of the table.

Gill's viscountess, his wife, and hostess presided over her end of the table looking as serene and lovely as any Greek goddess. Penelope had been a pretty girl, a diamond, an Incomparable, et cetera and so forth. She had matured from pretty to alluring in the ten bewildering years of their marriage.

An irony, that. When Gill had agreed to court her, he'd thought her an uncomplicated young lady, easy to look upon and easy to like, though in need of some self-confidence. She barely glanced at him now.

On the three occasions when Gill had made courting calls on his then-fiancée—meaning he'd sat in the garden with Penelope while an army of aunties had chaperoned from the nearby terrace—she'd worn her hair in a fussy concoction of ringlets and braids. He'd spent most of his brief visits wondering how her hair stayed up.

Such were the intellectual depths he'd plumbed as a very young man.

After speaking her vows, Penelope had gradually put aside the fancy styles and the fancy gowns. The result was feminine perfection planed down to the essentials. A tidy golden chignon, blue eyes full of intelligence rather than uncertainty, and a way of moving that was so quietly graceful, Gill was riveted simply watching his wife cross a room.

Her ladyship no longer tittered or giggled. She smiled graciously, and impecunious bachelors started composing bad poetry.

She no longer fretted over seating arrangements. She issued her invitations, and they were invariably accepted.

She no longer issued Gill invitations to her bedroom, though he knew he could present himself there at any point and receive a civil if puzzled welcome.

Penelope also no longer cried, as far as Gill knew, and neither did he.

"My lord, good morning."

He bowed over her proffered hand. "Good day to you, my lady. Might I have the business pages?"

She passed him the requisite section of the newspaper, which Gill tucked under his arm.

No footman stood sentry duty by the buffet. Penelope had issued that decree three years ago, and Gill had been relieved to no longer have a witness to the morning drill. He helped himself to eggs and bacon—a rack of toast already waited at the head of the table—and took his seat eight feet and three universes of marital civility from his wife.

"Any news worth repeating?" he asked, which was his way of inviting conversation on Saturdays. Friday's question had to do with what Penelope's friends might be getting up to. Monday's question dealt with social events at which Penelope would need Gill to appear.

She had escorts, flirts, and gallants by the dozen, a state of affairs toward which Gill had learned to manufacture benevolent indifference. Penelope would never play him false, of that he was certain. They had neither heir nor spare in their nursery—nor, at the present rate, would they ever—and thus the viscountess's behavior remained above reproach.

In the past several years, Gill's behavior had become rather monkish as well. He was plagued with desire, of course. What man in his prime was immune to animal spirits? But that desire focused on one, unattainable objective, and professional substitutes, no matter how skilled, would simply make the whole situation more complicated and sad.

Which ought not to have been possible.

Penelope resumed studying her newspaper. She had the ability to memorize the contents of the Society pages in five minutes, so Gill flattered himself that she used the paper as an excuse to linger over her morning tea.

Hope springs eternal, and all that.

"Town is filling up," she said. "A bit early this year, perhaps because of the mild weather. Did the kitchen give you enough butter?"

That was, as best Gill had established the pattern, her Thursday question to him, though today was Saturday.

"Quite enough, thank you. What do we hear from my dear

mama? Will she be gracing us with her presence soon?" An exploratory volley, because Gill was growing not desperate, but rather, determined.

Penelope took a sip of tea while perusing the *Times*. "I suspect she will, and thus I thought I'd fortify myself with a week or so at Summerton Hall before the whirlwind commences. Lady Stanthorpe is lending me her carriage so the traveling coach can remain with you here in Town."

What the bloody hell? Gill buttered his toast with every appearance of calm. "Shall I escort you to the Hall?"

"No need to trouble yourself. I should be back in Town in a fortnight or so."

"We have no social engagements to tend to in the next two weeks?"

The hated date lay two weeks hence, and as troubled as their marriage was, as empty and hollow as it had become, they had at least faced that date together.

Penelope turned a page. "I thought a respite was in order before the Season officially arrives. Do you mind, my lord?"

Yes, Gill minded. He minded anything that suggested Penelope had taken yet another step away from their marriage and away from him. He minded that she hadn't told him sooner of her plans. He minded that today *was* different and not in a good way at all.

"Do I mind? Of course not. I might follow your example and have a look in on Thomas and Cymbeline at Lychmont." To see an empty seat at the other end of the breakfast table, to rattle around this house alone as the date approached, and Mama descended...

Not to be borne.

Penelope took another sip of her tea. "Please do give Bella and Tommie my regards. Lychmont is so pretty in spring."

You are pretty. Now, nine years after that compliment might have done some good, Gill could not push the words out. Penelope would smile, nod, and return to her newspaper.

Gill consumed his breakfast when he wanted to rail at his wife:

Why leave Town now? Why desert him without warning? Why consign him to managing dear Mama without reinforcements at this most dreaded time of year?

"When do you leave?" he asked, as Penelope set aside her newspaper.

"This morning. I can tarry for a day or two in Town if you'd rather, but I've cleared our calendar and given some of the staff holidays."

"Don't let me keep you from your plans." Gill rose, needing to leave the breakfast parlor with her. He would not be that pathetic joke, the husband all alone with his newspaper, crumbs on his cravat, a smear of jam on his chin.

Not yet.

Penelope remained seated when he would have held her chair. "You will be at Lychmont, my lord?"

"Tommie and I can enjoy the country without Bella's supervision. She will doubtless be up to Town like a shot once Mama arrives." Though the last place Gill wanted to spend the next two weeks was at Lychmont, with not less than three nieces and four nephews, to say nothing of Tommie's dear but prattling company. For an idle younger brother, he could be positively pontifical on an astonishing variety of topics.

"Then I will wish you a pleasant visit with family," Penelope said, "and see you upon my return." She rose, and because Gill held her chair, he was afforded one blessed, wretched moment of closeness to his wife. He stepped away before Penelope could catch him closing his eyes and inhaling her honeysuckle scent.

She glided toward the door, and Gill had to put his hands behind his back to stop himself from reaching for her.

"I'll miss you, Pen."

He hadn't used her nickname in years, and it was enough to have her pausing and bracing a hand on the doorjamb, though she did not face him.

"I'll miss you too, my lord. My love to our nieces and nephews."

"Of course." Gill had no doubt Penelope did love those children. "Safe journey."

"And to you." She left him in the parlor, and he sank into her chair.

What the deuce was this about? Except he knew what the deuce. The awful anniversary approached, and this year, Penelope would fortify herself with a few days at Summerton before braving a return to Town, and to him.

Gill took an absent sip of Penelope's lukewarm tea.

"I am not subjecting myself to Lychmont." His ears, if not his heart, could not take that abuse at this time of year.

And yet, he needed to go somewhere. Somewhere that would aid him to plan the repair of his marriage, that would rekindle the useful parts of the old Gill, a fellow of overweening confidence and no little daring.

If next year was to be different, or next month was to be different, his strategy had to be different.

"Siren's Retreat." The first place—nearly the only place—he and Penelope had been deliriously happy as husband and wife. The seaside inn should be deserted this early in the year, despite how fashionable Brighton had become. He could be there by nightfall if he didn't dither around doubting himself.

The Siren's retreat was the subject of a quaint legend, which Gill had learned of from the proprietress herself. According to Mrs. Cartwright, all travelers who spent the night at her seaside hostelry would find true love before their stay was complete, provided they brought an open and willing heart to the search.

Gill's heart was open and willing—also determined—when it came to rekindling Penelope's regard.

The Summers family motto was *audax et fortis*. Bold and brave. For too long, Gill had been patient and bewildered. A week or so of contemplation and rest by the ocean, and he could return to Town with renewed purpose.

And maybe with a few husbandly bright ideas, because nine years was too long to pine for his own wife.

~

Penelope managed to leave the breakfast parlor at a dignified pace, but the consternation in Summerton's eyes when she'd told him she was leaving Town had nearly inspired her to sprint for the door.

She had thought herself well past the point when telling her husband a falsehood would bother her—their whole marriage was a falsehood—but no. Every day, she hid behind her newspaper, both dreading and longing for the moment when Vergilius strode into the room, his boots drumming confidently on the carpets, his sheer presence compelling notice.

He'd been a beautiful youth, and he was a magnificent man—to appearances. The dark Adonis, they'd called him. The Swoon-Worthy Swain. He was tall, devilish, and handsome, with exquisite manners, a substantial fortune, and excellent antecedents.

All quite true, though as a husband, Summerton had proved himself to be a spectacular mistake. Why, if a man had to be such a disappointing spouse, couldn't he extinguish the last of his wife's tender regard with some obvious failing? Something even his viscountess could see from across a crowded ballroom?

No such luck. Vergilius's shortcomings were private, gentlemanly, and of long standing. Penelope cared for him, was the problem. Mostly out of habit and not with the passionate devotion she'd fallen into as a new wife, but she did care for him.

Maybe that was why, as she made her way to her apartment, she felt not like a woman on the verge of attaining her freedom, but rather, like a schoolgirl sneaking off to read in the hermit's grotto when dear old Godmama was tooling up the drive.

"Almost done packing, ma'am." Silforth, Penelope's lady's maid, folded a plain nightgown into an open trunk. "I am looking forward to seeing my mum. You're sure you don't want me to come with you to the Hall?"

Penelope was very sure, and she wasn't traveling to the Hall. "You are kind to offer, but the staff will look after me adequately in your absence. You are due for a holiday."

Silforth, a plump, cheerful soul only a few years Penelope's senior, closed the trunk. "I saw the family at Yuletide, my lady. Mum asked if I'd been turned off when I told her I could visit again so soon."

"Mothers can be a tribulation, can't they?" Mothers-in-law could be, too, to say nothing of sisters-by-marriage.

Penelope resented her husband, but she understood why he behaved as he did. Summerton was that paragon of spouses, the wealthy, titled, handsome, robust man. Of course he would be unfaithful. Of course he'd lack patience with a woman's untidy emotions. Of course he would fall short of Penelope's idealized dreams of a husband. Considering his limitations—wealth, good looks, standing, pride—Summerton wasn't half as bothersome as he might have been.

That vexed Penelope too, of course. Had Vergilius been less considerate, less polite, less outwardly attentive, she could have ripped up at him. After a few porcelain-shattering rows, nobody would question why husband and wife operated in separate spheres.

And had that separation happened five years ago, what she had planned now would have raised a lot fewer eyebrows.

"My mum's a good sort," Silforth said. "Raised us to know our Bible and work hard. She doesn't see so well lately, but I swear that woman can hear halfway to France when one of her grandchildren is being naughty."

"How many is she up to?" Seventeen, with number eighteen due in two months. All healthy, every one of them, from birth onward.

"Seventeen, my lady. My youngest sister's confinement should end as summer arrives."

Silforth's sister already had four rambunctious boys. "Is she hoping for a girl?"

"Hoping and praying, my lady."

The true culprit in the whole melodrama of Penelope's marriage was Penelope's late mother. She'd built up marriage in Penelope's mind and sung the praises of the dashing Summerton heir, until no reality could possibly match the expectations created by the advertisements.

The one time Penelope had raised the topic of a marital separation with her mother, Mama had had a tantrum the size of Gibraltar, then lapsed into an injured silence that had been worse than all of her ranting lectures combined.

In the years since Mama's passing, Summerton had grown more distant—and inexplicably more attractive—while Mama-in-Law had become a hovering, intrusive presence in the London town house. And where Mama-in-Law went, Bella was sure to follow.

That thought put Penelope in a tearing hurry to climb into Lady Stanthorpe's traveling coach.

"Would you like to attend your sister's confinement, Silforth?"

"I couldn't leave you again so soon, my lady. People will think I'm not good at my job."

People will think... Three of the most useless words ever strung together in English.

"You are quite good at your job, but your sister is dear to you. The offer will remain open, Silforth. You earn your wages without complaining, and family is important." In fact, Penelope had already written out a character for Silforth and a bearer bank draft that would serve as lavish severance. Silforth could kick her heels at home for the next five years and still have funds on hand.

Looking after Silforth, who had tried hard to look after Penelope, was important.

A husband ought to be important to his wife, too, and conversely. Summerton had taken the news of Penelope's decision to travel—and at this time of year—with nary a word of protest. He'd been surprised, though—a petty and backhanded consolation when a wife was abandoning her marriage.

"Will you take your jewels, my lady?"

"I won't need them." Had never needed them, though Mama had gushed about the Summerton tiaras for the entire four weeks of Penelope's engagement. Vergilius had called upon her weekly, bringing gifts—a locket containing a curl of his dark hair and a painted miniature of him, a box of French chocolates, a book of Wordsworth's verse.

Penelope had shelved the book with the rest of the library's poetry and left the chocolates for her staff.

"What of your Sunday bonnets, ma'am? Just the one, or should I pack several?"

"I will choose from what's available at the Hall." A mere dozen, not to mention sun hats, skimmers, toques... The viscountess's dressing closet had struck a much younger Penelope as a hall of wonders.

I'll miss you, Pen. What did that mean? What had the look in Summerton's eyes signified when he'd said those words? Had he been concerned? When would it occur to him that Penelope had hit the end of her tether for the last time?

She must remain firm now, or the rest of her life would not hold a half-penny's worth of peace or contentment.

She'd given up on joy, but she could still aspire to freedom. Vergilius would be the aggrieved party, and after a suitable period of fuming and brooding—both of which he'd been quite good at as a younger man—he could get on with his life. Eventually, he'd see that Penelope had done him a final, sincere favor by leaving him.

Silforth went to the window and nudged aside the drapes. "Lady Stanthorpe's carriage is in the mews, ma'am. You'll soon be on your way."

Those words should have filled Penelope with relief, but all she felt as she changed into half boots and took a last look around her apartment, was guilt. She was slinking away under false pretenses, abandoning her marriage, and abandoning a good man, though a man who—after ten years—she hardly knew.

I am just too tired to keep trying. She'd been emotionally exhausted for years, and every so often, such as when Vergilius had looked at her this morning at the breakfast table, she suspected he was as weary as she.

She gathered up her reticule and gloves and made her way to the porte cochere. To her surprise and horror, Summerton waited on the steps in all his lordly glory.

"I will see you off," he said, smiling slightly. "The least I can do."

Why, oh, why, must he look so serious and dear in the morning sun? When had he traded the insouciance of youth for the gravitas of the mature man?

Two porters loaded the largest of Penelope's trunks onto the boot.

"I won't be far," she said. "Just down at the Hall." The lie made her bilious. Vergilius did not deserve to be lied to.

"You'll be back a fortnight hence?"

Why did he ask? "I hope to be." Penelope would never be back, and if Lady Stanthorpe's staff continued on to the Stanthorpe estate in Cornwall, Summerton would have no way of knowing precisely where his prodigal wife bided.

"Will you miss me?" he asked, with a ghost of his old devilment, though the look in his eyes was watchful.

What has become of us? Penelope wanted to ask that question aloud, even as a voice that sounded very like Mama clamored in her head that it wasn't too late to change her mind.

"I will miss you terribly." She leavened that truth with a smile of her own and went up on her toes to kiss her spouse farewell. God help her, in some corner of her heart, she *would* miss him terribly.

Summerton ambushed her, turning what should have been a kiss on the cheek into a lover's kiss, mouth upon mouth, body to body. Penelope hadn't kissed her husband in that manner for years, but she kissed him back.

Foolishness. Utter, sentimental, wasted, stupid foolishness, but parting foolishness and therefore forgivable.

"When you return to Town," Summerton said, stepping away as the last trunk was lashed to the boot, "I'd like to talk to you. I've been much preoccupied with voting my seat, the renovations at the Hall, and a few other matters. I see no need for us to do as much entertaining this spring as we usually do and wanted to assay your thoughts about a reduced social schedule."

And that was just like him. To offer her the first real kiss they'd shared in years and then start maundering on about household matters. How did he do that?

"We'll talk when I return," Penelope said, though those hours she'd spent planning dinners, musicales, and at homes had been intended to serve Summerton's political aspirations and to keep her own blue devils at bay.

The porters ambled off to the mews, and a footman opened the coach door.

Time to go. Time to take the first step toward freedom and away from failure.

"I really will miss you," Penelope said, the words bringing a lump to her throat. Vergilius was a fine man, he truly was, and in his way, he had tried.

"Then hurry home, my lady." He handed her up and closed the door after her.

The coach was soon tooling out of the porte cochere, and Penelope's last glimpse of her husband was of a tall, strikingly handsome man alone in the morning sun.

The coach hadn't reached the first tollbooth before she was in tears, damned stupid useless tears that she'd promised herself years ago she was done with for all time.

CHAPTER TWO

"Rose Cottage, if it's available." Silly, to ask for the very same cottage, but Gill didn't judge himself for wanting to return to a place where he'd made his happiest memories.

The inn's proprietress, Mrs. Cartwright, gave him a curious glance from behind her desk. "Of course, my lord. I hope your journey was uneventful?"

"The English countryside shows to good advantage this time of year." And the miles had given Gill time to think. His objective this spring was to reason and charm his way back into Penelope's good graces and, if possible, back into her bed.

She was no longer a shy schoolgirl who could be flattered with chocolates and poetry, but who was she? He would have to come up with a fairly good guess, or his attempts to woo his wife would make a bad situation worse. Penelope would be unimpressed by either begging or husbandly ultimatums, but what did that leave in the way of courting strategies?

"Shall I have a porter escort you to the cottage, my lord?" Mrs. Cartwright asked as a loud family party crowded through the inn's main entrance.

"I can find my way. I'll need a key, though."

She again looked slightly puzzled, but passed over an ornate key attached to a pink satin ribbon. "We start serving dinner at six, if you'd like to reserve a table?"

That would leave Gill two hours to grab a nap and go for a walk along the beach. "A table at six, then. I don't recall the Siren's Retreat being such a busy place."

"We are always busy, my lord. The sea air is said to work wonders on the humors, and if that doesn't suffice, good food and pleasant surrounds will."

The lady in charge of the noisy party all but shoved Gill aside as she demanded the best rooms in the house. Mrs. Cartwright politely asked if madam had a letter reserving those rooms for her use.

Rather than eavesdrop on what was bound to become an altercation, Gill slung his saddlebags over his shoulder and left the inn proper. Somebody had kept the Siren's Retreat in good trim, and as Gill made his way to the path that led to the elm grove, he wished Penelope could see how busy their sleepy little honeymoon destination had become.

The trees had been barely more than saplings ten years ago, and the tallest among them now reached nearly forty feet. As Gill wound along the shady path, he had the sense he was leaving the last of the bustle and hum of Town behind him—far behind—and arriving at a destination where contemplation and peace were possible.

On the far side of the elm grove, the sea stretched out in a vast sparkling vista, gulls wheeled on shore breezes, and along the beach below, a lone lady strolled at her leisure. Rose Cottage sat on its slight promontory, as snug and tidy as ever, and Gill felt a ridiculous sense of homecoming.

"We were happy here," he said to no one in particular, "and we can be happy again." He closed the distance to the cottage and used his key in the door, though somebody had apparently left the place unlocked in anticipation of his arrival. He'd sent an express, which should have reached the inn several hours before he had.

The interior of the cottage was still cozy and welcoming, with whitewashed walls, exposed beams, and a flagstone floor covered in slightly worn Axminster carpets. The color scheme was still blue and green with touches of white, and somebody had left a jar of daffodils on the sill of a window cracked open a mere inch. The fragrance of the flowers sweetened the scent of the sea.

Penelope loved daffodils. She said only the bravest of flowers bloomed when winter had yet to depart.

Gill took off his coat and hung it on a peg behind the door. His boots came next, a profound relief, and then he stretched out on the sofa. The sole bed in the main bedroom held memories, even if it wasn't the same bed after all these years.

The view from the bedroom window would be the same. The old wardrobe would still stand in the corner. Tonight was soon enough to face those memories, after a good meal and perhaps a game of cribbage with some other guest at the inn.

Gill jammed a pillow behind his head, tipped his hat down over his eyes, and within ten minutes was lulled to sleep by the soothing rhythm of the distant surf.

He awoke what felt like mere moments later.

"I don't know who you are, sir, or what you think you're doing here, but you will leave this instant, or I shall scream."

His first thought was that somebody was very angry with somebody else, then his sleep-drunk brain informed him that the person causing the lady such vexation was *him*. He lifted his hat from over his eyes and beheld *his wife*, a wrought-iron poker clutched in her upraised fist.

They spoke at the same time. "What are *you* doing here?"

"Ladies first," his lordship said, sitting up and scrubbing a hand over his face. He was in stockinged feet, no jacket, and his cravat was creased with dust. Penelope had not seen her husband in such dishabille since the last time they'd stayed at this cottage, and the sight was inexplicably unsettling.

"Have you taken to reading my mail, my lord?" How else could he have known she'd reserved this cottage for these dates?

He rose and eyed the poker in her hand. "I have not. You were on the beach."

"I was on the beach, and I saw some fellow spying on me from the path. I thought it best to retreat to the cottage before he intruded on my solitude, and now I find him intruding on my very sofa."

Penelope was being shrewish, but of all the inns on all the shores in all the realm... What was Summerton *doing* here?

He hung his hat on a peg near the door, then crossed the room to the window that overlooked the terrace. "You were supposed to be at the Hall. Are you expecting company, perhaps?"

"I came here for solitude."

"I'll leave you to your solitude, then, but first might you join me for supper at the inn?"

His lordship had always been one to mind appearances, and husband and wife eating separately would look uncongenial indeed.

"You rode down from London?"

He remained by the window, gazing out at a sparkling ocean. "My wife told me she was nipping off to the family seat, leaving me all alone as Town filled up. I bethought myself, 'I have no wish to idle about here on my own for the next fortnight.' I made up some taradiddle about visiting my brother and his yodeling horde of prodigies, whom I saw and heard plenty of at Yuletide. I took myself here instead."

Summerton looked tired, not merely road weary. "Why make up a taradiddle, my lord?"

He slanted a look at her over his shoulder, and why had the Almighty made Vergilius Summers equally attractive when viewed from any perspective? A raging injustice, that.

"Why did you make up a taradiddle, my lady?"

Because I could not tell you honestly that I was leaving you. "Easier, I suppose, than explaining why I'd want to be alone." *At this time of year*.

"It's still hard, isn't it?" He considered the sea as he posed his question. "I expect it always will be."

"But not as terrible a grief as it once was." *These things happen*. Penelope had nearly voiced the platitude that had driven her to thundering her way through Beethoven finales at the piano and poring over seating arrangements by the hour.

"You don't believe that." Summerton spoke quietly, and Penelope joined him at the window, the better to see his expression.

She resisted a wayward urge to slip an arm around his waist. She'd tried making overtures. Hugging Vergilius when he was all remote and broody was like hugging an obelisk. Granite was more inclined to cuddle than his lordship if he was preoccupied with his own concerns.

"I don't believe it," Penelope said, rather than argue for form's sake. They'd passed through an arguing phase many years ago. She hadn't cared for it at all. "I can leave you in peace to finish your nap. I will resume my constitutional and inquire at the inn about getting you a room for the night."

"I've slept enough for now. Might I join you on this constitutional?"

What was he up to? "I am truly here alone, my lord. The last thing I'd seek in this location is an adulterous assignation." The last thing she'd seek, *period*.

"Likewise, I'm sure. Let me get my boots, and we can take this discussion to the out of doors."

Penelope did not want to take *this discussion* anywhere, but perhaps fate had served her a good turn after all this time. Sneaking off to the coast under false colors had been intended to avoid an honest explanation to Summerton of her plans.

To avoid a final confrontation, even when confrontation was the more honorable course. Maybe here, at the Siren's Retreat, Penelope could find the courage to speak truthfully to her husband. They could not go on as they had been, and the time had come for them both to admit that.

His lordship pulled on his boots and donned his jacket. "I am not in the first stare, I know, but part of what I like about this place is its sense of informality. One feels welcome here, not on display for the benefit of the gossips."

"One does. You have dust..." Penelope swatted gently at his cravat, though the result was far from pristine. Too late she realized that her fussing was wifely, and she'd lost the habit of being wifely with his lordship.

This cottage, and the memories it held, were to blame for her lapse.

His lordship caught her hand, placed it on his arm, and swept a gesture toward the door. "The splendors of the sea await us, my lady. Let's hunt for pretty shells and get our toes wet."

He smiled as he extended that invitation, and when he smiled, Lord Summerton was powerfully attractive—also when he did not smile. Penelope decided to enjoy that attractiveness for just a little while on the beach, because tonight at supper was soon enough to inform her husband that their marriage—long over in truth—was past due to be officially interred.

I want us to start afresh. Gill mentally tried on those words as he and Penelope wound down the trail to the beach. Except that starting afresh implied erasing the past ten years, reducing them to a wrong turn on an unfamiliar bridle path.

I want us to try harder. Seeing the fatigue in Penelope's eyes and the sadness, Gill knew she'd been trying as hard as he had to keep their dealings civil. They were to have supper together, after all, something that hadn't happened outside of formal entertainments for years.

Inspiration struck as they gained the wide sandy beach. "I want to find you a pretty shell," Gill said. "Another ormer to go with the one I found last time."

"You were lucky last time," Penelope said, opening her parasol. "Though it was a very pretty shell."

"You no longer have it?" That hurt, more than it should.

"I do, somewhere. Bella suggested I give it to the jewelers to fashion all that nacre into a little box. I put the shell away rather than leave it out to tempt her."

"Because Bella might think to surprise you by taking the initiative with the jewelers. She excels at taking the initiative." Probably a matter of survival for a mother of seven, but not one of the lady's more likable qualities.

The tide was out, which was perfect for shell hunting. Gill perched on a handy rock and pulled off his boots, then his stockings. Penelope watched him, her expression pensive.

"Does the sight of my bare feet offend?" Gill asked, draping his stockings over his boots and adding his jacket to the pile. Because he was wearing his riding breeches, his ankles and calves were also on display.

Penelope looked away, far out to sea. "The sight of your bare feet tempts me, though sand on the toes has a way of ending up everywhere."

"You did not come all this way merely to gaze upon the ocean, my lady. Come wading with me. You were about to indulge in that very pleasure when you spotted me on the path."

"The water will be frigid at this time of year."

How many reasons could she concoct to avoid even the smallest detour from strict propriety?

"Not frigid," Gill said. "Refreshing. Hand me your parasol, and I promise not to peek."

As a new husband, he'd peeked. He'd casually strolled in and out of his wife's boudoir, handled her clothing, and handled *her*. She'd handled him, too, but they'd lost the knack. In recent years, Tommie had advised Gill to just set up a mistress and be done with it.

But Gill hadn't set up a mistress. He hadn't marched into Penelope's bedroom, and Penelope hadn't marched into Gill's bedroom either.

Penelope surrendered her parasol and dealt with her half boots and stockings. "The sand is warm," she said, wiggling bare toes. "But the water will be shockingly cold."

She hiked her skirts a few inches, left the dry sand, and let that water wash around her ankles. "And to think people immerse themselves entirely," she said. "It's a wonder they don't catch an ague on the spot."

"They sea-bathe later in the year," Gill replied, wading past her. "God, this feels good." Revitalizing, and not simply because the water was cold. The ocean had energy, movement, power... He'd forgotten that. Forgotten the pleasure of communing with the reality of living water.

Penelope stood in the shallows, the brim of her straw hat flapping in the breeze, while she held her bunched hems around her calves. She might have been her much younger self, except for the way she watched him.

"Find me a shell, my lady. A pretty shell to commemorate this lovely day."

To his surprise, Penelope began searching the damp sand, and soon they were comparing finds—a dog whelk was colorful but chipped, and several tellins were judged too small. Penelope decided to keep a painted top of a rosy hue, while Gill tossed every candidate back into the foaming surf.

"I'm holding out for an ormer," he said, "a beautiful, intact specimen for my lady. I'm hungry, and we have wandered quite a distance. Let's start back, before the tide comes in and washes away my favorite boots." Without thinking, he extended a hand to Penelope.

She took it, and sidled close enough to walk with him arm in arm down the strand. The late afternoon sunshine bathed the cottage upon its little overlook, and the larger edifice of the inn proper rose behind it on the far side of the elms.

"The trees surprised me," Gill said. "They are enormous, considering how poor coastal soil can be." The elms were native to the Low Countries, where thin soil and salty sea air were the norm.

"You surprised me," Penelope replied. "The last thing I expected to find on the cottage sofa was a man, much less my husband. I should have told you where I was going, my lord. I apologize for that."

Gill had always esteemed Penelope's sense of integrity. If she was wrong, she admitted it. If she was right, she did not back down except to protect another person's dignity. At some point in the last ten years, Lady Summerton had become formidable. She was an influential hostess, and she did not tolerate gossip or backbiting.

"I might have asked to come with you," Gill said, "and if you sought solitude, my presence would have been a burden."

"Town is a burden. As a girl, I longed to make my come out, then I longed to entertain. To plan the most spectacular menus, the most elegant centerpieces, but for what? To impress people who will forget what they ate before they have returned to their coaches?"

That sentiment was as shocking as the chill of the ocean surf. "I thought you enjoyed all the social whatnot, Penelope. You excel at it."

"You vote your seat, my lord. A peer who is active in Parliament should be able to rely on his wife to support his political goals."

Gill was stunned to think that all those elegant dinners, the musicales, the Venetian breakfasts had been... for him?

His pondering was cut short as a larger wave advanced toward the shore. He scooped up his wife and charged to higher ground with her in his arms while the surf soaked the knees of his breeches.

"My lord! This is very athletic of you."

He set her on the dry sand before he could turn a small gallantry into an embrace. "I didn't want your ruined hems on my conscience. Besides, I like being athletic for my wife's benefit. Do you suppose the dining room still serves those excellent little rolls fresh from the oven? I have dreamed of those rolls."

"I recall the champagne fondly and the chocolate cream parfait."

They'd shared one serving of parfait each night of their honeymoon and had spoon-fed each other on the last night on a blanket on the terrace. Gill had been all for making love under the stars. Penelope had insisted on the comfort—and privacy—of the bedroom.

"Your luggage, I presume," Penelope said when they reached the cottage and found a single trunk sitting in the middle of the front parlor.

"Just in time, though your dinner escort might be a bit rumpled, my lady. Where has Silforth got off to?"

Penelope took inordinate care fastening her parasol closed and still couldn't seem to get the button and loop to cooperate. "She's not with me on this trip."

"Let me do that." Gill plucked the parasol from Penelope's grasp and buttoned the damned button. "You truly did seek solitude, and I have wrecked that plan."

She shook her head, at exactly what, Gill could not fathom. The idea that Penelope had traveled without even a lady's maid was alarming. Gill had assumed Silforth had already been in the coach when Penelope had departed or had traveled in a lowlier vehicle with some extra baggage.

What the hell was Penelope up to? "My lady, are you well?"

She took back her parasol. "I enjoy excellent health, thank you, my lord. If we're to change for dinner, we'll have to take turns in the bedroom."

"Ladies first." Though since when had a husband and wife been forbidden to dress in each other's company?

She shot a fulminating glance at him and stalked off, leaving Gill standing just inside the front door, unwilling to track sand on milady's carpets. He went outside to the pump in the little garden and washed his feet off as best he could, then took a seat and waited his turn to enjoy the privacy of the blighted, benighted bedroom.

The same bedroom where he'd made passionate love to his wife long, long ago.

An hour had gone by, the sun was nearly set, and the air was growing chilly, and still Penelope hadn't summoned Gill back into the cottage. He rose, looking forward to a scolding for his presumption—Penelope had ceased scolding him years ago—and made his way to the bedroom door.

A light tap merited no response. He eased the door open and came upon Penelope, Viscountess Summerton, fast asleep on the bed, a quilt draped across her middle and her bare toes and damp hems peeking from beneath the blanket.

Gill was in a bedroom, alone save for his wife. He stared at those bare, feminine toes and had not the first clue how to go on.

CHAPTER THREE

Penelope dreamed a cruel dream, with the sound of the surf drifting in through an open window and gulls crying overhead. Gill was with her in the dream—when they'd been happy, she'd called him Gill in private—and he was sunburned, barefoot, and ambling hand in hand with her down the shore.

The dream was so real, she could smell his luscious shaving soap, and as always when these dreams came, she did not want to waken.

"My lady?"

"Not now, Silforth." *Please just another moment.*

"Penelope Ann?"

The dream evaporated as Penelope realized that Silforth had never before spoken with a man's voice—*with Gill's voice*—much less used familiar address. She tried to scramble to a sitting position, but her blanket was caught beneath her hips, and her chignon had come unraveled, leaving her half trapped by her braid as well.

"Penelope, it's only me. You thought to catch a nap, and instead the nap caught you." Summerton, looking amused and rumpled, lounged against the bedpost. "Should I have the inn send us down a supper to share here?"

The inn. The Siren's Retreat. A horrendously inconvenient coincidence. Penelope's sleep-muddled mind shoved aside the last cobwebs as reality crashed about her like a breaker hitting the shore.

His lordship... was real, and he was in the bedroom and barely dressed. Penelope watched while he unknotted his cravat and slipped his sleeve buttons into the pocket of his breeches.

"I fell asleep," she said, pulling her braid out from between two pillows. "The sea air does that. I always slept well here."

"We both slept well, as I recall, and not entirely as a result of the sea air. Shall we move our supper reservation back, or would you prefer to have them send us a basket?"

Thinking rationally while Summerton pulled his shirt over his head was nearly impossible. Penelope sat amid the covers, frankly gawping as he draped his clothing over the privacy screen.

He'd literally swept Penelope off her feet on the beach, hoisted her into his arms as if they were newlyweds frolicking in the surf. The sensation of being cradled against his chest had stolen Penelope's breath. Once upon a time...

But that time had come to an end. "If we hurry, we can keep our reservation. I'd rather not be at table when the dandies and gossips come down to dinner later in the evening."

"The Siren's Retreat attracts Brighton's dandies and gossips now? My, how things change." Summerton ambled behind the privacy screen. "Ye gods, I would turn the Medusa to stone in my present state. May I borrow your brush?"

"Of course." Penelope tossed the quilt aside and bounced and pushed her way to the edge of the bed. "I'll find you something to wear." Any excuse to leave the bedroom, to put distance between herself and that, that... paragon of masculine pulchritude strutting around in only his riding breeches.

Did he think she was made of stone? Think she no longer had eyes in her head?

Penelope rummaged in his lordship's trunk until she'd put together a proper evening kit. His cravat would not be starched to a knife edge, but Gill had never been one to fuss over his turnout. He managed to look scrumptious no matter what he wore—or didn't wear.

Penelope marched back into the bedroom and heard the sound of a cloth being wrung out behind the privacy screen.

"If you take down your hair," Summerton said, "I can help you pin it up again. I'm accounted competent at fashioning a coronet."

Penelope had said that to him when he'd played lady's maid for her *ten years ago.*

"As I recall, your skills are passable." She laid his clothing out on the bed and ducked into the dressing closet to hunt for clean stockings and a simple dinner dress. By dint of wiggling and tugging, she got the gown on over her jumps and found some heeled slippers that matched the embroidery around the gown's hem

Fastening the hooks was a lost cause.

Penelope sat on the dressing stool, feeling unaccountably worn out and teary. She did not want Summerton to be here, she did not want to ask him to help her dress, and she did not want to tell him that she was leaving him.

Worst of all, in some small, stupid corner of her heart, she did not want her marriage to be over.

"Shall I do up your hooks?" Summerton, looking delectable in his evening attire, stood in the doorway to the dressing closet.

"Please." Penelope rose and gave him her back. "I had not intended to take meals in the dining room, and if need be, I can request the services of a maid. I did not foresee..."

She fell silent as Summerton deftly fastened her dress closed. His touch was light, but not as impersonal as Silforth's, and when he finished, he smoothed both hands along Penelope's shoulders.

"On you, the simpler styles look more sophisticated. I've admired that about you. Let me brush out your hair, and we'll be very nearly on time for our meal."

"I can manage."

"Why should you have to?" Summerton preceded her into the

bedroom and patted the back of the vanity stool. "I have seen you with your hair down before."

Penelope acquiesced, because she was good at acquiescing and because arriving late to the meal would inconvenience the kitchen and cause talk.

"One braid," she said, sitting up very tall. "Over the left shoulder."

She endured as Summerton gently unraveled what remained of her plait. She endured when he used his fingers to spread the long skeins of hair down her back. She endured as he gently brushed out the tangles. By the time he'd fashioned a single braid over her left shoulder, Penelope could have cut the silence in the bedroom with her sewing scissors.

She pinned the braid into place in a double coronet, gave her appearance a final inspection, and rose.

"Will I do?" she asked.

"Splendidly, and just for tonight, Pen, might you pretend that we are an old married couple enjoying a respite from Town, happy to be away from London and all the busyness?"

Penelope had hoped to broach the topic of a marital separation with Summerton in the civilized surrounds of a private dining room. Hoped and feared, because once she confessed the true nature of her journey, the fabric of her marriage would be rent for all time, even more irreparably than it already was.

She and Summerton were not enemies, not yet, but by midnight, they might be.

"Just for tonight," she said, "I can support that fiction." She took his arm and said nothing more as he escorted her up the path.

Tomorrow she'd broach more difficult topics, when both she and Summerton were rested, and she'd had time to consider how to tell her husband he was about to suffer a betrayal worse than adultery.

The relatively early hour meant the dining room was half empty, and to Gill, that was a relief. If he was to share a meal with his wife, the other diners would provide fodder for small talk. Of course, the other diners would also remark the novelty of Lord and Lady Summerton sharing a seaside respite.

That talk would have pleased him, except Lady Summerton had planned a solitary holiday and had lied to ensure that result. In fact, they had both lied, which troubled Gill worse than a sore knee.

As the waiter led them to a table by the window, Gill was struck afresh by how little time alone together he and Penelope had had in their marriage. Mama tended to hover, Tommie and Bella were forever popping up to Town or down to the Hall. Gill's parliamentary duties were taxing, and Penelope kept her hand in with any number of charitable organizations.

"Do you have a private dining room?" Gill asked the waiter.

"We do, my lord."

"My lady," Gill said, "the choice is yours." Would Penelope decide to be seen publicly sharing a meal with her husband at a cozy seaside inn, or would she brave two hours alone in the same room with him, behind a closed door?

Her expression gave away nothing. "Does the private dining room have a view of the sea?"

"Yes, my lady. Up one floor, just off the south terrace."

"That sounds lovely. Today was long and wearying, and some peace and quiet with our meal will be appreciated."

They followed the waiter up the steps and along a corridor and were shown to a pretty little chamber that already had a fire burning on the grate. The wallpaper was lavender silk flocked with ivory fleur-de-lis, and the furnishings looked to have been chosen more for comfort than style.

"Would you prefer *service à la russe or à la française?*" the waiter asked, lighting a candelabrum in the middle of a small table draped with a lavender tablecloth.

"If you will set the dishes on the sideboard," Penelope said, slipping off her gloves and laying them on the mantel, "*à la française* will do. His lordship and I can serve ourselves."

More discussion followed, of wines and desserts, and then Gill was alone with his wife, by her choice, twice over.

That Penelope might want to avoid the gossips in the dining room made sense, but service *à la française*—with the food brought in all at once—meant they would dine without interruptions.

The waiter departed, closing the door silently.

"You don't mind putting up with me for the next two hours?" Gill asked.

"As I recall," Penelope said, "you can be charming."

Penelope went to the window, which overlooked the elm grove and had a view of the ocean beyond. Sunset streaked the eastern reaches of the sky with mauve and violet, and the breakers formed undulating lines of white surging onto the pale shore. The view had a restless quality, caught between daylight and darkness, between pretty and melancholy.

Gill joined his wife at the window, abruptly tired to his bones. "Are you scolding me because I have not been charming to you, my lady? I will exert myself to the utmost if you want witty banter and gossip, but I would really rather..." He'd rather sit with her on the terrace of the little cottage and watch the stars come out.

"My lord?"

When had Gill's viscountess become so adept at hiding her feelings? "How are you, Penelope? You came down here to be alone, and that is not how we've typically weathered this time of year. You did not feel you could inform me of your plans in advance, and that concerns me."

He thought she might come back with another brittle, ambiguous retort, but she instead cracked the window, letting in both a whiff of ocean and the faint, rhythmic sound of the surf.

"I hate this time of year."

She spoke mildly, but for Penelope, Lady Summerton, to use the word *hate* was surprising.

"I'm not too keen on it myself. All the socializing and engagements and crowds?"

She nodded. "All I want to do is hide, except one cannot, not in spring. Sometimes, I want to talk about the past, but Bella and Mama-in-Law made it plain one does not dwell on such things. Then I will be planning some dinner or musicale for your parliamentary cronies, and your mother will mention that Bella or some cousin is expecting again..."

Gill risked taking Penelope's hand. "Then, for just a moment, you hate Bella and Tommie and every stupidly contented couple in London."

"In the world," Penelope said. "Bella always means well, but she never seems to realize that her good news might bring something other than unmitigated joy to those who hear it."

Cymbeline was—not to put too fine a point on it—somewhat insensitive. She was energetic, practical to a fault, and dear to her husband, but Gill found small doses of his sister-in-law's company sufficient.

More than sufficient, particularly when she started haranguing him on the need to establish trusts for his nephews and set aside funds for his nieces. Tommie had inherited Lychmont, and the property was solvent, but according to Bella, the head of the family should *see to his heirs*.

"Was Bella threatening to come up to Town with Mama?" Mama and Bella got on amazingly well, considering both were outspoken and headstrong.

"They will arrive in London sometime after tomorrow," Penelope said. "Mama-in-Law does not feel it necessary to provide me an exact date. They leave you mostly in peace, while I cannot claim parliamentary duties or an appointment with the solicitors when I need a respite from them."

This made Penelope's flight more understandable, though it did not explain the need for secrecy. Gill would have understood her reasons better than she knew.

He was contemplating putting an arm around Penelope's shoulders when a discreet tap on the door heralded the arrival of the food. He seated his wife and took the place at her elbow so they both had a view of the ocean.

They started with a pepper pot soup, a good choice for a brisk spring evening, followed by ham, potatoes, and by some hothouse miracle, green beans *amandine*. The discussion was superficial—the inn appeared to be thriving, the weather agreeable, the countryside so pretty in spring. Gill was encouraged nonetheless, because it was *conversation*, and Gill exerted himself to go about his half of the dialogue as charmingly as he could.

Penelope had a lovely laugh, and he had not heard it in years, much less inspired her mirth.

"You aren't eating much," he said when they'd moved on to a tray of cheese, orange slices, and apple tarts.

"Travel truly does put me at sixes and sevens," Penelope said, passing him a tart. "Why did you suggest we simplify our calendar this year?"

The tarts were good. Still warm, an excellent complement to a tangy cheddar and a light Sauternes.

"I am out of patience with parliamentary nonsense," Gill said. "The intrigues and pettifogging and blatant corruption... So few citizens have the vote that the Commons gets away with nearly anything they please, and the Lords..."

He was complaining, and to his wife. Not very charming of him.

"I thought you liked all the"—Penelope waved a hand in circles—"horse trading and palaver and late nights. I thought you enjoyed wielding your influence for causes you believe in."

Gill liked sharing a simple meal alone with his wife. Why had he never insisted that he and Penelope stay home one night a week together? Other couples did that. His own parents had done that.

"I make little headway with my causes because I am unwilling to cheat, threaten, lie, or break the rules. I told myself that if I wasn't to have children of my own, I could at least do my bit for the children cast upon the streets of London. I had hoped..."

Penelope was looking at him as if he'd announced a plan to move to darkest Peru.

"*That's* what all your committees are about? Vergilius, I don't know what to say."

Gill had surprised his wife. Maybe alluding to the past wasn't always a bad idea. "I gave Parliament a good try, but I have no intention of spending another nine years beating my head against a wall of indifference and corruption. I will be conscientious and active, but not... not overly involved."

Penelope studied him by the flickering candlelight. "Your late father was always much taken up with duties in the Lords."

"After several years of voting my seat, I grasped that Papa was not *active* in the Lords, he was *social* in the Lords. He believed that by pouring enough good port down the throats of enough peers, he'd eventually see some bills passed. He was wrong, though by the time I realized the futility of his approach, you had a reputation as a hostess. I could not ask you to give up something that you seemed to enjoy."

Whatever reaction Gill expected—incredulity, resentment, ridicule—he did not expect Penelope to smile and salute him with her wineglass.

"You tried. You gave it your best effort, and you are blowing retreat now that it's clear the rules of engagement were not what you'd been led to believe. I do enjoy having some influence as a hostess, Vergilius, but I am glad you have decided to take a step back. Entertaining London year after year has paled, just as your enthusiasm for Parliament has paled."

Encouraged by that response, Gill rose and extended a hand to his wife. "I wish we'd had this discussion sooner, Pen. I can't say our time and effort were wasted, but we might have made a yearly sojourn here instead of bracing ourselves for the annual onslaught. Perhaps next year we'll plan accordingly."

Something about that little speech apparently did not agree with his wife, for when Penelope rose, she'd once again donned the mask of the gracious viscountess. Gill paused only long enough to wrap some apple tarts in a table napkin, before he held the door for her and escorted her down the steps.

They passed through the dining room, which was full of chattering guests and bustling waiters.

"The private dining room was a good choice," Gill said. "Shall we reserve one for tomorrow evening?"

Penelope withdrew the hand she'd wrapped around his arm. "I thought you were returning to Town?"

So much for making headway over a private meal. "Let's see about getting me a bed here at the inn," Gill said, "and we can make further plans in the morning."

Mrs. Cartwright, poring over a bound ledger, looked up as they approached the front desk. "My lord, my lady, I hope your meal was enjoyable."

Supper with Penelope had been beyond enjoyable, dammit. Gill added making her ladyship laugh again to his list of goals for this journey.

"Everything was quite in order," he said, "but I will need a room here at the inn for at least tonight."

Mrs. Cartwright's genial smile faded. "I'm sorry, my lord, that won't be possible. We had several parties arrive without reservations, and we're at our capacity. Over capacity, to be honest. By the end of the week, we should have some leeway."

A party of four emerged from the dining room, a young couple and two older women. They moved toward the main staircase, but paused as if to admire the paintings hanging in the inn's foyer.

"No matter," Penelope said, twining her hand over Gill's arm. "Please have breakfast for two delivered to the cottage at the usual hour." She smiled up at Gill with desperate ferocity, and he realized he'd just been delivered his cue in some farcical stage play.

He smiled back, letting all the genuine tenderness and longing he felt for his wife show in his eyes. "Better make that breakfast for four," he said. "Her ladyship and I find the sea air provokes powerful appetites."

They goggled at each other as they sauntered past the gaping buffoons in the foyer, and Penelope did not turn loose of Gill's arm even when they had gained the shadows of the elm grove.

As Summerton escorted Penelope through the shadowy woods, she wished she'd worn more than a light shawl to protect her from the bite of the seashore's damp, salty air.

"I love that sound," he said, steps slowing. "The whump-and-swoosh of the waves lapping at the shore after dark. The surf has moods, just as the sky does, and tonight all is at peace in Triton's realm."

All was not at peace with Penelope. She'd intended that a private meal aid a private, difficult conversation, but then Gill had started teasing her about the coiffure she'd worn on her wedding day. Mama-in-Law had sent her lady's maid to fashion Penelope's hair in the latest style, and undoing that monstrosity had taken an impatient bridegroom nearly an hour.

The bride had been impatient too. Penelope wanted to forget that, but she'd *liked* the person she'd married, as much as any girl could like any man whom she barely knew. Vergilius had gone out of his way to be endearing and made the whole wedding business very much a matter of bride and groom joining forces to endure the machinations of the meddling horde.

Penelope could still hear Bella warning her not to be too appalled by the wedding night, because, "You have no choice but to put up with it, sad to say. If he gets out of hand, just start crying, and he'll finish quickly enough."

By morning, Penelope hadn't wanted to leave the marital bed. Vergilius had known what he was about, and some stubborn, honest part of Penelope could admit she'd miss his lovemaking.

She *had* missed his lovemaking, though he apparently had not missed hers.

"Pen?" Summerton asked as the path emerged from the woods.

"My lord?"

"What was all that in aid of, back at the inn?"

At first, she thought he was alluding to the private dining room, but no. She'd given him a reason for that—to avoid the gossips. The gossips had been out in full force, alas, by the time she and her husband had crossed the dining room at the conclusion of their meal.

"You did not recognize Amaryllis Piper?"

Summerton stopped where the trail enjoyed a view of the beach and the moonlit sea. The vista was peaceful and, to Penelope, a little sad. As a new bride, she'd been passionately kissed on nights like this and along this very trail. She and her groom had been prodigiously prone to kissing in any romantic spot, and with Vergilius, a dressing closet could be romantic.

Which made the present topic all the more painful.

"Who is Amaryllis Piper?"

The breeze was livelier here beyond the woods, and Penelope again regretted her lack of a heavy cloak.

"Amaryllis Piper is Marie Chalfont's aunt." Penelope kept her voice even, as she had long learned to do when discussing an awkward topic, but the urge to shout, to shove Vergilius hard on the arm, was strong.

"Marie... Horace Chalfont's wife? Is that significant?" How innocent he sounded, how genuinely bewildered. "Didn't they remove to Paris immediately after the war? I'm sure I haven't seen Chalfont in the clubs for at least two years. I should look him up. We were good friends at university, to the extent a university scholar remains sober enough to be any sort of friend."

"My lord, if you are trying to be discreet or considerate or any of the other lies men tell themselves for their own convenience, you need not make the effort. I know you and Marie were *involved*."

Summerton stepped closer, and for a moment, Penelope was

confused as to his motive. Did he think to kiss her? Here, in the midst of *this* discussion?

He unbuttoned his coat and draped it around her shoulders, provoking more useless, sweet memories. "How the hell did you get that idea?" His lordship sounded perplexed and a little annoyed.

"You were her escort for most of a Season, Summerton. She could not go anywhere without you, and she positively hung all over you. I had it on good, trustworthy authority that she wasn't above sighing over your manly *prowess*, and she had to know such talk would get back to me."

Summerton peered down at Penelope. "Is this why you have such a reputation for rebuking the gossips, Pen? You fear to hear gossip about me?"

If a cold, stinging wave had crashed over Penelope out of nowhere, that quiet question could not have been more shocking—or insightful.

"Of course not. Nobody should encourage slander masquerading as idle talk. I do not begrudge you your diversions, my lord, and they are of no concern to me."

Summerton offered his arm, and Penelope took it out of habit—or something. She did not want to, not when she was so stupidly upset over ancient business.

"Penelope, listen to me. Horace was being a negligent husband. Marie asked me to do what I could to make him jealous. I explained to Horace what was afoot, because I had no wish to have my brains blown out over a silly marital spat. Horace confided in me that he was unwell and begged me to accommodate Marie's need for a flirt until his malady passed. I suspect he contracted an ailment that he dreaded passing along to his wife, and that's why the Chalfonts decamped for the Continent."

"Oh dear." The grim set to Amaryllis's mouth had not been because she judged Lord Summerton for his frolicking, but because she feared Lady Summerton knew of Horace's situation. "Poor Marie."

"Precisely. One cannot help but feel compassion for a couple in such a situation. I encouraged Horace to tell his lady the truth, because I wasn't comfortable playing the gallant for more than a few weeks. I did not want to cause precisely the sort of talk that reached you."

"There wasn't *much* talk. Most people know better than to spread nasty rumors in my direction." Though Bella was always a font of tattle when she came up to Town. She had a network of correspondents that would make a banker envious.

"I'm sorry there was any talk at all, my lady. I should have confided in you sooner."

They traversed the remaining distance to the cottage in silence, while Penelope wondered what other rumors had reached her in error, and had the same malicious gossips spread falsehoods about her?

"Did you ever hear talk about me?" Penelope asked, glad for the darkness.

"I did," his lordship replied mildly, "malign-thy-neighbor being one of Mayfair's most popular pastimes. You were Wellington's favorite a few years back. Before that, Lord Neville also held your interest for a time. While you tried to be discreet, Society also had its suspicions about you and Timothy Whitstable, as well as Monmouth Merrismith, and... Lord Cranford, I believe. There were others. You are a beautiful, poised, intelligent woman and very highly regarded among the gentlemen."

Penelope stood on the threshold of the cottage's front door and frankly stared at her husband. "Wellington, Whitstable, and Merrismith? I merely *danced* with them. I love to dance, and they are competent partners. Cranford is hopeless, though. He was a pity waltz. Those men could no more turn my head than... than..."

Vergilius drew her gently into the cottage, where only moonbeams slanting through the curtains provided any illumination.

"I know that, Pen. I know you would never stray, and thus I could not play you false. We have honored our vows, despite all. I cannot tell you how grateful I am to you for safeguarding that aspect of our dealings. I was much too young to be married, but in that at least, your example inspired some maturity in me."

Penelope stood in the darkness while her husband knelt to uncover the embers of the fire in the front parlor's hearth. He used a spill to light the candles on the mantel, then disappeared into the bedroom with a taper. Penelope was still standing in the shadows by the door, his coat about her shoulders, when he emerged.

"I built up your fire," he said. "You will find purloined apple tarts in my coat pocket. I thought they'd make a nice addition to breakfast." He resumed his efforts before the parlor hearth and had soon coaxed a merry blaze from the coals.

He is not who I thought he was. The thought kept Penelope fingering the fabric of the coat's lapels and inhaling the lovely scent only Vergilius wore.

How could she tell a husband who'd remained faithful *despite all* that she'd acceded to a private meal not so he could inspire her to laugh with him again, but so she could explain her reasons for leaving him?

"I'll undo your hooks," Vergilius said, rising. "If you are half as tired as I am, you are nearly asleep on your feet." He took his coat from Penelope's shoulders and hung it on a peg.

A terrible show of disrespect for Bond Street tailoring. How much more disrespectful had Penelope been, to believe rumors and whispers about her husband?

"I did not want to think you'd cavort with your friend's wife," Penelope said, "nor did I want to dignify the matter by admitting I'd noticed."

Vergilius gestured toward the bedroom. "But you were hurt nonetheless, and I'm sorry for that."

Penelope preceded him into the bedroom. Despite a few lit candles and the fire on the hearth, the chamber was shadowy and cool. Vergilius's fingers whispering over Penelope's nape provoked a shiver, and more memories.

"You could take the bed," she said when most of her hooks were undone. "I fit on the sofa, or I can take the smaller bedroom, whereas you..."

"I will manage."

"Don't give me that 'the subject is closed by decree of Lord Summerton' tone of voice, sir. I am nearly a foot shorter than you, and I will be perfectly—"

He laid a finger to her lips. "Take this bedroom, Pen. I am not being chivalrous when I make that request. I am honestly too tired to notice where I sleep tonight, and tomorrow we will find me a room of my own. For sufficient coin, one of those dandies or gossips at the inn can be inspired to remove to some other Brighton hostelry or take himself off to Bath."

Penelope did not typically argue with her spouse. They'd passed through that phase, and she had the sense neither she nor his lordship wanted to revisit it.

But he was being ridiculous, and arguing was better than being politely ignored. "Take the bed, Vergilius. Don't be a ninnyhammer."

"Penelope... *Not that bed. Not now. Not without you.*"

He strode out of the bedroom and closed the door quietly. Penelope finished undressing, took down and rebraided her hair.

Not that bed. Not now. Not without you.

Penelope expected to fall asleep the instant her eyes closed, but instead, she lay awake, Vergilius's parting words echoing in her head —and in her heart.

CHAPTER FOUR

"No green ormer," Gill said, bringing the bag of apple tarts to the table on the terrace. The morning was sunny, as only an oceanside morning could be, and in the bright light of day, Penelope still looked a bit tired. "I have asked Father Triton to surrender that boon to me, and I will continue searching until I find a shell worthy of my lady's notice. How did you sleep?"

Penelope was swaddled in a dressing gown that looked four sizes too large for her. She wore only old slippers, and her hair was still in its bedtime braid. An entire ocean of frigid water could not douse the interest she held for Gill in such dishabille.

"I slept," she said, "but I still feel the effects of yesterday's journey. You've been swimming."

"A refreshing dip to start the day." And to dash some frigid common sense on Gill's wayward imagination. "Shall I dress, Pen, or can you tolerate the sight of me in only breeches and shirt?"

She poured two cups of steaming tea. "I am less presentable than you are, and the morning is too pretty to quibble over fashion."

Gill hadn't remained in the water long, but the exertion had helped settle his mood. "I did not sleep as well as I'd anticipated," he said, watching as Penelope fixed his tea—a dash of sugar, a drop of milk. "I became preoccupied with the thought of the tabbies subjecting you to nasty rumors about your own husband. I am sorry for that, Penelope. I am equally sorry that I gave you reason to believe them."

She adjusted her dressing gown, though it enveloped her from chin to ankles. "For a man of your standing and means, to support a second household is expected."

Could she sound any more uninterested? "What would be the point?" Gill sipped his tea and wondered where Penelope was going with her observation.

"Pleasure?" she said, her cheeks coloring. "You are vigorous, my lord."

"There is no pleasure in broken vows, Penelope. Not for me." *Have you missed me?* When Gill would have posed the question, Penelope passed him an apple tart.

"Do you ever wish we'd never married?" she asked, gaze on the sea in the distance.

Good God, she was in a fearless mood. "No. I have other regrets —I wish the baby had lived. I wish we hadn't been so young when we married. I wish... many things, but I have *never* regretted being your husband."

And that, to his surprise, was true. He and Penelope had grown apart, but he esteemed her, desired her, and in some stubborn way, he loved her. She had been through the fires of sorrow and loss with him as nobody else had been, and that... that mattered.

Gill did not, however, ask her the reciprocal question. Seeing her impassively watch the distant horizon, he did not need to.

Though even as he watched her, her expression did not change, while her eyes filled with tears. "I loathe this time of year."

He'd mentioned the child. Not well done of him. Gill rose, intending only to pass her his handkerchief, though he wanted desperately to take her into his arms, into his lap, and simply hold her.

She put up a hand, and she might as well have slapped him.

"I hate that you suffer, my lady. I hate that we lost our son. I hate that my father had the bad grace to expire two weeks later, when I was already reeling and hardly in a position to... Damnation, Penelope."

The first tear trickled down her cheek. She wiped it away with her fingers. "I tend to forget that yours was a double loss. The baby and then his lordship. Bad timing, as you say. Terrible timing. The worst."

Gill switched seats so he was beside her, and they could both gaze upon the eternal vastness of the sea. He passed over his handkerchief.

"Papa was so happy to know we had a son," he said. "I worry that when the baby died, the old man gave up too. That, somehow, the two deaths were related."

Penelope frowned at him as she dabbed at her cheeks. "Your father had lived his three score and ten, Vergilius, and Bella and Tommie already had two sons. The succession was and is secure, and your father was not overly given to sentiment. Besides, your mother lost a child at six months of age. She has mentioned this repeatedly. His lordship of all people knew that such things happen."

Gill barely recalled the sibling who'd died. He recalled a small, wheezy scrap of an infant, one whose presence had inspired the nurserymaids to prayers and hushed voices. At least the sickliest one was a girl, they'd said, though Master Tommie had been none too robust. At least his lordship had his heir and spare.

At the time, Gill hadn't understood those comments. Now they offended him mightily.

"I abhor those words," he said. "'These things happen.' War happens, and nobody suggests that's a passing triviality. Famine, influenza epidemics. Just because something happens with tragic predictability doesn't mean it's of no moment."

Penelope folded up his handkerchief and offered him a small, sweet smile. "You are angry."

And *that* caused her to smile at him? "Furious. With nursery-maids who've probably long since gone to their Maker. With my father, for dying when I needed him terribly. With my mother, for being so casual about her own bereavement. This is not charming talk, though, and I promised myself that I would be a charming companion to you on this sortie."

Penelope passed him back his linen, her fingers brushing over his hand.

"Keep it, my lady. A wife should not be without a token of her husband's esteem."

That earned him another smile, this one sad, but Penelope tucked the handkerchief into a pocket of her dressing gown.

"I am angry too, Vergilius. There is strength in rage, and it means much to me that I am not the only one still caught in a whirlpool of fury from time to time. I swim free, but the currents are devious, and I never know when I will again be struggling against the tide."

"Well put. I can tell you this—parliamentary committees are no consolation when I'm caught in one of those whirlpools, Pen. None at all."

They ate side by side, simple fare—oranges, tea, and apple tarts with cream cheese—the most enjoyable breakfast Gill could recall sharing with his wife in years. Penelope had smiled at him, a special smile that suggested, with luck and effort, he might also make her laugh again soon.

"What shall we do with ourselves today?" he asked, pouring a second cup for them both. "Mrs. Cartwright claims we'll have clouds this afternoon, but the morning should be fair."

"You've been up to the inn already?"

"Wandered up there at first light."

Penelope resorted to brushing invisible crumbs from her voluminous dressing gown. "I thought perhaps you'd return to London today."

"Why would I...?"

Penelope's newfound fascination with the toes of her slippers answered that question plainly enough. Gill should return to London because Penelope was through tolerating his company.

"I'm sorry, Vergilius. This is awkward, and the awkwardness is my fault. I should have told you I was coming here, but I did not want the drama of a confrontation."

Gill's meal abruptly sat uneasily. "Why would I object to you taking a short repairing lease by the sea, Penelope? This is a hard time of year for us both, and we have good memories of this place."

"The best," Penelope said, brushing at her cheek and turning her head so Gill could not see her expression. "The very best."

She rose, her chair scraping loudly against the peace of the morning. "I came here because I am leaving you, Vergilius. I could not face one more year, one more Season, one more *anything*. Not our stilted breakfasts, not your polite smiles down a table set for thirty. Not your mother's blasted hovering or her great good cheer over Bella's every confinement. I'm done. I'm worn out. I have n-nothing more to give."

Gill was on his feet, and his arms were around his wife before she could hurl any more thunderbolts. He was no longer a young husband put off by tears. He had learned that *please don't cry* was the last thing a weeping wife needed to hear, but he had no idea what to say.

"You are *leaving* me?" he asked, drawing her close.

She nodded against his shoulder. "We are miserable, my lord. I thought I was the sole malcontent in our marriage, that you were making do with your politics and amusements, but I see now... We cannot go on like this, Vergilius. It's not fair to either of us, and you deserve a chance at a real marriage."

Couples lived apart, they cultivated different friends, they became cordially distant. Penelope wasn't talking about any of those accommodations.

She was talking about *leaving him*.

"You want an annulment?" he asked, even as he treasured the feel of Penelope burrowed against him.

"Tell the bishops I am barren, that I've become barren, that we were too young to knowingly consent to our vows, that your father objected to the match. There are ways to do this. I know there are."

Gill said the first, stupidest thing to pop into his head. "You are not barren."

Penelope stiffened and stepped back. "By now, I might be."

"You aren't yet thirty years old, Pen." *I don't want an annulment. I don't want to lose you.*

But perhaps he'd lost her long ago, and she'd simply been waiting for him to gather the strength to acknowledge that loss—that loss too.

"I'm crying," Penelope said. "I thought I was beyond tears. Must be the sea air."

"You have much to cry about, Penelope. But I had hoped..." Gill fell silent as a particularly loud wave crashed against the beach. The tide was coming in, and it would take any pretty green ormers out to sea when it receded.

"I had hoped too, Vergilius. I hoped and hoped and hoped, and now we have been married ten years, and I have no more hope in me. I am sorry. I am sorry for so much, but I cannot change the past."

When Gill wanted to upend the table, smash the teapot, and rant, he instead passed Penelope her tea cup.

"Send Silforth to me." Bella Summers spoke pleasantly, as always, but her first day back in London was not starting off pleasantly at all.

"I'm sorry, ma'am," the Summerton butler said, "but Miss Silforth has taken a holiday with her family." MacMillan's burr was ever so slightly in evidence, while his loyalty to the dignity of Lord Summerton's household radiated from his stately bearing. He was young to be a butler, with dark, curly hair and fierce eyebrows. He was sizable enough to have been a footman, though his coloring was wrong for such a post.

MacMillan had joined the household when Summerton had taken a wife. A young, handsome Scottish butler had been one of

Penelope's first blunders, though not even Mama-in-Law had been able to talk Penelope into sacking him. If Tommie were the viscount... Bella set that thought aside.

"What of Plover?" she asked.

"His lordship's valet is also on holiday."

Bella had not realized her host and hostess were from home. She and the dowager viscountess had arrived quite late last night to the Summerton town house, and such was the efficiency of the staff that the guests had been shown directly to commodious quarters.

Penelope had over the years learned the knack of managing her domestics. Bella had to concede that much, though the Summerton staff had been more than proficient before the present viscountess had begun swanning about the premises.

"Then you will please tell me where my brother-in-law and his wife have got off to," Bella said, lifting the covers from the dishes on the sideboard. A savory omelet redolent of chives and cheddar sat in one warming dish, sliced ham in another. In the center of the table, a platter held orange wedges artfully arranged in a circular fan and decorated with some sort of blossoms. Had Tommie been here, he'd have gobbled up the fruit, and Mama-in-Law would approve of the racks of golden toast slathered with butter.

Though any kitchen could put on a decent breakfast.

MacMillan waited until Bella had completed her inspection of the buffet. "I'm sorry, ma'am, but I cannot be specific regarding the whereabouts of his lordship and her ladyship."

Bella took up a plate. "Spatting, are they? You can tell me, MacMillan. The beginning of the Season is a strain on everybody's nerves. For the combatants to seek time in neutral corners would be understandable."

MacMillan's glance was almost... chiding? But no. He would not dare. "Perhaps his lordship and her ladyship sought to avoid that strain you allude to, but I honestly cannot tell you where they are, because I do not know, madam."

Bella had heaped some eggs upon her plate and was choosing her slices of ham when the inspiration for MacMillan's silent scold occurred to her.

Penelope and Summerton had married at the start of the season ten years ago. They had chosen to embark on married life rather than spend springtime courting before all of polite society, probably to save Penelope's family the expense of both bride clothes and an unmarried lady's spring wardrobe.

A year later, their firstborn child had had the bad form to expire on their wedding anniversary. Dreadful timing and beyond tragic, but so typical of children.

Perhaps Penelope had dragged Summerton off for some sort of marital mourning session. Bella did not particularly like her brother-in-law—he was too penny-pinching by half and always prosing on about some bill or legal precedent—but she would not wish such a dolorous interlude on anybody.

"I suppose in the absence of my host and hostess, the dowager viscountess and I will have to carry on as best we can. Let's plan for an at home on Friday, MacMillan. Cakes, sandwiches, and champagne, I think. Champagne is always a nice touch during daylight hours. I must let all and sundry know the dowager viscountess is in residence, and she will want to renew her acquaintances."

MacMillan narrowed arctic-blue eyes. "The pantries have not been stocked sufficiently to allow us to host an at home this week, madam."

My, my, my. The laird of the larders was quite on his mettle. "Will *you* explain to my mother-in-law that this household is unable to procure a single afternoon's worth of supplies even upon several days' notice?"

"I would be happy to. The present viscountess gave a large portion of the staff leave as well. If the *dowager* thinks to hold any entertainments, she should know that we are shorthanded and will be for the foreseeable future."

The Scots were so disagreeably stubborn, though as Bella took the place at the head of the table—why not, if Summerton wasn't underfoot?—she realized that MacMillan would marshal the whole household in opposition to her.

"How long are we to be without a full complement of domestics?" Bella checked the strength of the tea in the pot swaddled in linen at her elbow. "This is China black. I prefer gunpowder."

MacMillan took a pot glazed all over in greenery and pink blossoms from the sideboard and set it by Bella's elbow. "I know not how long Silforth will be gone, but half the footmen and maids were given a fortnight's holiday."

Two weeks! Two weeks to lark about London without dreary Penelope to preempt Bella's use of the town coach, without Summerton's grim political droning. And yet, where *had* those two got off to?

"You may leave the China black at the far end of the table," Bella said. "Mama-in-Law prefers it, and she will be down any moment."

MacMillan did as he'd been told, for once, but then took up a post by the sideboard.

"You may be excused, MacMillan."

"In the absence of a footman, I will tend the sideboard, madam. Lady Summerton would insist that her guests be shown the courtesy of proper service at breakfast."

He had a way of making *proper service*—prrrroper sairvice—into another scold. Perhaps Tommie could be talked into hiring a Scottish butler for Lychmont. An older fellow... but no. If one was to have a Scottish butler, then one should have the pleasure of parading him about in his native dress, and older fellows did not do justice to the kilt as the younger men did.

"Do you have a formal kilt, MacMillan?"

He set the plate of oranges at Bella's elbow. "I do not, madam."

He was probably lying. The Scots were known for their mendacity. Worse than a lot of eight-year-old boys. At least they were good at fighting. Wellington had found their bellicose tendencies well worth the bother when Napoleon was being so odious.

Mama-in-Law sailed into the breakfast parlor looking enviably refreshed. "Bella, good morning. You will never regain your figure if you indulge your appetites to such an extent."

Bella would never regain her figure, *ever*, because when it came to indulging his marital appetites, Tommie Summers knew no restraint. Somewhere between babies four and five, Bella had realized that the price of motherhood—another price of motherhood—was a wrecked figure. Would that Tommie could afford a few mistresses, but no. Tommie lacked the head for budgeting his means and lacked the heart to stray, more's the pity.

"Travel taxes me," Bella said, "and ham and eggs are hardly a royal repast, Mama-in-Law. MacMillan tells me the household is at half-staff, and Summerton and his lady are from home."

MacMillan seated her ladyship, who had—predictably—taken her old place at the foot of the table.

"From home? MacMillan, whatever do you mean?"

MacMillan resumed his place by the sideboard. "Both his lordship and her ladyship gave instructions that they would be traveling. Plover and Silforth are among those on holiday."

Mama-in-Law waved a slender, beringed hand. "The oranges, MacMillan. Did either Summerton or his lady indicate where they'd traveled to?"

"They left no direction, my lady."

Bella had the oddest sense MacMillan was telling the truth. "Perhaps they've gone down to the Hall," she said. "The outside renovations are starting up again now that we have better weather."

"They aren't at the Hall," her ladyship said, choosing two orange slices. "I have reliable sources there, and nobody has indicated that preparations were made for Summerton to be in residence."

"Perhaps the trip was spontaneous?"

Her ladyship tucked into her eggs. "Not as hot as they should be," she murmured. "When the cat's away... Summerton would not abandon his committees and speeches simply to discuss gutters and downspouts with his architect. I cannot fathom that he'd leave Town just as the social calendars are filling up either. They must have had a blazing row."

Bella hoped so, which was bad of her, but for a married couple to be polite to each other for ten years was unnatural. Mama-in-Law did not look particularly distressed to think the head of the family and his wife were at odds.

"A mystery, as you say," Bella murmured, slicing into perfectly cooked ham. "But meanwhile, there is shopping to be done." She deliberately patronized the same shops Penelope used, and from time to time, she even got away with charging an order to Penelope's account.

If Penelope noticed, she never mentioned it—another addition to the long list of reasons to resent her.

"Is the traveling coach in the mews, MacMillan?" the viscountess asked.

"I would not know, my lady."

He knew, and he wasn't saying, and that confirmed Mama-in-Law's conjecture that Summerton and his lady were spatting.

What a pity, but in a long and unhappy marriage, these things happened.

Here at the Siren's Retreat, where Gill had passed some of the happiest hours of his entire life, he was apparently to know profound sorrow as well.

"We cannot change the past," he said, "and we might have considerable difficulty changing the immediate future too, Penelope."

She sipped her tea, which had to be cooling. "In what sense?"

"Some young sprig played too deeply at the inn last night and decamped by moonlight without paying his bill. I have booked his room for the next week. If I turn around and leave hours after making that reservation, Amaryllis Piper and her ilk will want to know why."

And yet, simply bowing to his wife and departing—from the

Siren's Retreat, from Penelope's presence, from the marriage—seemed the only sensible course. Gill could not order Penelope to keep trying, could not order her to love him.

"Amaryllis and all of London will know soon enough that I've left you," Penelope said. "I'm sorry. I don't see how biding together here for a fortnight, or a week, or another day will change that. We've had ten years, Vergilius, and I could not find a way back to you."

"Did you want to?" he asked, because a suffering man must double the agonies inflicted upon him.

"Yes," Penelope said. "I was told men grieve differently and that the responsibilities of the peerage must have your first loyalty. I was to be patient, bide my time, and allow you privacy with your sorrow."

The same advice Gill had been given. Why had he listened—to Mama, to Tommie, to his late father's lonely old friends at the clubs—when year after year, that strategy had yielded nothing but stilted breakfasts and stilted smiles down the length of a lavish supper table?

A young family emerged onto the beach from a path to the west—two loud children, a lady in a wide-brimmed hat carrying a blanket, and a young father hauling two hampers and bellowing uselessly at his children.

That should have been us. Gill wanted to take Penelope in his arms again, and Penelope wanted to be free of him for all time.

"How long have you been contemplating this decision?"

"Years, my lord. Not the done thing, and I will be ruined in polite society, but neither of us can make a fresh start as long as we're wed to each other. I dread your mother's attempts to reconcile us, Vergilius. Promise me you won't let her meddle again."

Mama, oddly enough, had been skeptical of Penelope's fitness as a bride for the Summerton heir from the beginning. Too pale, too quiet, too unlike dear, robust Bella, who had made Tommie *so* happy. Mama had even, once or twice, hinted that Penelope had fulfilled the worst of Mama's predictions, for which Gill had wanted to disown his only surviving parent.

"I can no more control my mother's mischief than I can control the tides, Penelope. As you say, half of London will soon know our business." *All* of London would know their business. A peer did not dissolve his marriage unless the succession was imperiled, and then the matter was still an enormous scandal.

"All it takes to thwart the tides is a stout seawall, Vergilius. I plan to spend spring traveling in the north."

Gill would probably spend spring in a drunken stupor. "The Lakes?"

"Too crowded. I've always wanted to see the Highlands."

That was news to him, as this whole damnable disaster was news to him, and yet, for once, years of parliamentary wrangling came to his aid. When caught in an ambush, *parlay*. Bargain. Ask questions. Offer terms, and the ambush could become a negotiation.

"This will be complicated, Penelope. Legally complicated." Was she relieved that he wasn't refusing her demand? Gill didn't think so, but then, he hardly knew his wife.

"You could divorce me, though I know that's beastly expensive. I'm sure some obliging fellow would be willing to play the role of my paramour for a sum certain."

"The courts won't stand for perjury, and neither will I. Unless you are willing to commit adultery in truth, divorce is not an option."

For a fraught, hideous moment, while the children on the beach appeared to argue over where to lay the blankets, Gill feared Penelope was about to shatter his already broken heart.

"Adultery is beyond me," she said tiredly. "The bishops will have to sort this out."

What the hell good had the bishops been when Gill's beautiful, perfect firstborn had breathed his last after only a few days in the world? When his wife had retreated into a silence that had lasted months? When he'd wanted to tell Parliament and Tommie and the whole blasted peerage to leap into the Thames on an outgoing tide?

We must soldier on as best we can, my lord. Except there had been no *we* about it. Gill had soldiered on in one direction, and now

Penelope planned to do her soldiering on in the bedamned Highlands.

Men ran around in skirts in the Highlands. Reivers and outlaws and such.

"The lawyers will sort it out, or pretend to," Gill said. "Mostly, they will send me enormous bills for a lot of talk that won't result in an agreement for years." Penelope must want her freedom very badly to inflict that penance on a man who had never wished her ill.

"I don't need much," she said. "My pin money will be sufficient... You won't begrudge me my pin money, will you?"

Gill's list of hates was growing faster than his list of goals, for he hated the uncertainty in Penelope's voice.

"You haven't thought this through," Gill said, while the little family settled on a spot above the tide line and fairly near the rocks where tide pools collected. "You will need a property of your own, Penelope. A place to live, and for the sake of your security, I want that property to be owned by a trust answerable only to you. Tommie might have to serve as one of the trustees for appearances' sake, but I do not—"

"*Not* Tommie. Anybody but Tommie. Some of your father's friends will do."

Gill had always thought Penelope and Tommie were reasonably friendly, but perhaps her objection was based simply on Tommie's status as Gill's brother. Gill had his own reasons for wanting Tommie's involvement to be merely for show.

"Papa's friends are elderly, Pen. You need trustees likely to be around for the next forty years at least. I will come up with a list of names, and you will choose among them."

She nodded, brushing a strand of hair back. "Why do happy families always intrude on one's peace at the worst times?"

Happy families, like Tommie and Bella's? "That young father detests this outing because the children will soon descend into more bickering, the sun will grow too hot, and the picnic will feature sand in every bite. The mother is worried for her complexion, and the children will try her nerves all morning with attempts to swim in a surf that could drown them. Those people only *look* happy."

Penelope surprised him by leaning against his side. "Thank you, Vergilius."

She was not thanking him merely for disparaging the foursome on the beach. Gill conjured up some of the daring he'd claimed as a younger man and slipped an arm around Penelope's shoulders.

"I need time, Pen. Time to get our affairs in order—between us—before I broach this topic with the solicitors. I want as little opportunity for them to meddle as possible. You should have the dower house, but I'm sure—"

"*Not* the dower house. Your mother considers that hers, and it's half a mile from the Hall."

"But I'm sure," Gill went on, "we can find a better arrangement for you. We should draft a budget so you know precisely what you have to spend and what your expenses are likely to be. You will need your own carriages and teams, though that's a significant expense, and we should probably keep the whole matter quiet until summer at least. By next spring, you might well be free of me, but not if we let the lawyers start brangling."

Penelope turned into his side so he was half embracing her. "I had not considered... I thought I'd simply receive a packet from the lawyers each quarter."

"Like a pensioner? And if I should die, and you are left to Tommie's sense of organization to ensure that packet reaches you regularly?"

A small shudder passed through her, and she looped her arms around his waist. "Very well, stay on here at the inn for a bit. We will make the budget and find me some trustees. You are being very decent about this, Vergilius. I do appreciate it."

Gill rested his chin against the silky warmth of Penelope's hair. The family on the beach had removed their shoes and stockings, and they were wading in the shallows, hand in hand. The wind must have picked up, because Gill's vision blurred as he stood wrapped around his wife—and she, finally, wrapped about him—as he offered to finance her abandonment of him.

"I will stay the week," he said, "and we will come up with a plan. We will be so civil and friendly for the next six days that all of Society will admit that we parted on the most cordial of terms."

Penelope tucked closer. "I am sorry, Gill. I am abjectly sorry."

"So am I."

She was apparently content—*now*—to be held, while Gill admitted that his apology was not entirely in good faith. He was being decent—he would be decent, if it came to that—but he was also being devious.

For the next week, he would be the most charming, endearing, pleasant, soon-to-be-rejected husband in the history of husbands, and if luck was with him, Penelope would rethink this infernal annulment.

He'd tried being patient.

He'd tried allowing her to come to terms with her disappointment in private.

He'd tried soldiering on.

To blazes with all of that. The time had come to woo his wife, and the stakes could not be higher.

CHAPTER FIVE

Penelope gained a new appreciation for why Summerton was so effective in the Lords.

Vergilius was able to use his mind like a clothes press. He opened one drawer—planning a picnic on the beach—and that task commanded his complete attention. When the picnic had been organized to the last detail—the menu, some towels for drying feet, and a good vintage to go with beef sandwiches—he closed that drawer and opened another.

At his request, the drawer labeled *marital dissolution* was not to be opened until after luncheon, and it was to be closed before supper each day. Several hours of negotiations, he claimed, were enough to curdle anybody's mood, though a week of afternoons spent in that endeavor should see the task completed.

Had Vergilius subjected his grief to the same degree of organization, locked it away until he had privacy and a glass of brandy at the end of the day? Until Parliament was no longer sitting? Until another round of house parties had concluded?

Would he understand that for Penelope, sorrow had taken eternities to recede, and without warning, it could still cast a shadow over every moment of her day?

Perhaps, later in the week, Penelope would ask her husband those questions. She did not need six more days to say, *I will manage on what you give me*, but his lordship had genuinely been ambushed by her request for an annulment.

She owed him a week to find his bearings.

Besides, what harm could a picnic on the beach be, when she and Summerton were also intent on projecting an air of calm good cheer to any and all gossips?

"They're packing up," Penelope said, peering down at the shore. "The invaders."

"The happy family?" Summerton replied. "Then let's storm the beach, as it were, before anybody else can claim the best territory." He hefted the hamper, tossed the blanket over his shoulder, and still managed to offer Penelope his arm.

"How can you be so polite?" she muttered, wrapping her fingers about his elbow. "I have asked to end our marriage."

"First, I esteem you. That hasn't changed just because you are no longer interested in being married to me. That will never change." He set a leisurely pace down the trail, and his tone suggested they were discussing the progress of the renovations at the Hall. "Second, my honor as a gentleman requires civility of me. Your decision is not made out of spite. I know that. You're just... done in. Knackered. At your wits' end. I can hardly blame you for that. Somebody forgot a ball."

On the sand below, a bright red ball remained, like a treasure washed in on the tide. "There will be recriminations in the nursery," Penelope said. "Lectures and promises to do better."

"Or nobody will notice. I have to ask, Pen. Could I do anything to change your mind?"

She hadn't expected that question, so she gave it honest consideration as they wound their way down to the water.

"Years ago," she said, "we both might have done things differently. But your father died, you had to see to the estate, and I… I was not at my best. We were dealing with double grief, a relatively new marriage, your mother's adjustment to widowhood, finances in a muddle, and we were both *so young*, Vergilius. Perhaps it's a wonder we did not end up in separate countries years ago."

"Don't expect me to hare off to Paris, Penelope. It's more crowded than the Lakes."

"I thought we were not to discuss the terms of our separation until after luncheon."

"Whose idea was that?" He grinned and gave the red ball a gentle kick across the sand. "Choose our spot, my lady, for as surely as God made sunrises and sunsets, wherever I lay this blanket, you will tell me to move it."

Oh God. When Vergilius smiled like that… Penelope was reminded of why, as a new bride, she'd been absolutely dazzled by her husband. She chose a place away from the rocks, but not too near the trail. As Summerton was arranging the blanket, the young father returned to the beach.

"There it is," he said. "Beg pardon for intruding, but the children do set store by their playthings."

Summerton kicked the ball to him. "They will sleep well tonight for having enjoyed some fresh air."

"That was the idea," the man said, his smile beaming from beneath a slightly reddened nose. He had sandy hair and a pleasant face, though his accent was public school rather than local for all that his dress was on the rustic side. "We take our niece and nephew to the shore every year for a week and give my brother and his wife a parental respite. We wear the children out, and they go home ready to take any and all naps and even sit quietly in the schoolroom for a few days. You're Summerton?"

Vergilius bowed slightly. "At your service."

The fellow bowed to Penelope, then to Vergilius. "Tregoning, at your service. I must say, Summerton, I was impressed with your speech about the tailors' apprentice bill. Reform is meaningless without funds to enforce the measures passed. How many in the Lords have been trying to dodge *that* little detail?"

"Uncle!" The boy, barefoot, his hair a riot, stood where the western path met the sand. "Auntie says you must come and leave others to enjoy the shore."

Lord Tregoning tossed the ball to the child. "Tell Auntie I'm merely exchanging pleasantries with a fellow guest. I have not been kidnapped by pirates."

"You're staying at the inn?" Penelope asked.

"We come every year," Tregoning replied. "The children love it. Perhaps you'd like to dine with us this evening? Amanda would be very pleased to have a conversation that isn't about who went first last time and whether licorice is better than lemon drops. We love the children dearly, but they are children."

"Uncle! You aren't *coming*!"

"We will be happy to join you for an early supper," Penelope said, though she had no idea what prompted that acceptance. A desire to avoid any more private dining rooms, perhaps. "Shall we say six of the clock?"

"I will make the reservations, and Amanda will be very pleased." He nodded briskly and jogged off as his nephew tore up the path ahead of them.

"I should know him," Penelope said. "He's Northford's heir, isn't he?"

"He is. The old marquess is too infirm to vote his seat. I've been told Tregoning is his uncle's eyes and ears in the Lords, though Tregoning is only observing. It had not occurred to me that his situation is not unlike our own."

The earl or viscount, or whatever his courtesy title, disappeared up the path, hand in hand with the boy clutching the red ball.

"They are dissolving their marriage? Perhaps the Siren's Retreat has something to answer for."

"They have no children," Vergilius said gently. "He is the heir, he is without progeny, and yet, his younger brother's union has been fruitful."

That observation added to the undercurrent of sadness that never ran far from Penelope's awareness of late.

"They are gracious in their affliction." Could *she* have been more gracious? Bella and Tommie were awash in children, and Penelope kept her distance from their nursery. She was godmother to the second-oldest girl and conscientiously recalled the children's birthdays. She did not take her nieces for ices, and she did not join in their nursery tea parties.

"You are frowning," Vergilius said.

"Bella always seems so blithe in her mothering. She has all in hand, no need for assistance or respite or adult conversation."

"If she wanted adult conversation," Vergilius said, setting the hamper at the end of the blanket, "she ought not to have married my brother."

Penelope could not help herself. She laughed—quietly, though she did laugh. Tommie was charming, but he was a fribbling dandy who could barely keep his children's names straight.

"Guard the fort," Vergilius said, pulling off his boots and stockings. "I am off to search for the holy grail."

"I beg your pardon?"

"A green ormer," he replied, setting off down the strand.

"Watch out for pirates," Penelope called after him. "I would not want to lose you to the foul clutches of the Barbary corsairs."

His lordship stalked back across the beach, kissed Penelope on the mouth, and then marched on at the tide line.

Her teasing had been meant as just that, but Summerton's kiss had been in earnest. Penelope watched him walk away, an ache starting up in her chest. A new ache, one sharp with regret, for she did esteem her husband too.

She always had. She took off her own footwear and was assailed by the thought that she hadn't realized how much she'd lose when she set Vergilius free, but by the end of this week, she would be intimately acquainted with the magnitude of that loss—that loss too.

Gill had wanted to reserve mornings for wooing, but he'd been unable to abide by his own rules. On a blanket on the beach, over a tray of sandwiches on the terrace, at breakfast in bright seaside sunshine, he and Penelope considered finances, who should be told what, and other details of untangling a long and public marriage.

He had the sense that much of what they discussed should have been covered earlier—years earlier. Penelope was appalled by the sums the dowager viscountess and the Lychmont household drained from Gill's exchequer. He had not known the extent of her charitable efforts, nor how much she genuinely took them to heart.

Children in the mines. Children in the mills. Children on the streets. The pattern was clear and laudable—and closely mirrored Gill's agenda in the Lords. How had he not known this about his own wife?

Or—more accurately—how had he not *appreciated* it about her? All he'd noticed was that she was often from home during the day, attending committee meetings. Parliament did its work mostly in the evening, and thus husband and wife had seen little of each other for much of the year.

"Did you want to marry me?" Penelope asked as Gill did up her hooks. He had changed for supper in his room at the inn, a pleasant little chamber with a view of the elm grove. He'd then come to the cottage to escort Penelope to dinner.

Gill paused, batting aside a now habitual urge to kiss Penelope's nape. This was their fourth day by the sea, and they were again dining with Lord and Lady Tregoning. Gill had thought separate quarters a terrible idea, but he'd been wrong.

Taking meals together, spending mornings wandering the beaches and paths, and afternoons sipping tea and making lists on the terrace had provided both proximity and privacy. No servants hovering to carry tales belowstairs. No social whirl keeping everybody up until all hours—and no stilted breakfasts either.

By degrees, conversation had wandered, from Gill's resentment of his mother's extravagance, to questions like the one Penelope had just posed. *Had* he wanted to marry Penelope?

"With the general caveat that young men are often idiots," he said, finishing up her hooks, "I did very much want to marry you."

Penelope gestured toward the bed. "For the usual reason?"

Gill took up the shawl she'd draped over the back of a wing chair. "That figured heavily in my longings, of course, but you were not exactly a retiring bride. Not once we came here for our wedding journey. I went from being relieved at having the whole matchmaking ordeal behind me and being rather pleased to have a pretty, sweet wife, to being..."

He wrapped the shawl around her and sneaked in a little pat to her shoulder.

"Vergilius?"

"Besotted," he said. "I became besotted with you. You had read so many books, and you remembered what you'd read. You argued with me over battles and statutes, and you expected no quarter when I returned fire. Then we'd end up in bed, and I realized..."

Penelope faced him and fluffed his cravat. "You realized how lonely you'd been." She leaned in, only for a moment, and Gill was assailed again by the knowledge that this talking, this discussing and revisiting and recollecting, should have been part of their marriage all along.

But how was he to have known that? "Did you want to marry me? I hardly exerted myself to court you, but then, Mama said I must not pester you when you had a trousseau to pack up and daily fittings to endure." Mama had had much to say. Papa had observed that arguing with a woman might not be precisely rude, but it was most often pointless, and thus a gentleman spared himself the bother.

"I did want to marry you," Penelope said, "though let it be said that young women can be idiots too. You were gorgeous and so self-possessed. You always knew what to say, you knew and were liked by everybody, and you had such grand ideas."

"Ah, youth," he said, and they shared a smile both sweet and sad. "I will miss you, Penelope."

These expressions of regret had become a wistful counterpoint to the pragmatic lists and schedules and budgets. And really, who else could share these regrets, but the other party to the marital bereavement?

"I will miss you too, and, Vergilius, may I say something awful?"

"Of course." *But only to me, because a wife should be able to confide in her husband.* Why had he not made earning Penelope's confidences a priority after the baby had died? They'd certainly traded confidences before that.

"I will not miss your mother. I will not miss Bella, and I will miss Tommie only a little. I don't want to have to *deal* with them over this annulment. I don't want them telling me how to comport myself, where I must appear in public, with whom I may not be seen, and how I am to dress."

Gill retrieved Penelope's reticule from the vanity. "They've presumed to that extent in the past?"

Penelope assessed her appearance in the cheval mirror and met Gill's gaze in their reflection before turning from the glass.

"After we lost our son, you went to the Hall to contend with your father's death. Bella came up to Town to *comfort* me. If anything in the whole world could cut through my sorrow, it was the certain knowledge that I must not toss Bella bodily from the house, or I would create one of those insufferable family rifts that echoes for generations."

"She did something terrible, if she vexed you to that degree." Something he and Penelope had never discussed.

"Bella would not leave me alone when I craved solitude. She would not allow me out of the house when I needed fresh air. She forbid even my closest friends to call and nearly stopped me from going to divine services. She countermanded my orders to the servants, decided I should have only bland food when I craved a good spicy curry. Her meddling was without end, and had it not been for MacMillan quoting orders to Bella that I doubt you had left in truth, that woman would have sent me to Bedlam."

"I'm sorry." Gill thought back to those miserable, dark weeks, when the grief had still borne a leavening portion of shock. "I don't recall how Bella ended up in Town. I certainly did not send her to you." Though Tommie had repeatedly told Gill not to thank him for making the sacrifice of parting from Bella *at such a time.*

"She just presented herself, uninvited, because 'family doesn't need an invitation.' She turned away my sister's offer to visit, and I would not have learned of that perfidy except that my sister mentioned it several years later. I longed for you, Vergilius, not because I could be any sort of comfort to you, but because if you were on hand, you could make Bella *go away.*"

Gill wrapped his arms around his wife. "Mama and Tommie would not let me leave the Hall. They had one excuse after another for why I had to meet with the solicitors again, the steward, the vicar. Then it was planting, the condolence calls... and Mama was insistent that I leave you privacy in which to recover from both the ordeal of birth and the loss of our son."

Penelope gave him her weight. "I'm sorry, Vergilius. I should have told MacMillan to have the horses put to and taken myself down to the Hall, without a word to Bella."

"I should have had my horse saddled and come home to you, without a word to anybody."

This, too, had become part of their conversations—regrets, increasingly sharp. *Shoulds* and *oughts* and *why didn't I's* along with many, many apologies, freely given and freely reciprocated.

"Promise me something," Gill said, keeping his embrace loose. "Promise me that if you should ever be in need, if you don't trust your solicitors, if you aren't getting along with whatever trustees we choose, you will let me help. Send for me, drop me a note. Don't be all noble and distant and stubborn."

She eased away, her expression hard to read. "That is an odd request to make of the woman who is precipitating the most monumental scandal ever to sully the Summers escutcheon."

"Promise me, Pen. Please. I cannot keep you trapped in a marriage that has failed you, but I cannot ignore that, for ten years, we were man and wife, and marriage to me has cost you much."

"I cost you as well, Vergilius."

That was the sort of comment that begged for a change of subject, but if Gill did not pursue the topic now, he might never learn what had prompted such an outlandish observation.

He led Penelope by the hand to the cottage's front door. "What did you cost me?"

"Another woman, a stronger woman, would not have been laid so low by the baby's death. Bella has had disappointments. Your mother lost a child. They both assured me that my grief was unnaturally intense, selfish even, and I must..."

"Soldier on?" Gill said, finding a new least-favorite phrase. "Bella and Mama both had other children, other sons. They had been married much longer than a year when their losses befell them, and they weren't twenty years old and wed to a man stumbling into a title when his wife needed him by her side." He opened the front door, wishing good manners allowed last-minute cancellation of their dinner plans. "A stronger, wiser husband would not have left you to contend on your own for so long, Penelope."

That had needed to be said aloud. Gill had chided himself in the odd moment for those months apart, but had followed his moments of self-doubt with reassurances that Penelope could have come down to the Hall if she'd wished. He'd invited her to often enough, while she had returned his invitations with silence.

"It's chillier than I expected," Penelope said, joining Gill on the front terrace. "I should wear my cloak."

"I'll fetch it." Gill left her by the door and went to the wardrobe in the bedroom. Penelope's purple merino cloak hung next to her old dressing gown, some sort of metaphor for the woman versus the viscountess.

Gill took out the cloak and draped it around Penelope's shoulders and let the stroll up the path put distance between sad, intimate discussions and an hour intended to be social. At the dinner table, he exerted himself to be pleasant to Lord Tregoning and his lady. Gill smiled, he listened politely, and in the back of his mind, he turned over a puzzle.

That old dressing gown, the one that was four sizes too big for Penelope, had belonged to Gill long ago. The elbows were worn, and one lapel was frayed, suggesting regular use. Penelope's jewelry box had been open, and atop her trinkets and earbobs had been Gill's embroidered handkerchief. A shiny green ormer shell had glinted among her necklaces and bracelets, the thin chain of a golden locket wrapped about the shell.

Unless Gill was mistaken, that locket held a curl of his hair and his likeness.

Penelope's determination to end the marriage was at least tinged with regret, which broke Gill's heart all over again, yet some more.

"I had not appreciated how much of a service the present marquess has done us by living into great old age," Amanda, Lady Tregoning, said. "We had a chance to find our balance as husband and wife and to weather a few storms before William had to start taking on the duties that go with the title."

She gazed fondly at her husband's retreating form. The waiter who'd brought out the fruit-and-cheese course had informed Vergilius of a note arriving for him at the front desk. Lord Tregoning had excused himself to have a word with old friends seated nearer the veranda, and thus the ladies had a moment to themselves.

"How long have you been married?" Penelope asked.

"Ten years," Lady Tregoning replied. "Arranged, though we were cordially acquainted prior to the betrothal. We finished growing up together, to the extent anyone ever finishes growing up. You and Summerton seem quite settled."

That erroneous observation was kindly meant. "We are contemplating a separation." Penelope should probably have kept that admission to herself, except the knowledge of what lay in store at week's end loomed larger and larger in her awareness.

Summerton was granting her wish, her dearest, most heartfelt wish, and now... she wasn't sure her wish made such great good sense after all.

"I'm sorry," Lady Tregoning said. "William and I reached the same point after the second miscarriage. We raised the topic of a separation gingerly at first, but then realized that it wouldn't solve anything. We'd still be childless, we'd still be relying on the younger brothers to see to the succession, but we'd..."

Penelope wrapped four small raspberry tarts in a linen napkin and slipped them into her reticule. Vergilius liked them with his breakfast.

"You'd be giving up?" Penelope suggested. "Creating a scandal, fueling gossip?" She'd be doing all of that in spectacular fashion once word got out that the lawyers were involved.

"We'd be compounding our losses," Amanda said. "I'd reached the point that when I looked at William, all I could see was the man to whom I *owed sons*, not my friend, not my partner in mischief, not a fellow who'd need allies when his father died. Not the only person who knows just by looking at me that my dancing slippers are pinching. I had to widen my focus to encompass all of him again. That was work, but work worth doing, and he had to see in me more than an unhappy wife."

"But two miscarriages... How can you face the prospect of the same thing happening yet again?"

"We are careful, and whether to try again is an ongoing discussion. When I'm ready, William isn't. When he's feeling courageous,

I'm not. We have three nephews. Children for us would be a blessing, but they are not a necessity. Being honest and kind with each other is what matters."

Elsewhere in the dining room, people were laughing and talking, while in Penelope's mind, ten years of marital history were taking on a very different aspect. Lady Tregoning and her husband had been talking *for years* about whether to try for more children, while Penelope had been hiding behind the Society pages and stuffing her calendar with committee meetings.

"How did you cope?" she asked, keeping her voice down. "When you felt you no longer knew your husband, when you wanted to stay home yet again, when the sight of family coming to roost in your home for the Season made you bilious?"

Lady Tregoning's smile was wistful. "We didn't cope very well at the start. We muddled along for the first couple years, and everybody told us to try again. To put the past behind us. Carry on, and don't dwell on what cannot be changed. I hate those words—'don't dwell.' It felt as if they were telling me to ignore my own broken heart. Then I lost the second baby—a boy—and *carrying on* was beyond me."

Penelope sipped her wine, a pleasant white. "Precisely. I sometimes hate my sister-in-law."

Amanda bit into an orange tart. "How many?"

"Seven. Four boys, three girls, and I suspect she's not done. She pops them out like some broodmare. At her oats for breakfast, a baby in the straw by noon, at grass an hour later."

"We hate them, the broodmares, and then we feel guilty because we aren't among them, and we know nobody *pops out* a baby without considerable pain, danger, and struggle. But if I'm a broodmare, is my dear William merely a stud colt? I will never forget the day he asked me that, and I had no answer for him."

"It's different for men." Penelope was horrified to hear herself quoting her mother-in-law.

"It could well be worse," Amanda replied, selecting a chocolate from the arrangement on the platter. "The fellows are supposed to be strong, stoic, *manly*. Impervious to suffering. How lonely that must be."

"We don't think of them as lonely." Vergilius had been the most generous and tender of lovers, and good God, Penelope missed him intimately. They had made passionate love, but they had also talked in bed. Long, thoughtful conversations punctuated by rest and affection. Did his lordship have anybody else to simply talk to?

Penelope certainly didn't. Vergilius had never asked to resume relations, and she hadn't either. *Give him time,* Mama-in-Law had said. *Don't nag. Don't impose.*

Penelope was abruptly tempted to gulp her wine. She instead put the glass down and pretended to consider a plum tart.

"William took me away from Town when things were at their darkest," Amanda said. "Took me to Cornwall for a summer, of all places. We walked all over the countryside, read to each other, went fishing and never caught anything, rode horseback to nowhere in particular. We'd sometimes go for hours without speaking a word to each other, but we needed the closeness to be had even in silence."

"What gave you the idea to do that, to turn your backs on all of Society and your families and...?" Penelope waved her hand in the general direction of the other diners.

"I don't know," Amanda replied, holding the platter out to Penelope. "When William suggested it, my first reaction was that I did not want to spend a summer weeping in some dreary cottage by the sea. I nonetheless suspected William needed the respite, and I do love him. We wept, some, but we also napped, and wandered, and talked. We needed time, and we made some wrong turns, but we knit ourselves back together more securely than we'd been knitted together before."

Penelope took a pretty little chocolate pressed into the shape of a rose. "You had a foundation to build on." And the leisure time and means to do the rebuilding. Perhaps most couples soldiered on because Society and limited means gave them no choice, and thus that tactic became the standard.

"You have a foundation too, my lady," Amanda replied, setting a chocolate on her absent husband's plate. "I see how Summerton looks at you. The viscount is not simply your stud colt, and you are not simply his broodmare."

Penelope let the smooth, rich sweetness of the chocolate dissolve on her tongue and selected a sweet to put on the edge of Vergilius's plate. He wound his way back from the foyer, a scrap of paper in hand, while Penelope allowed herself to simply appreciate him.

She could not knit herself back together with Summerton, but she could admit that she'd grieve the loss of him. They did have a foundation, but a couple could not dwell in peace and safety without walls and a roof too.

"Bad news?" she asked as Summerton resumed his seat.

Amanda excused herself and joined her husband at the table closer to the window.

"I don't know. My mother and Bella have arrived in Town, and they are asking after our whereabouts. MacMillan recalled where my trunk had been sent and thought I should know of the invasion."

"He is a treasure."

"He will miss you," Vergilius said. "You might consider taking him with you."

Penelope was assailed by the temptation to cry, right there in the dining room, but that would cause talk. Though what did *talk* matter when she was about to cause *scandal*?

"Pen? Are you well?"

He knows just by looking at me that my dancing slippers are pinching. "I am being ridiculous."

Vergilius held out the chocolate she'd chosen for him. "Tell me."

She took it and set it on her plate. "I don't want your mother and Bella in my house. It's not my house, it was never my house. I left that place with an intention to never return there, but I don't want those women making free with *your* wine, inviting their friends into *your* parlor, and driving *your* horses in the park."

Vergilius rose and held Penelope's chair for her. He was quiet as they made their way past the reception desk and out the front door, pausing only long enough to drape Penelope's cloak over her shoulders.

"A question for you, my lady." He strolled arm in arm with her to the elm grove, the laughter and noise of the inn fading with each step. "What would have made it *our* house, *our* wine, and *our* horses?"

It was on the tip of Penelope's tongue to answer with one word: children. Children would have changed everything. Even daughters would have changed everything, but again, she heard her mother-in-law and sister-in-law echoing in that reply. According to those two, *even a daughter* would have proved Vergilius's virility, though not as effectively as a nursery full of sons would.

Vergilius's *virility* was not now, nor had it ever been, in doubt.

"I have seen myself as a failed broodmare," Penelope said, "and thus a failed wife, but there's more to it than that. I failed to listen to my own instincts, and in a way, Vergilius, I have failed my vows."

He shifted his hold so they walked hand in hand. "That is utter rot, Penelope. Tell me you know that reasoning to be the rankest tripe."

"It's not reasoning," she said as they emerged from the trees to behold the vast sea undulating beneath a rising moon. "It's how I feel, Vergilius. I suspect you have felt likewise, but we have not shared how we feel. We've shared formal dinners and lonely breakfasts."

He was quiet all the way to the cottage, then he again opened the door and lit the various candles. When he'd also poked up the fire, he bowed his good-night over Penelope's hand, as he had for the past several nights.

They had two more days before he would return to Town, two more nights before he would stride out of Penelope's life.

"I'll see you in the morning," Vergilius said, "but before I go, I will tell you, my lady, that if I had to marry again, that if I was once more that strutting young fellow determined to catch up to his younger brother's marital accomplishments, I would still account myself the luckiest of bridegrooms to end up married to you."

He kissed her lingeringly on the mouth, then walked off into the darkness. Penelope caught sight of him half an hour later when she'd made herself a last cup of tea to take out to the terrace. She was swaddled in his old dressing gown, a habit she'd acquired after the baby had died, and she'd waited in vain, for months, to be summoned to the Hall.

Down on the beach, Vergilius sat upon a rock, his knees drawn up, his boots beside him on the sand.

"Good-bye." Penelope tried the word out at a whisper, and even that was enough to bring tears to her eyes. She grew cold keeping the vigil on the terrace, and when she eventually went inside, her husband was still alone on the distant beach.

Her last thought before drifting off in a bed where she still couldn't get warm was that she'd left a perfectly luscious chocolate sitting on the edge of her plate.

What manner of fool wasted perfectly luscious chocolate?

CHAPTER SIX

Gill's mind was accepting what his heart refused to admit: Penelope had made her decision, and she would not be charmed away from it. She'd suffered in silence for years from a marriage that had, as Gill had said, failed her.

He had failed her. She'd never refused him anything—save for not joining him at the Hall after Papa's death, and she'd had her reasons, of course—and Gill wasn't about to refuse her anything now. She had asked him to take her riding along a wide, sandy expanse of beach, and he had rented her a handsome mare so they could gallop along the waves. She had asked him to read to her, and he'd done his best with bucolic Wordsworth.

Then he'd trotted out, from memory, some of the naughty old John Wilmot verse he'd picked up at university—the man had been a stranger to euphemism—and Penelope had descended into outright laughter. One goal attained.

She'd retaliated with a limerick about old Friar Tuck that had astonished Gill with its vulgarity and left him wondering what other treasures his wife had kept hidden from him.

"Have we resolved where I'm to live?" Penelope said as they returned from a final afternoon spent on the beach.

"I thought you were taking Antrim Cottage? It's unentailed, available now, and well maintained."

Antrim Cottage was also just outside a pretty little village in Berkshire, not halfway to the benighted Highlands, which had been Penelope's original choice of abode.

"Antrim Cottage is lovely," she said, "but it's the former gatehouse for Antrim House. You enjoy spending time at Antrim House in the autumn."

He'd thought *she* enjoyed those weeks away from both Town and Hall in autumn. "Then I will promise to avoid Antrim House," Gill said, "or I can break the entail on Antrim House—Tommie will have a price for that, but he'll agree as my heir—and you can have Antrim House."

Penelope preceded him into the cottage, something about her posture suggesting that, like many negotiations, this one was coming spectacularly unraveled just as the opposing parties ought to be shaking hands on an understanding that met all needs.

"If you think," Gill said, stalking into the cottage behind her, "that some cow byre in the Hebrides will suffice for my viscountess's abode, you are sadly in error."

"Vergilius, hush."

In ten years of marriage, Penelope had never once told him to hush. He kept his mouth shut out of sheer curiosity.

"I will no longer be your viscountess," Penelope said gently. "You will remarry, and when you do, *you* might well be able to forget that your former wife is living in the gatehouse when you bide at Antrim House. Your next viscountess, however, will wonder about me and about why you offered me that property. For me to put her in that position would be unkind."

Gill knew Penelope's cool, self-possessed expression, but he'd also spent most of a week paying closer attention to what she did not say and what she did not allow to reflect in her eyes.

To expect Penelope to watch Gill and his new wife riding about the Antrim House park would *upset Penelope*, an odd vestige of the marital bond for a woman who'd longed for years to dissolve it.

And she worried for nothing. "I will never remarry, Penelope. You are leaving me because you must, but spare yourself any gracious gestures undertaken for the benefit of my next wife."

She pokered up, blinked, and blinked again. "You must remarry, Vergilius. Tommie won't make any sort of viscount, and Bella will squander the family fortune on outlandish hats if your mother doesn't beat her past the post in a procession of new carriages. I knew they were spendthrifts, but the figures you've shown me this week... Tommie and Bella are appallingly irresponsible for a couple with seven children."

"Tommie takes after Mama when it comes to finances," Gill said. "If you don't want Antrim Cottage, what about Patchwork Cottage? It's not as grand, but those tenants are some of our finest farmers, and the house itself is lovely." Then too, Patchwork Cottage was in Sussex, the next county over from the Hall.

"Patchwork Cottage is lovely," Penelope said, worrying a nail. "I think Bella had her eye on it as a dower property for one of her girls."

Gill took off his hat and shrugged out of his jacket. "She has a list? She's seen me dead and buried, such that properties that are no concern of hers have already been parceled out to her nursery full of children?"

Penelope nodded. "Mama-in-Law is nothing if not concerned for her progeny. She and Bella frequently discuss what's to be done for each of the children."

"When Mama isn't noticing how behind the current fashion the cabriolet I bought her last year is, and Bella isn't sneaking her millinery onto your accounts."

Penelope hung up her bonnet. "Bella knows not to abuse that privilege, and I haven't wanted to antagonize her. I'll put the kettle on and tell you what I know of their plans."

End of day approached, the sun low on the water, and Gill really ought to be heading up to the inn to dress for dinner and pack his trunk. He would leave in the morning, and he needed solitude to come to terms with that awful reality.

He instead undid his sleeve buttons and rolled up his cuffs, prepared for more tallies and lists.

Penelope might never again share a cup of tea with him, much less at a humble kitchen table where nobody could hover or intrude. If sharing that final cup of tea meant Gill was treated to a litany of Bella's and Mama's ambitions, so be it.

The second pot was half empty by the time Penelope had finished summarizing Bella's plans for the Hall and the further renovations to be made there. If Bella, Mama, and Tommie had their way, more than a half-dozen functional estates would end up in the hands of children raised by a pair of profligates, and some of the viscountcy's most valuable acreage would be sold off.

For years, Penelope had been silently enduring speculation about how the family would go on after Gill's death, and of all the trespasses Gill could lay at his mother's feet, that one was near the top of the list. Bella was thoughtless and outspoken by nature. Mama was a widow herself and one who'd not coped well immediately following her spouse's death.

"The dowager will take over Lychmont when I die?" Gill muttered. "Has it occurred to her I am barely thirty?"

"Her ladyship will live forever," Penelope said. "Doesn't seem fair when others..." She fell silent.

Gill covered her hand with his. "When others live for only a few days. You can say that to me, and I will agree with you. Don't think to spare my blushes because these people are my family. They are also the source of some of my greatest frustrations."

To what extent was Penelope demanding an annulment because Gill had failed to protect her from his family and had instead expected Penelope to guard *him* from Mama's and Bella's meddling?

Penelope hunched forward. "I have the sense there's much I should have said to you in years gone by, Vergilius, but I can't change the past. I want to say something to you now, if my courage does not desert me."

Gill had thought himself fairly familiar with his wife, a sweet woman grown withdrawn and serious as a result of a tragic loss. Now, he wasn't half so confident of his assessment, and he wished to his soul that he'd had an opportunity to truly learn to whom he was married.

Except he'd had that very opportunity and squandered it on committee meetings and suppers at the club.

"I'm listening," Gill said, "and I want to hear whatever you need to say."

Penelope set her tea cup back on the tray. "Promise me an honest answer, Vergilius."

What on earth was she about? "I promise."

Penelope left the table and went to the window. The moon had yet to rise, and she stared out at the vast undulating shadow that was the sea.

"I would like you to spend the night here at the cottage."

A cool feeling shivered through him. "With you? In the same bed?"

"With me. In the same bed, as man and wife."

Vergilius had never asked Penelope for anything, and she had tried not to impose on him either. He was a busy man, with even more responsibilities than she'd realized. He was putting enough money and property into her hands that she could maintain her dignity and her charitable contributions, as well as a pleasant if retiring lifestyle.

That dignity hung by a slender thread braided of determination, selfishness, and—this astonished her—gratitude.

"What are you asking me, Penelope?" Vergilius stood beside her, and Penelope was as aware of him as if she were a new bride, or a wife whose husband was soon to march off to battle.

"I am asking you for a farewell to treasure. A send-off, a fond remembrance." Penelope fumbled for those words, because she truly had no coherent answer. She had missed Vergilius for so long, the Vergilius she'd loved and respected and *liked.*

Of all places, she'd found him here, where she'd found him once before.

"You are sure?" he asked, his tone giving away nothing.

"We tried, Vergilius. We tried, and tried, and tried. Are we to have no reward for all that effort save some stilted meetings with stilted lawyers? When I run into you five years from now on some busy London street, may I not have one sweet, private memory to share with you as we nod and pass without speaking?"

"You might have one more regret too, Penelope."

She rounded on him, abruptly out of patience with the tactful negotiator he'd become. "What of you, my lord? In the past nine years, have you never once been tempted to tap on my bedroom door? For old times' sake, for a lark, in a moment of weakness, for any reason at all? We knew such pleasure before the heartache got the better of us. I want that again, if only for one night."

Vergilius looked out to sea, and in the utter impassivity of his expression, Penelope saw one final, grand, implacable rejection. That it should come from him was fitting, when she'd been the one to give up on the marriage.

"You ask much, Penelope."

I wish I had asked much years ago. "It's the wrong time for me to conceive, if that's what concerns you."

He slanted her a puzzled glance. "And if you did conceive?"

"I suppose we'd have to remain married, but I won't conceive. My courses are predictable." And every month, they still made her unhappy. How much unhappier would she be as a woman who had abandoned her vows?

"This week has been..." Vergilius took her hand. "I was delighted to find you here. I saw an opportunity to bring everything right between us at last. I would be gallant and attentive and flirt my boots off, not that I know how to do that. You would fall into my lap, grateful and pleased to finally have harmony restored between us."

She slipped her arms around his waist. "Vergilius, I am sorry."

He held her loosely. "We are both sorry until we're sick with it, but that, as you say, does not change the past. When you told me you were leaving me, my first thought was, 'What took you so long?' I know it's been hard for me, and doubtless harder for you. My next reaction to your decision was simply to redouble my efforts to court you back into love with me. I leave tomorrow, and we must conclude that my efforts to woo you were in vain."

"Not entirely in vain, certainly."

"Right, we have made our final arrangements, as it were, and I do take some satisfaction from having kept the lawyers out of it thus far."

"But I'm asking too much when I invite you to stay with me tonight?"

His embrace changed, no longer the comforting passive stance couples indulged in that had little of the erotic about it. For the first time in years, Penelope felt from her spouse not merely a husband's touch, but a lover's.

"I fear," he said, "that much of what we regret is because we did not ask enough from each other. Enough honesty, enough trust, enough determination, enough ingenuity. If you want me in your bed tonight, Penelope, then in your bed, I shall be."

A weight of self-judgment, loneliness, *something*, fell from Penelope's heart. Truly, Vergilius understood the situation and had, like Penelope, reached a place of acceptance. That was sad, but it was necessary if either of them were to know peace and contentment going forward.

"I will return to the inn and order us some supper," Vergilius said. "I will also pack for my departure in the morning, then I will join you for supper, and we shall all the pleasures prove."

He'd used that phrase once before, as they'd bounced and kissed and cuddled their way along the king's highway on their wedding journey. Penelope had wondered what a quaint little inn by the sea could possibly offer that was worth all that bother.

"I'll see you in an hour or so," she said, stepping back, "and lest the obvious go unsaid, thank you, Vergilius, for everything."

A ghost of a smile touched his eyes. "And thank you, Penelope. For everything." He bowed, gathered up his hat and coat, and left Penelope standing by the window, counting the minutes and wondering what in the name of holy matrimony she'd got herself into.

Gill would not try to trap Penelope with a child, of that much he was certain.

Over the past days, the longer he'd listened to her recount the sheer misery she'd endured with Mama and Bella taking turns disrespecting her authority, invading her household, and imposing patently stupid advice on her, the more he'd realized that Penelope's depths of self-restraint rivaled the ocean itself.

Equally bad advice had come to Gill from Tommie, *old married man* that he'd claimed to be at barely twenty. Papa's friends had been similarly backward in their suggestions for how to deal with a bereaved wife, and Gill—regret piled upon woe placed atop self-recrimination—had listened to them.

He did not dress for dinner, but instead donned the riding attire he'd wear in the morning, a reminder of where this final interlude with Penelope would end. He also did not question his motives for agreeing to her proposition.

For selfish reasons, for stupid reasons, for no reasons at all, he wanted to be what she'd asked him to be—her lover—if only for one night.

The meal was simple—cold ham-and-cheese sandwiches, apple tarts, a bottle of Merlot. Gill appropriated the hamper from the porter when he met that good soul on the path under the elms.

"And her ladyship will want breakfast brought over, as usual,"

Gill said. "Leave it outside the door, for she might not rise with the sun."

The porter winked and trotted back to the inn. Gill had already settled up both his account and Penelope's, because it was still his privilege to see to her financial needs. Three months hence...

He knocked on the cottage door, which opened almost immediately. Penelope was in an old morning gown, a shawl about her shoulders. She looked tired, dear, and determined as she stepped back to let him into the cottage.

"Do we fortify ourselves with sustenance first," Gill asked, "or fortify ourselves with pleasure and eat later?"

If he'd shocked his wife, the only sign was a slight raising of her brows. "I suppose the wine should breathe."

Gill set the hamper on the kitchen table. "Merlot typically breathes for less than an hour, Penelope. I have missed you for nine years, and I will not be rushed once we are in the bedroom."

She blushed even as her chin came up. "Nor will I. We can eat later. A midnight snack."

Oh ho. Gill followed her into the bedroom, though doing so felt precipitous. "I did not mean that I'd fall upon you like a plundering barbarian."

"I was rather hoping you would, because now that the moment is here..." Penelope halted before the cheval mirror. "I did not exactly dress for the occasion, did I?"

Gill came up behind her and slipped his arms around her waist. "Now that you are about to have your wish come true—and one of my wishes, too, lest there be any doubt—you feel awkward. You are suffering cold feet and doubting yourself, but let's not take that path tonight, Penelope. Let's not be so polite and careful and proper. Let's take the other path, the one where we speak honestly with each other, we show some trust and patience, and we listen without leaping to conclusions."

They'd made a start down that other, wilder path in the past week. Too little, too late, but not in vain. Not entirely in vain. Even without this last night of passion, Gill would treasure the memory of this week for the rest of his life.

Penelope turned to embrace him. For a moment, they simply held each other, and for Gill, that was a time to relearn the pleasure of having his wife near. She was petite but sturdy, curved in all the right places, and she always smelled of flowers.

He paid attention to the exact texture of her hair, so thick and fine.

To the rhythm of her breathing, to the moment when she finally let herself lean into him.

"I am afraid, Gill."

So am I. "What scares you the most?"

"The fear that I am making the worst mistake of my life."

He realized two heartbeats after she'd spoken that she did not refer to a night beneath the covers. She referred to giving up on a ten-year marriage, very likely the only marriage she would have.

Gill set aside the rising joy of sexual anticipation and set aside his own myriad fears as well.

"I suspect had we been more willing to err, to share doubts and worries, we might not have come to this moment. But we were not brave the way we might have been. We were... proper, correct, tidy. We minded our elders and the etiquette books instead of minding each other. We were as we thought we should be, and now you want to live as your heart tells you to. That adjustment will take time."

"And you?" she asked, stepping back. "What adjustments will you make?"

Gill had thought about this during the late-evening hours in his solitary room. "I will be more ruthless in the Lords. I won't abandon my scruples, but I will take the gloves off, Pen. The world is changing, and change for the better in the midst of upheaval will take concerted effort."

He sat on the vanity stool to pull off his boots. "The same with Bella, Mama, and Tommie. You have kept them from plaguing me too awfully, but they will descend upon me, expecting to get the same reception they had from me when I was one-and-twenty and new to the title. They are in for a polite, stern awakening."

"Good," Penelope said, turning down the bedcovers. "Long overdue, and if you truly wanted a challenge, you could have MacMillan take a look at the Lychmont account books."

Gill stripped off his stockings and draped them over his boots. "A daunting thought, but of course the creditors will expect me to cover my brother's debts."

"Cover them once if you must, then put the trades on notice that Tommie has been cut off. I will do the same with the modistes and so forth, because Bella won't allow a little thing like an annulment to interfere with her larceny."

"You sound very determined." While Penelope looked quite fetching, sitting on the bed steps, her slippers in her hand.

"I will no longer have the threat of your intervention to hold Bella or the trades or anybody in check. I must learn to be ruthless, too, and I suppose that is another fear I have about living on my own."

"Let me undo your hooks," Gill said, shrugging out of his jacket and draping it over the back of the wing chair. "And for your information, you are already quite formidable. Ask anybody who has ever tried to bring you a bit of tattle, anybody on your charitable committees. You are a force to be reckoned with, do you but know it."

This time, he did kiss Penelope's nape and had the satisfaction of knowing he'd earned her attention.

"I've always enjoyed that particular preliminary," she said, making no move to march off to the wardrobe and hang up her dress.

Gill was out of practice, but he wasn't stupid. He lavished kisses on his wife's nape and on her shoulders while he eased the dress down to her waist. Penelope wore no stays, bless her foresight, and thus he could gently cup the lovely shape and weight of her breasts through her chemise.

He would have been content to go slowly, to let desire build gradually, but Penelope wasn't having any of that. She rounded on him, lashed her arms around his waist, and fused her mouth to his. The shock of her passion rocked through Gill, stirring his own ardor from embers to flames in moments.

"Penelope... There's no..."

"Nine years, Gill. Nine years I've waited to taste you again, and they have been long years."

The gleam in her eye did not bode well for Gill's buttons. He fumbled out of his waistcoat and shirt, but kept his breeches on lest he disgrace himself.

"We have all night," he said as Penelope wiggled out of her dress and tossed it—*tossed it*—atop the vanity stool. "We need not—"

"I need," Penelope said. "I need and I want and yearn, Vergilius. For you."

A tempest blew through the bedroom in the next quarter hour. Penelope had Gill on his back atop the covers, his breeches unbuttoned, and his hands pinned to the pillow. She sank onto his erect cock with the confidence of a woman who knew absolutely who and what she wanted.

As a new wife, Penelope had been sweet, playful, ardent, funny... but nine years had taught her how to *take* what she needed, how to demand her lover's cooperation.

Gill gloried in her newfound wisdom. Nine years had taught him a thing or two as well, about strategy and patience. When Penelope was riding him hard, satisfaction eluding her by the smallest, most frustrating increment, he wrapped his arms around her, rolled with her on the bed, and drove into her with all the passion in him.

The tempest became a one-woman gale, a silent, thrashing force of nature determined to seize her pleasure and hold it fast. By some miracle of marital devotion, Gill managed not to spend—perhaps the shock of Penelope's loving had done that for him—but they remained joined as her hips slowed, and her arms eased from about his neck.

"*Good God*, Vergilius. Almighty, everlasting, merciful *God*."

"Catch your breath," he whispered, resting his cheek against hers. "We're just getting started."

He caught *his* breath, and the second loving was gentler but no less passionate. Gill managed to hold out once more, though the third time capsized his self-restraint as effectively as it sank Penelope's.

He was vaguely aware of hunger as his wife drowsed against his side and also of a creeping sadness. In the coming weeks and years, he'd stay busy, he'd maintain decorum when anybody was watching, and he'd find ways to distract himself from this new version of his ongoing marital sorrow.

He'd learned all of those skills years ago.

But as he held Penelope in the shadowy bedroom where they'd first fallen in love, his grief was as vast as the ocean. They had both tried so hard for so long. He could not ask Penelope to keep trying now.

"It wasn't like this before," Penelope murmured.

"It wasn't," Gill replied, kissing her brow and needing desperately to avoid a discussion of the differences between honeymoon lovemaking and farewell lovemaking. "Are you hungry?"

"Famished."

Penelope was allowing him to change the subject, to call an intermission to the pleasure and the pain. They ate companionably in the kitchen, Penelope wearing nothing but Gill's old dressing gown. He decided that this would be his favorite memory of her, eating sandwiches by candlelight, looking well loved and tired.

"You will wake me before you go?" Penelope asked.

"I will love you before I go," Gill replied, offering her a smile and a wink.

She smiled back, though neither one of them was quite able to make those smiles merry. Penelope had spoken the truth when she'd said the lovemaking had never been like this. Never been this intense, this honest, this emotional.

This sad and wonderful.

When they'd finished eating and tidied up, Gill wrapped himself around Penelope beneath the covers, determined to stay awake, a feat he managed for five entire minutes. His last thought before drifting off was that the lovemaking had never been like this before, and it would never be like this—like anything—ever again.

Sneaking away from Vergilius back in London had felt wrong, and as Penelope drowsed beside him, she understood why. Giving up on her marriage was the lesser of two pains—another nine years like the last nine would be unbearable—but she had failed to acknowledge precisely what she was giving up on.

She'd dodged that bit of honesty with herself, and this week with her husband had held her accountable.

Vergilius was, if anything, a more impressive man than he'd been ten years ago. He had grown into his title and now wielded it for the benefit of others. He was stalwart in the face of family members who took his generosity for granted. He was kind, humble, hardworking, and entirely deserving of a second chance with another woman.

He was also breathtakingly desirable.

If-onlys multiplied in Penelope's head, and her dreams were troubled. She woke at one point in darkness to find herself alone in bed, and in her panic to locate her husband, she banged her elbow and barked her shin.

She finally caught sight of him, wandering alone in the moonlight down along the shore. The sight was so dear and sad Penelope nearly shouted at him to come back to the cottage and back to bed.

Back to her. He'd said he would not leave her without waking her, so she instead waited on the terrace, swaddled in blankets, until he turned his steps in the direction of the path.

She had learned too well how to wait for him, more's the pity.

When Gill again wrapped himself around her beneath the covers, she feigned sleep, though she was in truth exhausted. She let the rise and fall of his breathing soothe her back into dreams, and when she awoke, faint light seeped through the curtains.

Gill was still abed with her, and she could tell he was awake even before she opened her eyes. The awful hour of parting had arrived, as it must.

"You said you'd love me before you leave," she whispered.

Vergilius could have put her off with vague excuses meant to be kind. Instead, he loved her in silent splendor, rising above her and looking directly into her eyes as passion ignited. Penelope tried to hold his gaze, to return his regard, but as the yearning crested higher, so did heartache. When the end came, she closed her eyes and clung as she had longed to cling for so many years.

Gill held her gently, then withdrew and spent on her belly. He dealt with the mess and did Penelope the great kindness of curling up beside her and tucking her close.

"You will stay here for the next week?" he asked.

"I will." She'd need to. "I'll send word to Patchwork Cottage to expect me and give the staff some warning before I descend. You're for London?"

"London and the solicitors. I will send the traveling coach for your journey to the cottage. I will also boot Mama and Bella from the town house. Mama can stay with friends if she must bide in Town, and as for Bella..."

"Be not merely firm, Vergilius, be ruthless. Bella cannot be allowed to destroy your peace as she has so often tried to destroy mine. Give her an inch, and she will have appointed herself your hostess by Friday."

Vergilius shuddered. "Tommie married somebody very like our mother. Will you help me to dress?"

"Of course." A wife often valeted her husband, and he served as her lady's maid. Penelope tried to view passing Vergilius his sleeve buttons, tying his cravat, and straightening his watch chain as final mementos of a lovely week, but those small acts mostly just made her sad.

Sadder.

He was leaving because she'd asked him to leave. She *needed* him to leave.

When he was dressed, had downed two cups of tea, and tarried over the last of the apple tarts, there was nothing more to say or do that would not be a blatant delay of the inevitable. Penelope belted her old dressing gown more tightly about her middle and accompanied Vergilius to the door.

"Thank you for this week," she said. "And for last night."

He drew her into his arms, and she went willingly. "Last night was magnificent, Penelope, as you are magnificent. Let me know when you are settled at the cottage. There will be agreements to sign, affidavits, and so forth. All tedious, but we'll get through it."

They would. Now, when it was too late, she and Gill had developed sufficient trust and shared purpose to weather the impending storm. She walked with him to the door, the flagstones of the floor cold through the thin soles of her slippers. Vergilius donned his hat and coat, then dipped his head to kiss her cheek.

"Platitudes would be blasphemous," he said, pausing just outside the front door, "but silence won't do either. Promise me again you will let me know if you need anything. Don't go through the lawyers. Just drop me a note and be blunt. I will worry about you, and I will..."

Penelope nodded, crossing the threshold to take his hand. "Miss you. I will miss you as well, Vergilius." She hugged him, all of her fears welling up into one great big ball of sorrow lodged in her throat. What did *he* fear? What nightmares haunted *him*? Too late to ask that now.

"Will you write back?" she murmured, breathing him in, memorizing his wondrous male shape. "I always wondered why you never wrote back to me, Vergilius. I know you were busy, but... I should not ask."

Penelope's husband stared down at her in the predawn gloom. "Write back to you?"

"All those years ago, when you had to be at the Hall, and I was still too unwell from childbed to travel from Town. I wrote to you, and my letters went unanswered."

He looked at her as if he had no clue what she was going on about.

"Never mind," Penelope said. "I should not have asked, and you must be going."

He studied her, then he kissed her again, this time on the mouth. "Be well, Penelope, and if you can, be happy. Perhaps I did not answer your letters for the same reason you did not answer mine."

He was out the door and striding up the path in the next instant, though she did not understand his explanation. At that moment, Penelope understood little except that Vergilius was leaving, her great freedom was at hand, and all she felt was devastating loss.

Penelope watched her husband until he disappeared into the elm grove, and still she stood on the cold stones, staring at the morning mist. When she stepped back inside the cottage, she was shivering, but she could not bestir herself to put the kettle on, or to do much of anything.

A marriage long over had just ended in truth, and only in the past week had she realized the magnitude of the defeat that represented. Penelope returned to the bedroom, struck by the disarray she and Gill had created the previous night.

Her dress was in a heap, one slipper peeked from beneath the bed skirt, the indent of Gill's head still shaped the pillow. Penelope moved forward, intent on smoothing her hand over that pillow, when something solid bumped against her thigh.

Something in the pocket of her dressing gown. She did not recall that weight being there when she'd put the dressing gown on, but then, her powers of perception were not at their most acute. Gill had found the strength to leave her, and she must be grateful to him for that consideration.

She withdrew a perfect, iridescently beautiful ormer shell from the dressing gown's pocket. This specimen was smaller than the first one Vergilius had given her, though it gleamed even more brightly.

He must have slipped the shell into her pocket as they'd parted. A memento, a treasure. Penelope climbed beneath the quilts, the shell clutched in her hand, and curled up on her husband's side of the bed.

She held firm against all the voices clamoring in her head—the commands to soldier on, to put the past aside, to consider her blessings. On and on the lectures and sermons would go, if she allowed them to.

Instead, Penelope gripped her green ormer, clung to her pillow, and cried like a childless mother.

CHAPTER SEVEN

Gill could not ride like the demons of hell were after him, because he valued his horse. He also needed time to think, to start this new phase of grieving, and to plan. He made the journey to London in reasonable stages, and all the while, he considered options.

I've always wondered why you never wrote back to me. One small, passing admission, upon which his whole marriage might well have turned.

Disowning Mama would not do. That would compound the scandal of the annulment, but then, in for a penny... And he could disown Tommie and Bella, too, though Tommie would still be heir to the title. The unentailed wealth could go to Penelope's charities, or to Penelope herself...

A packet of old letters—if they still existed—could not make much difference at this late date, but he wanted Penelope to have them, just the same. Such thoughts saw him through one turnpike after another, and by late afternoon, he was passing his hat to MacMillan.

"Where are they?" Gill asked.

"Perhaps you'd like to freshen up first, my lord. I believe the ladies have company. They are entertaining in the formal parlor."

The formal parlor, where Penelope alone had authority to receive guests as the lady of the house. "Of course they are. How have you not tossed them bodily into the street?"

"Certain privileges are uniquely yours, my lord, though I would give a fortnight's wages to watch the eviction, as would the entire staff. The week has been trying, especially for Cook." MacMillan's gaze held a hint of humor, but only a hint.

"I will make use of soap and water. The instant the guests leave, please let me know, and do not warn the ladies that I have returned."

"Very good, sir." MacMillan's smile would have done a border reiver proud.

Gill used the next quarter hour to bring some order to his appearance, and to his thoughts. Something about the past week, as difficult as it had been, had fortified him. What had Penelope told him?

Be ruthless. He'd manage that much easily, but *ruthless* did not mean *uncivilized.* A tap on the bedroom door was followed by MacMillan's soft voice.

"The guests are gone, sir. The ladies are alone in the formal parlor."

Alone, finishing off a lavish tea tray and planning their next raid on Gill's finances and his consequence. Before he went downstairs, he crossed the hallway into Penelope's suite. Her presence permeated her apartment, in the soft colors and pretty seascapes, in the scent of fresh flowers, and in the perfect balance between order and comfort. A portrait of the Summerton bride and groom hung in her sitting room, a pair of innocents who'd deserved much more loyalty from family than they'd had.

Well, Gill could still be loyal to his wife. He owed her that much and more.

He bowed to the image of his bride, then took himself down to the formal parlor at a dignified, businesslike pace. When he opened the door, he caught Bella stuffing a tea cake into her mouth and Mama reaching for the plate of sandwiches.

Gill had left the door open and had left MacMillan at the ready in the corridor.

"All I want to know," he said, "is which one of you stole the letters?"

Mama and Bella traded a look thieves exchanged when the constable came upon them dividing up their loot.

"Summerton, how dare you greet us in all your dirt?" Mama began. "Where have you been, by the way? A thoughtful man leaves word of his whereabouts when others are depending upon him, and we have been worried—"

"Which one of you stole my letters to Penelope and hers to me? You either give me the truth now, or the pair of you will never set foot in London again. You will not be received, the shops will not accept your custom, you will be as ignored as if you were in deepest, perpetual mourning."

Which was exactly what they deserved—nine years of it, without respite or comfort.

Bella chewed with the dispatch of a rodent before launching her volley. "Summerton, have you taken a fall from your horse? I tear myself away from my children and husband and travel all the way from Lychmont to ensure Penelope is not overwhelmed by the duties that come with the Season, and you strut in here making wild accusations. One worries for your sanity."

"One does," Mama added. "But then, you always were a difficult boy."

"While you, my lady," he retorted, "are insufferable."

The old Gill, the Gill who'd kept the peace and remained above the affray, would have turned her insult into a joke, or announced a pressing appointment at the club.

The Gill who'd been advised to be ruthless had more to say. "The pair of you are no longer welcome in this house. I don't care which of you took those letters. You have both overstepped often enough, with me and with Penelope, that you are to pack your things and leave. You will be gone in the next hour and can make the twenty miles to Lychmont easily before nightfall. I would bid you good day, except you don't deserve a good day. You deserve nine years of despair and bewilderment and misery, and I hope they befall you starting now."

He spun on his heel and was halfway to the door before Mama spoke.

"I never tampered with any letters from Penelope, Summerton. You insult me to suggest as much."

Gill studied his mother, whose righteous bearing would make the queen look like a trembling lackey by comparison. Mama was prevaricating or bluffing. She wasn't *quite* lying.

"I never tampered with any letters from you, Summerton," Bella added, though like Mama, her declaration carried an undertone of bravado. "You never wrote to Penelope, as far as I knew. Too busy, I told her. Taking over a title and dealing with a house of mourning aren't the work of a moment. She eventually understood."

The truth snapped into Gill's awareness as Mama and Bella exchanged another one of those caught-red-handed looks.

"I never saw a single letter from Penelope arrive at the Hall," Mama said. "Why should you be writing daily to a wife who could not bother to write to you and at such a time? A better son would appreciate my efforts to look after his wellbeing."

Gill wanted to upend the tea tray, smash the mirror over the sideboard, and toss both Mama and Bella into the garden.

"Bella withheld Penelope's letters from the post here in Town," he said, "while you, Mama, made sure my letters to my wife never left the Hall. You saw an opportunity to tear me and Penelope apart, to weaken a marriage that was off to a roaring fine start. Both of you committed enormous harm to a young couple who needed your support and compassion." Who had needed each other, desperately.

In that moment, Gill hated his mother and hated his sister-in-law. He loathed their stupid, venal, selfish schemes. Their small-minded fixation on bonnets and cabriolets and spending money they had not earned. Penelope spent her pin money on orphanages and soup kitchens. Bella and Mama were parasites.

"I was protecting Penelope," Bella said, her voice for once lacking confidence. "Nary a word from you, and her still recovering from childbed. I had no idea Mama-in-Law was drawing a similar conclusion at the Hall. We meant well, Summerton. You must believe that."

"And I could not possibly realize that Bella had taken it upon herself to meddle," Mama said, a touch of her usual asperity returning. "Very forward of you, Bella, to presume to that extent. Had you not been so—"

"Mama-in-Law, you are not thinking clearly. Surely had you allowed even one letter to leave the Hall... but no. As always, you fail to consult me, when my judgment—"

"Hush." Gill spoke sharply and softly. "Where are the letters? If you have destroyed them, be assured I will destroy you both. I will look after the children, but the two of you will be consigned to a cottage on some sheep farm in the Outer Hebrides."

A fraught silence took hold, though Gill was no longer being ruthless. He was simply being honest.

Perhaps Mama grasped the depths of his ire, because some of the righteous conviction left her posture. "The letters are at the Hall," she said. "When Bella and I realized what had happened, we meant to attribute the situation to a problem with the post, to have the correspondence found without explanation, something. But the opportunity did not arise."

"It has been years, Summerton," Bella said, shoving to her feet. "What can a lot of old drivel mean now? You and Penelope lead separate lives, *there have been no children*, and Tommie and I are resigned to stepping into the title when the time comes. Do you think it's easy, being brought to bed with a child every eighteen months? Watching yourself lose any semblance of a figure and any will to maintain one? My days are full of feuding nurserymaids, and my nights are an inescapable exercise in duty. I almost wish... but no matter. I am a loyal wife. I know my duty."

She smiled at Gill, as if trying to will him to accede to her version of events. "You have nothing to worry about, Summerton, and nothing to be upset about."

Bella, Gill realized, was profoundly, wretchedly bitter, and in her mind, that bitterness was justified.

Penelope had doubtless grasped the depth of Bella's unhappiness, but Penelope had also been more egregiously wronged by Gill's family than she knew.

"You are both leaving for Lychmont in the next hour," he said, "and you will tell me exactly where the letters are. I will send word through the solicitors regarding new budgetary arrangements to be enforced going forward. What you two have cost me and my wife is incalculable, and you will not be received in this house in future should you presume to call. MacMillan will have the cabriolet brought around."

"Not the traveling coach?" Mama asked. "You insult your mother, Summerton."

"Madam, if you do not want to walk to Lychmont in your slippers, you will cease harping like the fishwife you so readily impersonate. Pack your things and be grateful I do not sell the cabriolet to pay your millinery bills. Mrs. Summers," Gill said, turning to Bella. "I will write to your husband and explain this situation to him. Do not call at the Hall. Do not show your face on any Summerton property other than the one where you bide. You and Tommie should have sorted yourselves out years ago—*tell him* if you are done with childbearing—but don't take your frustrations out on others. I will see you off in an hour."

To their credit, both ladies were in the porte cochere forty-five minutes later, the silence between them as cold as the Thames in winter.

"My lady, where exactly are the letters?" Gill asked as the cabriolet clattered around from the mews.

He saw his mother weigh the possibility of bargaining with him, saw her discard the notion. Penelope had been right. Ruthlessness worked.

"In the escritoire in my sitting room," Mama said, "bundled beneath some old letters you wrote to your father from university. Bottom right-hand drawer. Penelope's are there as well. We were going to get them to you, one way or another, but the moment was never right, and then the whole business lost any significance."

"No, it did not. Safe journey to you both." He stepped back so the first footman could hand the ladies up. Gill wasn't about to touch either woman even while wearing his gloves. A groom took the perch at the back of the vehicle.

"They are to arrive in one piece at Lychmont tonight," Gill said to the groom. "No detouring to call on friends, no circling back to retrieve a forgotten reticule. Get them out of my sight and treat this trip to Lychmont as if you were delivering felons to the hulks. No delays, no frolics, no excuses."

"Of course, my lord." The groom was smiling. "One change of horses, and we'll have them back where they... We'll have them safely at Lychmont."

The cabriolet trotted off, and Gill considered whooping with relief. He also considered getting drunk, but no. He had too many notes to write to the shop owners and tradesmen, informing them that further expenses incurred by the dowager or Mr. or Mrs. Thomas Summers would be the sole debt of the relevant party and no responsibility of the Lord Summerton's.

Over the next two days, he wrote dozens of those notes, in his own hand because his secretary was among the employees given holiday. He went around to Tommie's clubs and had a quiet word with the relevant staff and did the same at several gaming hells and Bond Street shops.

By midweek, Gill was ready to take himself to the family seat, read what Penelope had written all those years ago, and send the traveling coach to take her to her next abode. But when he finally sat down with a glass of brandy and letters nearly a decade old, he decided on a slight modification to that plan.

The packet arrived at the Siren's Retreat just as Penelope had run out of excuses to dither and dawdle. The time had come to take up life as a former wife who'd demanded to be set aside. Vergilius had considerately sent the traveling coach, as he'd promised he would.

A brief note accompanied a bundle of what appeared to be old letters:

My lady,

I have evicted Mama and Bella from Town and forbidden them to set foot on any Summerton property save Lychmont. Between the two of them, they waylaid letters you and I meant to exchange years ago. Bella and the dowager appear to have meddled independently, to disastrous effect, another example of the interference that has plagued us since the day we spoke our vows.

I am at the Hall and finally in possession of the missives you wrote to me all those years ago. They will always number among my dearest treasures.

Godspeed,
All my love,
Vergilius

He'd *never* received her letters? Penelope took the forward-facing seat in the traveling coach, and when the beautiful spring scenery should have claimed her attention, she was instead cast back nine years, to the loneliest, most heartbroken months of her life.

She'd lost a child. Vergilius had lost a child *and* his father within a fortnight. The old viscount's death had meant Vergilius had been compelled to leave Penelope's side and thus part from the only real support he'd had.

Penelope had written to Vergilius as a means of comforting them both, sending her love, recounting small moments filled with both grief and hope. Wishing him fortitude and expressing all of her longing for the consolation of his simple presence. *I'll come if you send for me, my lord. Physically, I am recovering from my travail, but my heart yearns for the balm of your embrace.*

She'd written to him every day for nearly a month, and all the while, Bella had told her not to pester a man newly coping with a peer's responsibilities. *Don't cling. Don't impose. Don't whine. Nobody respects a woman who's always sniffling into her handkerchief.*

"Damn her," Penelope muttered. "Damn them both to the foulest privy in hell." Penelope's anger was on behalf of herself as a much younger wife and—more significantly—on behalf of her husband. Vergilius had doubtless been told not to bother his frail, sad wife, and by the time Penelope had eventually left Town for the Hall, she *had* been frail and sad.

She'd been hurt at Gill's apparent silence, and he had been hurt at what he'd thought was her cold, self-absorbed indifference.

Not merely hurt. Husband and wife had been quietly devastated. A wedge of spite, greed, and selfishness had been driven through their marriage at the worst possible time. She read Gill's letters over twice, murmuring passages aloud.

Nighttime is the worst, when I miss you unbearably. I refuse the lure of the decanters only because I know you would be disappointed in me for indulging in temporary oblivion. You haven't that comfort, so I will borrow strength from your example.

When nobody is looking, I hug my horse, Pen. I would feel pathetic, except I know you understand what drives that impulse.

Tommie brought his oldest son along with him to the Hall. I had to leave the room when I realized the boy was on hand. I will apologize to our nephew, but I was ready to throttle Tommie. Tell me you'd have throttled him too. I am dying for word from you, Pen, any word at all.

The letters had grown shorter and shorter and less and less intimate. The last one was dated a month after the baby had died. Penelope hadn't joined her husband at the Hall for more than a month after that. Bella had had one excuse after another for why a woman recovering from childbirth must remain in Town, and by then, Penelope had long since stopped writing too.

The coach drew into an innyard, one of several stops necessary to change horses.

"The kitchen here is trustworthy, my lady," the groom told her as he handed her down. "They'd pack you some good tucker for the rest of the journey."

He was dusty from hat to boots, and Penelope realized that they'd traveled better than half the day without pausing for more than five minutes here and there to change teams. She recognized the inn—The Jolly Farmwife—as one of the usual stopping points along the route from London to the seaside.

"You and John Coachman should take some sustenance," Penelope said amid the bustle and clatter of coaches coming and going. A whip snapped as a four-in-hand left the yard, and a horse whinnied in the distance. All was commotion, shouting, trunks flying through the air, children goggling at the liveried coachmen, and riding horses swishing their tails in impatience.

Life went on, time flew, but Penelope was no longer in a tearing hurry to complete her journey.

I am dying for word from you Pen. Any word at all. She'd written nearly the same plea to her husband, along with others of the same ilk:

If you cannot see fit to summon me to the Hall, sir, at least have Tommie recall Bella to Lychmont. I am begging you, Vergilius. She said I must donate all the baby's things to the poor, and I wanted to throttle her with my bare hands.

Our bed has become too large, my darling. As lonely and vast as the sea, and—without you—nearly as cold. I climb beneath the covers and toss and turn in the darkness, because my compass and lodestone, my one sure beacon, is parted from me.

Please write, Vergilius. I am desperate for the sight of even your penmanship.

"How far are we from Summerton Hall?" she asked the groom.

"We could make it from here without another change of teams, ma'am. The distance is a little less than twelve miles. The Hall is lovely this time of year."

"It is." Penelope and her husband, ably assisted by a devoted and respected staff, had made sure of that, and yet, they always spent early spring in Town.

Not this year. Penelope had known this year had to be different, but she hadn't quite sorted out the nature of that difference. Standing in that busy innyard, Vergilius's letters now among *her* dearest treasures, she knew that Patchwork Cottage was not the change her heart had longed for.

Vergilius had read her letters. He treasured them, even now. He'd told her that for a reason. *I am dying for word from you, Pen, any word at all.*

Very well. He would have some words from her. Some more words. "Please inform John Coachman there's been a change of plans. When you and he have refreshed yourselves, we'll make for the Hall."

The groom tugged his cap. "Aye, milady. A fine idea."

A fine idea—or a completely cork-brained notion. Penelope wasn't sure which, but she could always travel on to Patchwork Cottage some other day.

As the coach passed through a familiar crossroad and journeyed onto smaller byways, Penelope turned her thoughts to the why of it all. Bella clearly wanted her oldest to become the titleholder, her next-born to be the spare. Mama-in-Law had easily fallen in with that agenda, because if Tommie was raising the heir, he'd have greater influence over and access to the viscountcy's resources.

Or perhaps the dowager simply cared more for Tommie and Bella than she did for Summerton and his lady. Perhaps Mama-in-Law resented the fall from power that dowager status implied. No matter. Vergilius had banished the interlopers, and Penelope wished them the joy of Lychmont's chaos and noise.

By late afternoon, the coach was trotting up the lime alley to Summerton Hall's front door, and some of Penelope's resolve deserted her. The Hall was so stately, situated beneath enormous maples now luminous with new foliage, its façade stretching across sixteen gleaming windows on each side of an imposing three-story portico.

According to Vergilius, a previous titleholder had decided that the road to an earldom lay in the direction of expensive architecture. An earldom had eluded the family, while the house had acquired sprawling wings, formal grounds, and other lofty honors.

A man emerged from the front door. Not the butler, not a footman.

Summerton. Penelope knew her husband's bearing, knew his stride, even knew the particular manner in which he held himself motionless. She descended from the coach without aid, because she was too impatient to wait on decorum.

"I got your letters," she said, marching up to her spouse. "After all this time..." She slowed because Vergilius was very much on his dignity. Very much. "Might we talk, my lord?"

Good God. Was he *entertaining*? Penelope abruptly felt most foolish, then chided herself for that lapse. Summerton had sent her the letters, *and all his love*. That had to count for something.

He gestured toward the door. "This is still your home, my lady."

Was there a scold in that observation? An invitation? A reassurance? Penelope could not tell, but she did know that she had things to say to the man she was still married to. She preceded him into the Hall and kept right on going, up to the suite reserved for the lord and lady of the manor.

Vergilius followed her, his mood impossible to read.

When Penelope reached the sitting room that connected the lord's bedroom and the lady's, she could barely contain herself until her husband closed the door.

"We were besieged, weren't we?" she said. "Bella was the one who told me that you were dallying with Marie Chalfont, though my dear sister-in-law was careful to never make outright accusations. She hinted, she dangled innuendo, and when she saw how upset I became, she started a regular habit of speculation about your amorous recreations."

"Until you put your foot down and stopped her from bearing more tales."

Penelope stomped across the carpet, for the first time in her life tempted to smash any handy breakables. "Your mother took up the campaign in the general case. 'A wife must not be tiresomely demanding. She must overlook her husband's passing fancies. She must hold her head up at all times.'"

"Tommie took the same tack," Vergilius said slowly. "He started with, 'Penelope is a high-strung filly,' and when I nearly gelded him for comparing you to a nervous horse, he switched to random musings on the patience a husband owes a difficult wife."

"I have been difficult," Penelope said. "I am sorry for that, my lord, but I am not sorry you tossed those women from our home."

Vergilius cocked his head, his expression wary. "*Our* home, Penelope?"

Penelope had put that caution in his eyes, that guarded, weary self-possession, though her folly had been aided by a trio of worthless bounders and some very bad marital luck.

"I found the green ormer. It's gorgeous." She'd spent many a passing mile holding the seashell in one hand and the letters in the other.

"Our week by the sea deserved a memento."

"Our marriage deserved a chance, Vergilius. Our love deserved a chance."

He came a few steps closer, but remained out of hugging range.

"No argument there, my lady. I am still too angry to write to my brother. Tommie might not have hatched up the mischief that was unleashed against us, but neither did he stop it."

"I think I am calmed down," Penelope said, "then I recall another comment Bella made, about what a comfort it must be to you to know that the succession is secure. About how ladies cannot resist a handsome man with wealth and a title. I vow I will plant her a facer if ever I should meet her again."

This was not what Penelope had come here to say, and yet, she was *so angry.*

"Say something, Vergilius. I am spouting off like a temperance preacher amid a flock of gin drunks, and you are back to being your silent, lordly self. I already miss the man who joined me for a week by the sea, and I am very much afraid I will miss him for the rest of my life."

Penelope's husband studied her for a long, silent moment, then held out his hand. "I've missed you too. Let's repair to the balcony, shall we? Spring can be such a pretty time here at the Hall. I'd forgotten that."

Penelope let him lead her to the balcony. For the first year of their marriage, they'd practically lived on that balcony. Taken morning tea out there, watched the moon rise, chosen names for the baby...

Penelope took the wicker chair on the shady end, while Vergilius remained standing. He faced her, his hips braced against the railing. He was a strikingly handsome man, but the setting sun also revealed him to be tired.

"I'm glad you came, Penelope, but why are you here?"

This was not the reception of a man who'd made one last, dramatic bid to save his marriage and who was overjoyed to see his errant wife on his doorstep. This was an honest question, and it deserved an honest answer. In the past week, Penelope had learned that such discussions, while painful, could also heal and nourish the spirit.

"I am here because I love you, and because... because I hope you still love me."

Summerton sank into the other chair. "I do love you, Penelope. I absolutely do. I love you, I admire you, and I will pray for your well-being every night so long as there is breath in my body."

"Is there a 'but,' my lord?"

He scrubbed a hand over his face. Somewhere in the vast wood that flanked the far side of the deer park, a nightingale was anticipating nightfall. A doe grazed along the tree line, and in the flower beds lining the path to the stable, tulips were putting on a colorful display.

The scene was lovely and peaceful, and Penelope would miss it for the rest of her life. "Tell me, Vergilius. We've come far in the past week. Please just tell me the truth."

Gill's heart beat a slow tattoo, and the moment—just another pretty spring evening in the English countryside—took on solemn significance. Despite having spent hours in a rocking coach, despite being in a long-overdue temper, Penelope looked as serene and sweet as ever. The sunshine turned her hair coppery. An errant breeze teased at wisps that had escaped her chignon.

She was beautiful, but was she *his*? "Do you recall telling me that you were afraid, Penelope?"

She nodded. "Of making the biggest mistake of my life."

"Your courage and honesty have always been dear to me. I will try to be equally brave and honest now. I am afraid too."

"Afraid to trust me?"

"In a sense, but mostly afraid to trust myself. To give you privacy was hard, Pen. To spend night after night listening to windy speeches about nothing, or standing up with women who now look young enough to be my daughters... That was hard. Lonely. I know now that you were lonely too."

"Vastly." She let that one word speak volumes. Her letters had referred to loneliness as vast as the sea, and she'd navigated that ocean without him.

"Every time I found myself outside your door late at night, I'd confront a question: Could I stand to lose another child? Could I ask you to face that possibility? I would wait there, hoping and wishing that the door would be opened from the other side, because I wanted you to find the answer for me."

"That door never opened."

"Today, you did not wait for me to hand you down from the traveling coach, my lady."

Something shifted in Penelope's gaze. "I stood outside your bedroom door too. Waiting, wishing, praying. I never want to lose another child, Vergilius."

"Is there a 'but,' Penelope? I can live with you in a chaste relationship, if that's what you want."

She made a face that suggested somebody had boiled the tea, *and* the cakes were stale. "That is not what I want. I want to be brave and married. One or the other won't serve."

"I want to be brave and married, too, Penelope, because I realized that what I truly feared was losing *you*. Losing a child is awful, losing a parent is sad, no matter that it's nigh inevitable. But I got it into my head that if you and I reconciled, and life handed us another blow, then the last of your formidable strength would give way. The last of my strength. I could have the ceasefire we called a marriage, or I could risk losing even that. I took the inadequate sure thing over the greater, riskier prize."

Penelope regarded him as if he were a work of art, a sculpture full of subtle complexities, not merely a husband trying to speak from the heart to his wife.

"Half a love," she said. "Like half a loaf being better than none. And we had a Greek chorus to remind us that a ceasefire was all we could hope for. Do you want more children?"

Gill had pondered that question until his heart ached with it. "I want *you*, Penelope. We honestly do not need to have children. Tommie and Bella have at least spared us that burden."

He scrubbed a hand over his face. "I want a marriage where you and I can discuss that issue," he went on, "among many others. How much we entertain and why. Who our friends are—our real friends, not merely the acquaintances happy to show up for fancy dinners that leave us both exhausted. I want your help with the renovations here at the Hall, because I have no head for what makes a space pretty. I want your friendship and your trust, and if that means I cannot have your body, I will be grateful for the bounty you do share with me."

"But what do you *need*, Vergilius? What do you dream of?"

"You," he said, going down on one knee beside her chair. "To have and to hold, for richer or for poorer, in sickness and in health. We have suffered much, Penelope, and I'm sure if we remain together, we will encounter more storms. I am asking..." He took her hand and kept his grip light by effort. "I am *imploring* you for a chance to weather those storms together. If we are joined in love and courage, then I am confident that we can always find our way safely to shore, together."

He had not answered her question about children, but Gill realized his answer did not signify. *Their* answer signified, the one they arrived at *together*, the one that felt right to *both of them*.

Penelope stroked her fingers through his hair. "I will not know how to go on, Vergilius. What shall we say to each other at breakfast?"

"Pass the butter? You look lovely this morning? I don't expect we will ever again be that besotted young couple who honeymooned by the sea, Penelope, but we can be us." He was about to get to his feet, bid her to consider the notion of a reconciliation, and inform her of his decision, but that wasn't right.

This was not a choice one of them made and the other yielded to, but what did that leave for a couple who had nearly parted for all time?

Gill had no answers. He had only the abiding conviction that losing Penelope would wound him beyond bearing, and yet, he would never force her to remain by his side. The silence stretched, and Gill learned what true heartbreak meant. The inability to rise, the inability to reason. The inability to struggle on for even one more moment.

Losing Penelope had been his worst fear. Now it was to be his never-ending reality. He dragged a breath in, his surrender that of a drowning man yielding to the embrace of the unrelenting sea.

Penelope slid to her knees beside him. She was quiet for a moment, her head on Gill's shoulder.

"I think of those two young people who married ten years ago," she said softly. "That pair had no idea of the tempests they would face, or the forces that would conspire against them. I am so angry and heartbroken for that young couple, I can barely speak."

She did fall silent, and Gill put his arms around her. She was on her knees, curled against his side, and that allowed his heart to keep beating.

"Those young lovers would tell me," she went on, "to let my heartache go out on the receding tide. To reach again for the lovely man I married, the brave man I married, the man with whom I can share a wonderful future if I am courageous, and honest, and true to him."

They clung to each other for a small eternity, both joy and trepidation trickling into Gill's soul, along with a new kind of peace. Not the peace of a quiet, private moment, but the peace of having come safely into port after a long, stormy crossing.

A peace earned through courage and tribulation, through love and fortitude.

"I am still afraid," Penelope said, wiping at her cheek. "What if we were to lose a toddler? A son gone off to war? A daughter in childbirth? Life presents a series of potential terrors once tragedy has struck."

Gill helped her to her feet, took one of the chairs, and pulled her into his lap. "Then we must love as fiercely as we can and seize our joys with both hands, Pen. I would not want to erase the past, because I learned much in the years of our estrangement, but I promise you, *I vow to you*, nothing and nobody will ever again distract me from guarding our marriage. If we do lose another child—God forbid—then we will endure the loss together."

"We are agreed," she said. "Nothing and nobody will ever again distract me from guarding our marriage and guarding you. I could not stand to lose you again, Vergilius. Not ever."

They cuddled in the chair until Penelope had taken a catnap, and Gill had begun composing a letter to MacMillan, explaining that the staff could have the rest of the Season off, with pay, because Lord and Lady Summerton were taking an extended holiday.

When Penelope woke up, Gill put that idea to her. They watched the sun set as they discussed an itinerary that included the Lakes, the Scottish Borders, and even the Highlands and Hebrides.

Gill did not particularly care where they went, and he sensed Penelope's ideas were more suggestions than goals, but that was not the point. The point was that wherever they traveled—on a second wedding journey, to look in on their various holdings, or simply to hack out on a spring morning—they would make the journey together, hand in hand, husband and wife, best friends and lovers, forever and ever, amen.

A SPINSTER BY THE SEA

To those who dwell in hope

The Siren's Retreat Novella Quartet

A Tryst by the Sea—Grace Burrowes
An Affair by the Sea—Erica Ridley
A Spinster by the Sea—Grace Burrowes
Love Letters by the Sea—Erica Ridley

CHAPTER ONE

"Can't fault Miss Baxter's bloodlines." Lord Corbett Hobbs held up an amethyst-encrusted hand mirror and ran his tongue over his teeth. "Related to two earls, one on each side. Mama says she has good hips. The fellows admit she has a delectable arse."

Augustus, Duke of Tindale, glanced at the clock. "If you are mentioning your bride's fundament to me less than an hour before the wedding, you are at least half foxed." Were Hobbs sober, Augustus might have bothered to remonstrate with him further.

Hobbs passed the hand mirror to a silent valet. "Last night's celebration became this morning's fortification. You must agree that my bride is not the stuff of love's young dreams. Five-and-twenty if she's a day, and appallingly well-read."

Augustus took the blue delphinium boutonniere from the valet. "Your bride is intelligent, which gives me some hope for your progeny. Hold still." Miss Anne Baxter was not only intelligent, she also had a good sense of humor, plenty of patience—she'd need a generous supply married to Hobbs—and a dowry that had earned her the hand of no less than a ducal spare.

"Mama said the same thing." Hobbs tipped up his chin as

Augustus affixed the flower to the groom's lapel. "That my children will need to inherit their wits from their mama, to which Papa replied that I would supply the looks. I do cut quite a fine figure, don't I?"

Physically, Lord Corbett Hobbs was masculine perfection. Just over six feet, blond, broad-shouldered, and blessed with exquisite features right down to a nose that knew to keep to the noble side of aquiline. Compared to his lordship, Augustus felt like a plow horse trudging beside a prancing thoroughbred colt.

Miss Baxter had earned the enmity of every matchmaker in Mayfair, Paris, and Berlin by snapping up that ducal colt. How did the young lady feel about her supposed good fortune?

"You are all that is manly perfection," Augustus said. "Where's your hat?"

Hobbs looked to his valet, who bowed. "A moment, Your Grace. His lordship has yet to decide between the cooing dove and the Spanish moonbeams."

"I'm not manly perfection," Hobbs said when the valet had closed the door. "I'm nervous as hell, Tindale. I esteem Miss Baxter greatly and all that, but Marie is threatening to toss me over, and Papa has said he won't pay my gambling debts until I produce a son. Do you know how long it takes for a baby to show up? And the first three will likely be girls, and that means Miss Baxter and I cannot live entirely apart, and this whole marriage business rather overwhelms one."

Hobbs's mistress was said to keep her jewelry not in a pretty little box, but rather, in a sizable sea chest, so skillfully did she play upon her current protector's insecurities. She threatened twice a week to toss Hobbs over, and the betting books were full of wagers on the topic of her next protector.

"You could be a father by this time next year," Augustus said, "and prenuptial jitters are to be expected. Besides, once you're married, you can pay off your own gambling debts."

Miss Baxter's settlements were yet one more reason the matchmakers resented her, though a fortune that size ought to have inspired Corbett to *attempt* a period of fidelity.

Augustus, having come into his title unexpectedly, knew all about polite society's cruelty to those they deemed outsiders. Miss Baxter bore up with good grace, and Augustus had often wanted to ask her how she remained so civil in the face of such meanness.

"Besides," Augustus added, "marriage should be overwhelming."

"But in a good way." Hobbs surveyed himself in the cheval mirror. "In a wonderful way. One ought to be at least friends with one's spouse. I realize I'm being romantic—Mama says I'm being ridiculous—except that Miss Baxter is always reading, and she doesn't let a fellow win any verbal horse races just because he's the fellow. I have this dreadful sense that I amuse her." Hobbs shifted his stance, presenting his left side to the mirror. "You wouldn't understand."

Augustus understood all too well. Hobbs was no scholar, nor was he cruel by nature, but from boyhood on, he'd expected the privileges of his station to precede him.

And they had, until he'd been matched with Miss Baxter. She was kind, but she did not suffer fools, did not dissemble for the sake of currying favor, and did not simper and blush the better to impersonate a harmless nitwit.

"I understand that you and Miss Baxter are to wed, and I have less than one hour to get you to the altar."

Hobbs took out a silver flask embossed with the ducal crest and tipped it to his lips. "Damned thing is empty. Spare a fellow a nip, Tindale. Gin would be best—doesn't linger on the breath."

"I have no spirits with me. You'll find plenty to drink at the wedding breakfast."

The valet returned, carrying a pair of identical gray hats. "Spanish moonbeams," he said, holding up one on the right. "Cooing dove."

"The cooing dove has a bit of pink to it." Hobbs said, fingering the brim. "Does that clash with my boutonniere?"

Gray did not clash with blue. Even Augustus knew that much. "You won't be wearing the hat during the ceremony, Hobbs."

"Give me the Spanish moonbeams," Hobbs said, holding still so the valet could place the hat just so upon his head. "That will do. You may be excused, Benner."

"Congratulations on the happy occasion, my lord." Benner bowed and withdrew.

"Let's be off, shall we?" Augustus said, resisting the urge to toss Hobbs over his shoulder and convey him bodily into the coach that had been waiting out front for nearly twenty minutes.

"I don't have a good feeling about this," Hobbs said, pulling on a pair of gloves from the half dozen laid out on his vanity. "Truly, I do not, Tindale. I'm only the spare. Why should I have to marry so soon?"

Augustus suspected that Hobbs's nuptials were intended to save his parents the bother of managing an easily bored spare-about-Town. Miss Baxter could be trusted to take on that thankless task, though it would be a waste of her talents.

"You are nearly thirty years of age. Time to settle down," Augustus replied. "Besides, your brother has no sons yet. Do your bit, and your parents will spoil your offspring rotten."

"They no longer spoil *me* rotten," Hobbs said, stalking along beside Augustus. "My quarterly allowance wouldn't keep a Quaker in cravats. It's humiliating."

"Miss Baxter's settlements will buy you all the cravats you could ever wear." Augustus offered that placatory observation when he instead wanted to knock some sense into his friend. Hobbs, though, had been the sole hand extended to Augustus in welcome at public school.

Augustus knew now that Hobbs had been indulging in a whim. The expected thing would have been for Hobbs to sneer at Augustus, as all the other lordlings had. But Hobbs was a *ducal* lordling, and thus when he decided to take a benevolent interest in the hulking new boy, the rest of the pecking order had moderated their insults.

"Do you ever wish you were still just a solicitor?" Hobbs asked as he accepted a walking stick from the butler at the door. "Ever wish you were still a plain mister?"

"If I were a plain mister, then two of my cousins would still be extant, so yes, I often wish I'd been spared the title."

Both of those cousins had been healthy young men, but only the elder, Charles, had taken a wife. She'd not provided him with an heir in the short years of their marriage, and thus Augustus, a lowly if ambitious solicitor, had been elevated to the peerage.

"I wish I could be spared matrimony," Hobbs said, glancing around the soaring white marble foyer of his parents' home. "Wish I could take Marie by the hand and spirit her across the border. We'd live in a cottage, and everybody would secretly envy me for my boldness."

What sort of society allowed a ducal spare nearing thirty to remain as self-centered and ignorant as an eight-year-old?

"You can spirit Miss Baxter across the border on your wedding journey," Augustus said as the clocks in the house all started bonging the half hour. "Right now, let's get you as far as the church."

The butler held the door open, his expression beaming genial respect.

"Let me refill my flask," Hobbs said. "The decanters in the library will do. Won't be a moment." He spun away and jogged down the carpeted corridor.

Augustus waited five interminable minutes, while the butler held the door open, and the horses at the foot of the steps stomped the occasional hoof. Three streets away, Miss Anne Baxter was doubtless expressing her own impatience in a far more genteel manner.

"Best fetch him, Your Grace," the butler said. "Lord Corbett was never quite as stalwart as his brother. Always wanted a bit of encouragement."

"He wants a good hiding," Augustus muttered. He made his way to the library, all manner of threats piling up in his head, *I'll marry her myself* at the top of the list, not that Anne Baxter deserved such a fate.

Augustus yanked open the library door and was greeted with the utter silence of thick carpets, venerable portraiture, and thousands of books that hadn't been read in the past fifty years. The sole movement in the cavernous room was a white lace curtain wafting gently before the open French doors.

The incoming tide created an undulating line of white against the sand, while gulls wheeling overhead flashed white in the brilliant blue sky. Anne's wedding dress had been white, an unusual color and the very worst choice Aunt Daphne could have made.

White for innocence. Anne had vowed never to wear white again, not that she'd be donning any more wedding dresses.

"You will ruin your complexion." Cousin Helen plunked a wide-brimmed hat on Anne's head. "I understand the need to blow retreat, and I grasp why you chose the seaside to regroup, but if you neglect your appearance, Lord Corbett's defection will become an insurmountable setback."

Helen had not neglected her appearance. She was widowed and past thirty, but had the complexion of a renaissance maiden and a willowy figure any debutante would envy. Helen was a benevolent golden goddess, while Anne's hair could aspire to being blondish only in strong sunlight. Anne was also too curvy and incapable of simpering.

A maid emerged from the cottage and set a tea tray on the terrace's wrought-iron table. She bobbed a curtsey and withdrew without tarrying. Rejected brides did not exactly trail streams of glory compared to some of the dashing blades and merry widows staying at the Siren's Retreat inn itself.

"I tell you these things," Helen went on, taking the other seat at the table, "because I love you, and I hate Lord Corbett Hobbs. I am your most loyal cousin. We must make a list of eligibles who also hate him."

Helen was Anne's only cousin. "Nobody hates Lord Corbett." Anne certainly didn't. His lordship had shown some spine for once and run off with his mistress. For him, that would become an amusing peccadillo, while Anne's future lay in tatters.

Three days after having abandoned London, Anne was trying to care about that future and not having much luck. The sea was better company than polite society could ever be—the sea and some good books—and the whole match with Lord Corbett had been Aunt Daphne's plan.

Her *best plan yet*, as if the disaster with Lord Hume Billingsley hadn't been fiasco enough.

"Eat something," Helen said. "You must keep up your strength. You think this is the end of the world, and I grant you the situation is dire, but you are nothing if not resilient."

Anne took a bite of some sort of fruit tart, mostly to placate Helen. "Resilience has lost its appeal, my dear. Maybe next year, maybe in five years, I will venture forth again, but for now, all I want is to be left in peace."

Helen poured out, chose a tart for herself, and sat back with the sort of measuring expression that boded ill for any cousin craving solitude.

"You will not be left in peace," she said. "You will be left in disgrace. Twice jilted, despite your fortune. This is not a matter to be shrugged aside like a misplaced hatpin."

The tide was coming in, the waves crashing onshore growing louder, and how Anne loved to watch the relentless, restless power of the sea. Perhaps she'd take an ocean voyage or go exploring as Lady Hester Stanhope had.

"It has been three days," Anne said, as patiently as she could. "Less than seventy-two hours since I was left literally at the altar. Will you not give me a week, a fortnight, any time at all to regain my bearings?"

Helen, though a cousin, had graciously taken on the role of older sister when Anne had been orphaned. That Helen was now also widowed and a mother twice over had at some point made her a universal authority on Anne's best interests, even eclipsing Aunt Daphne's expertise on the same difficult subject.

A woman of five-and-twenty did not need a big sister as a child of thirteen had. Anne was also growing skeptical of universal authorities in general, particularly when their solution to every problem was an advantageous match.

Helen stirred her tea. "But you must get back on the horse, Anne. Surely you see that. The longer you hide here at the seashore, the worse the talk will grow. Brighton is nothing if not rife with gossips."

"Precisely. While I am enjoying my seaside respite, some other unfortunate lady will be jilted, or a lordling will be hounded from England by his duns, and I will be forgotten."

Helen set down her tea cup and rose. "You will be forgotten, but never forgiven. You know what they'll say, Anne. A woman with *that much money* couldn't bring even a dunderheaded spare up to scratch. Jilted twice. You aren't hideous to look upon or given to tippling, and you haven't any vices, other than your books. Society will conclude you are used goods or worse."

"Worse? Does that imply that I perhaps occasionally think for myself? That my fortune has thrived quite well in my own hands? That the dangers and suffering of repeated confinements—the mortal dangers—have not enticed me into becoming a husband's convenience-in-residence?"

In the midst of that tirade, Anne had snatched off her hat and pushed to her feet, though she was tired to her bones and had been forever.

"You are bitter," Helen said, a hint of relenting in her tone. "I was bitter, too, when Horace died. The nerve of the man, falling from his horse and breaking his neck, leaving me alone with two babies. The anger carried me through much, but then the sorrow and the solicitors had to be dealt with. I know you are disappointed, Anne, but this, too, shall pass."

No, it would not. As Helen had said, if Anne walked into a ballroom five years hence and was as yet unmarried, she would still be the subject of whispers and speculation. Why had two men, both in need of her fortune, spectacularly rejected a wellborn, reasonably comely heiress?

The fault surely had to be with the heiress. Of course it must. It had to be.

"This, too, shall not pass in three days," Anne said, "and I deserve at least a fortnight to decide upon my next steps. The Season will still be in progress, and God knows I will still be an object of talk two weeks hence."

Helen considered her, a humor-the-difficult-cousin sort of inspection. "Very well, a fortnight here at Rose Cottage, and then once more unto the breach. Do put on your hat, dearest. You will never successfully storm Mayfair sporting a crop of freckles. I'm off to make up a foursome with some other ladies in the inn's cardroom. I will see you in time to change for supper."

"Enjoy the whist," Anne said, setting the hat on the table. Helen let that petty display go unremarked and took herself off to gossip and gamble away the afternoon.

"I am an ungrateful wretch," Anne muttered, wrapping four small tarts in a linen napkin and tucking them into her pocket. "Helen will try to limit the damage the best she can, while I..."

Anne's gaze went to the surf pounding the beach below the cottage. How lucky men were that they could take ship, sail away, and see the wonders of the world. Anne could not go to sea, but she could go for a walk. She wasn't quite foolish enough to venture down to the beach without a hat, though she did leave her ribbons trailing and eschewed a parasol.

Once on the sand, she took off her shoes and stockings and was lost in the sensation of the water lapping at her ankles when a vigorous gust of wind tore the straw hat from her head. In a stroke of divine benevolence, her millinery came to rest on dry sand.

Anne gathered up her hems and was waiting for the most recent wave to recede when she noticed that a man stood two yards from her wayward hat. His dark hair riffled in the breeze, and he, too, had discarded boots and stockings.

Anne's next impression was one of size. This fellow was tall even standing barefoot, and he bristled with muscle and confidence. Not a farm lad, not with that fine lawn shirt and those exquisitely tailored riding breeches. He'd draped his coat over his arm—a beautiful dark blue merino—and his cravat sported a touch more lace than strictest fashion dictated.

Anne shaded her eyes with her hand as the intruder sketched her a slight bow.

"Miss Baxter, good day."

Oh, ye gods and little fishes. That Hades-at-his-forge voice, which all the public school education in England could not make into a gentlemanly drawl.

"Tindale," Anne said, her minuscule store of pleasure in the day washing straight out to sea. "Of all the dukes in all of creation, why must you be the one to disturb my solitude?"

He snatched up her hat and tossed it to her with a flick of his wrist. Anne caught it, though she nearly had to give up her grip on her skirts to do so.

"Your lucky day, Miss Baxter, and before you go storming off in high dudgeon, allow me to say that you're better off without him, and he would have bored you silly."

That was not what Anne had expected Tindale to say, but then, Tindale was a quiet sort, new to his title, and he seldom said much of anything.

"We are on a beach, Your Grace. High dudgeon with my skirts bunched up and my feet bare is beyond me." To say nothing of a nose likely turning redder by the moment.

Anne waded free of the water and let those skirts drop. "You truly think I'm better off in disgrace?"

"Not in disgrace," he said. "*Free*, and how I envy you that privilege. You must be profoundly relieved not to face a lifetime of humoring Lord Corbett's endless conceits. Let's walk, shall we?"

The beach was in plain sight of Rose Cottage, where Anne and Helen were biding, and also visible from the inn itself. Walking with Tindale would in no way be improper.

Nor, Anne suspected, would it be wise. He'd offered her the one gift she'd never thought to have from Lord Corbett's best man and the Season's most eligible peer—the truth.

"I am mortally relieved," she said, taking the duke's arm, "and I cannot muster even a scintilla of guilt about that. What brings you to the shore, Your Grace, and how long are you staying?"

He ambled along, as relaxed as if they promenaded around a drawing room at Devonshire House. "Not long enough, Miss Baxter. When I contemplate what awaits me back in Mayfair, I must admit I'm not staying at the shore nearly long enough."

"That makes two of us."

CHAPTER TWO

If Augustus lived to be a doddering old man, he would never forget the sight of Anne Baxter wading in the surf, her skirts bunched not decorously at midcalf, but drawn clear up to her knees. Her legs were muscular and shapely, though Tindale had spared them only a glance.

Her face had captured his whole attention. She was not classically beautiful—no delicate retroussé nose, porcelain complexion, or limpid blue eyes. Miss Baxter was a honey-blonde with a strong nose and a direct emerald gaze.

Her eyes had been closed, her face tipped up to the breeze, her whole being absorbed with the sensations of cold salt water and brilliant spring sunshine on bare skin. She had been both worshipping nature and a testament to its glories.

Odd thoughts for a duke who still had the mind of a solicitor, and Augustus had stood gaping on the beach much longer than either a duke or a solicitor—or a gentleman—should have.

"I ought to have left you your privacy," he said as they ambled along the packed sand near the water's edge. "I had no idea you'd come to the Siren's Retreat to hide."

"I am not hiding, Your Grace. I am pondering my course going forward."

She was hiding, of a certainty, and doing it properly—with lots of pride and a few handy euphemisms. "The ocean makes pondering easy," Augustus replied. "Puts matters in perspective. We see but a tiny sliver of its horizon. How grand are the troubles we contemplate compared to such vast splendor?"

"Are you trying to console me, Your Grace?"

Augustus had acquired the ducal title months ago—or it had acquired him—and he still found formal address jarring. A plain mister knew his place in the world, while a duke was an oddity even in that rarefied collection of decorative specimens known as the British peerage.

"I am trying," Augustus said, "to make polite conversation with you. Be patient with me, Miss Baxter. I am new to my honors."

"Polite conversation goes like this, Your Grace. 'Miss Baxter, what a pleasure to see you. The sunshine at the shore is always so bright, isn't it?' Then I say, 'Wonderfully so after a London winter.' You reply, 'But the breeze can be a trifle brisk, don't you agree?' And I respond... Come, Your Grace, give it a go. What would I say if I were being polite?"

She described polite conversation like a barrister's courtroom debate with king's counsel. Everybody taking a turn bloviating about the obvious. Whack the shuttlecock, air the counterargument.

"You say," he replied, "that you find fresh air in moderation invigorating. Then somebody brings up the topic of the last time it rained or the next time it might rain or the possibility that we need rain, and we all smile inanely."

"It will get easier," Miss Baxter said. "My parents had the bad grace to depart the earthly realm when I was thirteen. I was the much-indulged only child of a pair of unconventional thinkers. In the summer, I seldom wore shoes between one Sunday service and the next. I went from that to... Aunt Daphne and Uncle Potter, who set great store by order and decorum."

"You do not?" Anne Baxter had stood up with fortune hunters, bachelor peers, and everything in between and treated them all to the same lovely smile. Augustus had never asked her to dance, in part because he did not want that smile aimed at him.

Distant and gracious both, with only a hint of arch humor. A sword and shield. A strategy produced for a battlefield populated with gossips, matchmakers, and rakes.

"I am an heiress," Miss Baxter said. "This fate befell me when I turned fifteen, and my uncle Thomas went to his reward. I had had a decent portion before that from my parents. I wasn't a charity case, but I went from marginalized to ostracized. One learns to be unobtrusive at the watering hole, whether one is an antelope or a lioness."

What an odd—and apt—analogy.

"And how does one go on at the watering hole if one is an elephant?" Augustus asked as they approached the rocks that defined the western end of the beach. "I walk into a room, and it's as if the very clocks change how they tick because a duke has arrived."

"The elephants are invariably dignified, but I suspect they go on however they please to. We have established that I have come to the seaside to plan my strategy for dealing with Lord Corbett's defection. What brings you here, Your Grace?"

"You might not admit to hiding, but I will," Augustus said. "My godmother is holding a house party, an intermission in the social Season. Her entertainments are an exclusive respite for those who can eschew the Mayfair whirl for a fortnight—or so she claimed when I was fool enough to accept her invitation."

"Your godmother is Lady Deschamps?"

"None other, but too late, I realized I am not attending a house party, Miss Baxter. I have arrived at a horse auction. A dozen heiresses are accosting me on the way to breakfast and squeezing my arm as if considering whether to bet on me in tomorrow's fourth race. I cannot walk into the conservatory or read a single paragraph on the terrace without... I am whining."

"Lamenting," Miss Baxter said, clapping a hand over the crown of her hat as a strong gust blew past. "Lady Deschamps is a noted matchmaker. Surely you grasped that when you agreed to attend this horse auction?"

"Are you laughing at me?"

"Yes, and at the situation. I am now the twice-jilted pariah who will be invited everywhere to provide fuel for gossip, but nobody will ever again offer for me. You are the former solicitor raised to the peerage, and any woman in Mayfair would be delighted to accept your proposal for reasons that likely baffle the solicitor. We will both have many opportunities to socialize, and we would both rather not. What is it you'd be reading if the ladies left you in peace long enough to finish a paragraph?"

"Restoration comedies," Augustus replied. "Such wit and insight all dressed up as shockingly vulgar farce. Charles II was right to reopen the theaters, and for that alone, I respect him."

"Few do, at least not for that. Who is your favorite playwright?"

As Augustus and Miss Baxter wandered down the shore, the discussion wandered as well, from the witty Aphra Behn to William Wycherley to John Vanbrugh. Miss Baxter was thunderously well-read and a strong advocate for the theater as a means of empowering women.

Not an aspect of dramatic history Augustus had considered previously. "We have debated away half the afternoon," he said as he and Miss Baxter sat side by side on his coat.

They occupied a sun-warmed rock at the western end of the beach, and Augustus was pathetically sorry to see the discussion end.

"And a pleasant afternoon it has been, Your Grace." Miss Baxter rose and swatted at her skirts. "You've helped me forget for a time that I have a muddle to sort out. I wish you luck with the heiresses."

"I will need more than luck to evade capture, Miss Baxter. They are an enterprising lot."

"Are you being polite, Your Grace?" Miss Baxter resumed her place beside him, her gaze on the little cottage that occupied the promontory over the beach.

"Yes. These women are determined and arrogant, as if I should be thrilled to have gained their notice."

"They dance exquisitely," Miss Baxter said. "They dress in the first stare, and they speak a language of innuendo and insult that you can barely grasp. Put them in breeches, and they'd be polite society's eligibles. I'm sorry, Your Grace. Nobody should have to spend two minutes, much less two weeks, in such company. Perhaps if you put it about that you have a dread disease, they might desist."

She was serious, and the idea actually had some merit. "You considered that strategy?"

"Briefly. One must not tempt fate."

Her gaze went to the distant silvery horizon, and for a moment, Augustus would swear the ruthlessly self-possessed Miss Baxter was near tears. Then the breeze lashed the scarlet ribbon of her hat across her cheek, and her expression became again the serene regard of a woman whose affairs were quite in order.

"Who was he?" Augustus asked.

She shook her head. "Just a lovely fellow, a long time ago. Consumption. Once he realized he would not recover, he took himself off to some Greek island and told me to think of him fondly."

"You would have gone to that Greek island with him."

"I begged..." Miss Baxter fell silent, and Augustus was certain she had never begged anybody for anything since parting from that ailing young man. "So you see, Your Grace, I am, in fact, thrice-jilted. Lord Corbett decamping with the fair Marie was simply tradition upheld, though it's not a tradition I intend to participate in any longer."

Augustus wanted to take Miss Baxter's hand, to put an arm around her shoulders. He settled for patting her wrist.

"When Marie—whom we ought not to be mentioning—realizes that her devoted swain is pockets to let, she'll toss him aside like last week's porridge. He'll come crawling back to Town, hat in hand—the Spanish moonbeams top hat, not the cooing dove—and you will have a good laugh at his expense."

"No, I will not," Miss Baxter said, getting to her feet and

collecting her boots and stockings. "I wish him well, and I wish you well too, Your Grace. Thank you again for a lovely chat."

"I am new to my honors," Augustus said, rising, "but I know enough to see you to your door, Miss Baxter."

"Afraid the coastal trade will haul me off to the Barbary pirates?" She gazed out to sea, where not so much as a dinghy sailed the ocean blue.

Augustus was not afraid of pirates, but neither did he want to part company with Miss Baxter, and he positively loathed the thought of returning to dear Godmama's horse auction.

"There is no coastal trade in these parts," he said, gathering up boots and jacket to fall in beside her. "Nowhere to reliably hide the goods close to shore without being seen, and the tides and reefs make landing on the available beaches difficult. You are safe from pirates, Miss Baxter." But not from fortune hunters, impecunious spares, or malicious gossips. "I'd like your word on something."

She marched along the waterline, a far cry from the meandering pace they'd set before. "I am fresh out of vows, Your Grace."

"Assure me you won't do anything rash, Miss Baxter. Don't think to go sea-bathing with rocks sewn into your pockets or toss yourself from the nearest cliff."

She paused at the foot of the trail that led up to the pretty cottage. "If I were that given to melodrama, I would have tried swimming to Greece."

"You loved him?"

"I was seventeen. I loved him with the desperation that typically afflicts people of that age." A statement of fact, with a hint of old bewilderment beneath it. "Gossip and slander do not trouble me, Your Grace. I will find a way forward eventually. You must assure me you will not do anything rash at your godmother's house party."

He did take her hand, the better to assist her up the slope of the path. "Such as?"

"Proposing to the least vexatious of the lot. If you are presented with a half-dozen possibilities, you begin to think that one or two of them *might* do, and then you become so weary of being chased that might-do becomes won't-be-so-bad. Next thing you know, you've pledged yourself for life to a henwit whose best features are good personal hygiene and an excellent singing voice."

The fair Lady Arethusa Hambleton was a fine soprano. That Augustus had noticed this detail suggested Miss Baxter's warning was timely.

"I will do nothing rash," he said. "You will do nothing rash. Will you walk again by the shore tomorrow, Miss Baxter?"

They approached the small stone dwelling where she'd come to do her seaside pondering. Rose Cottage, one of several on the grounds of the Siren's Retreat inn, which sat on the far side of a grove of handsome elms.

"Tomorrow at, say, two of the clock, Your Grace?"

"Weather permitting. The young ladies are napping at that hour, or off conjuring spells to part me from my bachelorhood."

Augustus escorted Miss Baxter up the steps to her front door. The view here was peaceful and the feeling quite private. The property was likely in demand for honeymooning couples, which was neither here nor there. The Siren's Retreat was said to be a place to find true love, though Miss Baxter was proof that for some, peace and privacy were the more powerful draw.

"Another walk by the water would be lovely," Miss Baxter said. "In fact, I will look forward to it. Thank you for the discussion of Restoration comedies. The topic is relevant to my current circumstances." She kissed Augustus's cheek and disappeared into her cottage.

He stood on the covered porch, considering the sea below and what had just passed between him and Miss Anne Baxter. They had merely talked, mostly about old plays, but also about... life. About lost love, scheming heiresses, and compromises regretted.

Augustus wandered back down to the beach, in no particular hurry. Not until he was once again properly attired in boots and morning coat and making his way through Godmama's formal garden did he have a label for what he was feeling.

For months, his internal landscape had been painted in colors of resignation. He'd resigned himself to attending committee meetings, London entertainments, and even—what *had* he been thinking?—a house party by the sea. He was resigned, which was a careful way of saying he lived in dread. Some obligations were more onerous than others, but for more than half a year, he'd missed the sense of anticipation that a solicitor's work had given him.

Solve the client's problem.

Negotiate an agreement.

Render the terms in unassailably precise language.

Instead, his life had become Your-Grace-must-this, and but-of-course-a-duke-would-never-do-that. His valet and secretary, employees of the previous duke, spewed a litany of rules, restrictions, and obligations.

A house party by the sea had offered him hope of a respite, a fiction that had doubtless figured in Godmama's strategy.

For an hour on the beach, Augustus had forgotten he was a duke, and when he contemplated another hour in Miss Baxter's company, his anticipation was laced with that almost forgotten boon, *joy*. He *rejoiced* to think of his plans for tomorrow afternoon and would count the hours until he could once again walk along the shore with Miss Anne Baxter.

"A house party mid-Season," Helen said, pacing the confines of the cottage's front sitting room as a maid cleared away the lunch dishes. "That takes daring. Two weeks of fresh air is supposed to provide an intermission to the Mayfair madness." She sent Anne a brooding look. "Lady Deschamps has doubtless established a new trend. Only the most select guests can afford to miss an entire fortnight of the Season."

The design of Rose Cottage was simple. A sitting room/kitchen served as the humble equivalent of a great hall, while two bedrooms—one commodious, the other smaller—flanked the central space. A terrace on the seaward side of the building was both sheltered from the wind and blessed with a magnificent view.

Anne liked Rose Cottage's compactness and practicality, while Helen described it as poky and quaint. The maid bobbed a silent curtsey and disappeared through the side door with her basket of dishes.

Anne had taken supper in the main dining room last evening—showing the flag, according to Helen—but one meal a day in public was enough for Anne.

"We will wish her ladyship the joy of her new trend," Anne said, opening her workbasket. "We will also hope her bold idea garners more notice than my little contretemps with Lord Corbett."

"He's heading for Scotland, according to my whist partners." Helen regarded Anne, who sat on the sofa beneath the windows. "You do not seem upset, my dear."

I am relieved. Anne could admit that to Augustus, His Grace of Tindale, who'd been Lord Corbett's best man. She would never hint as much to Helen.

"We all grieve differently."

That observation seemed to placate Helen, who went to the front door. "Don't grieve for too long, Anne. That house party has possibilities, even for you. You are still an heiress, and you will add a certain backhanded cachet to Lady Deschamps's gathering if you appear at a few suppers or card nights. We can get you back on the horse without all of Mayfair looking on. I will see what I can do."

Anne rose, her embroidery forgotten. "Helen, you must not meddle. For me to invite myself to a choice gathering of Society's darlings would be the outside of desperate."

"No, it would not. It would be a coup. You must see that."

What Anne saw was two weeks of sly looks, knowing smiles, and half-overheard whispers, all of them malicious. She had run that same gamut when the betrothal to Lord Hume had come unraveled, and she had no stomach for such an ordeal now.

"It's too soon, Helen. I was *engaged* to Lord Corbett. I am beyond being smitten with any man, but I was somewhat fond of him and prepared to build a future with him. I cannot simply hand off my morning horse, climb upon my choice for the afternoon, and get back to the hunt field."

Helen swirled a green merino wool cloak about her shoulders. "Corbett Hobbs is on the way to Scotland with his *chère amie*. You not only discard him like a spent mount, you let it be known his gaits were bone-racking, and he shied at puddles. That's how this is done. Wish me luck at the card table. Mrs. Colonel Farragut is cousin to Lady Deschamps by marriage. A word in the right ear might see you invited to a luncheon, at least."

"Do not do this," Anne said. "I will look desperate, and desperation gives all the worst sorts of men ambitions that bode ill for my composure." More plainspoken than that, she could not be.

"Lady Deschamps does not invite the desperate to her gatherings. That's the beauty of this situation. You won't be importuned, but you will be an object of curiosity. A perfect place to resume socializing. I'll see you in time to change for supper."

Helen wafted out the door on a swish of green elegance, while Anne wanted to hurl her workbasket through the window.

No. No. No. If invited to a pity luncheon or a curiosity musicale, she would decline. She had few suitable dresses with her, for one thing, and she had no intention of attaching a man's interest ever again. No afternoon horses, no following the hounds, no being followed *by* the hounds.

What she craved was the peace and majesty of ocean views, the delight of the surf splashing her ankles, the benevolence of sunshine on her closed eyelids. Not a jolly good gallop down the buffet line.

Anne was still fretting and fuming when she made her way to the beach at two of the clock. Tindale occupied the same rock where they'd sat the previous day, but he'd spread a soft wool blanket, doubled up to four thicknesses.

He was not an elegant man, but rather, impressive. Substantial, with features more rugged than refined and enough muscle to make any Corinthian envious. The fashion for dandies was languid indifference to life at large unless involved in actual athletic pursuits. Tindale, even sitting still, his gaze upon the sea, could never be mistaken for languid or indifferent.

"Miss Baxter, good day." He rose and bowed. "You are punctual."

"As are you. You brought us a blanket." Inane thing to say, but Anne refused to discuss the weather with this man.

"If we are to devote ourselves to serious discussion of weighty matters, we must have a comfortable perch from which to exchange our profundities." He offered her his hand, and when Anne sat, he came down immediately beside her. "Also, a rock makes a hard bench, and a lady deserves her comforts."

The blanket was soft, and Tindale's bulk offered protection from a brisk breeze. "How goes the horse auction?"

"We're having a bit of drama, though if an event is both predictable and tiresome, can it qualify as drama? Miss Maybelline Carruthers has sent regrets, and Lady Deschamps is in high dudgeon. Miss Carruthers claims a spring cold has laid her low, but her ladyship knows that Maybelline has designs on Lord Andrew Postlebottom—I think that's his name. Her ladyship has chosen Postlebottom for some goddaughter or niece-by-marriage, and the perfidy of the Carruthers Creature—taking advantage of the field Godmama so graciously thinned for Miss Carruthers in Town—is the subject of much muttering."

"It's Postle*botham*, Your Grace." Though, of course, a former solicitor knew that. "You are relieved that Miss Carruthers is not underfoot?"

"I am terrified. The unlucky goddaughter or niece-by-marriage from whose clutches Postlebother was snatched will turn her sights on me, the consolation duke. I overheard a pair of chaperones planning strategy last evening. My antecedents are lowly, alas, but ducal enough, and 'when darkness falls,' a duke is a duke, no matter how unfashionable his looks might be."

"They seek a peer with impressive tailoring, Your Grace, while you boast impressive insights into society's foibles. The hostesses know you were a solicitor, and solicitors hear all the best secrets. If the chaperones tread warily around you, it's because they are accustomed to respecting the title rather than respecting the man himself. In your case, they must reckon with both."

Tindale was quiet for a moment, while the waves danced along the shoreline, and the breeze teased at his hair.

"You understand these people," he said. "I understood them as a lawyer understands difficult clients, not as a duke understands the society he's expected to favor. How are you faring at the inn?"

"Not well." The honesty of Anne's answer surprised her, but Tindale had asked, and he was owed the truth from her. "My cousin is plotting to see me engaged again, as quickly as possible, and I can't seem to convince her that three times is the limit of my fortitude."

"The first was the ailing youth. Who was the second?"

"Lord Hume Billingsley. The settlement discussions could not be brought to a satisfactory conclusion. The general conclusion is that I cried off because we would not suit."

Tindale shifted to consider her. "He was in debt up to his gold cravat pin, and your aunt and uncle came to their senses in time."

"My solicitors brought me to my senses. They sat me down outside my guardians' hearing and explained the numbers to me. Billingsley's debts were just shy of staggering because the whole family was trading on his expectations, and his mother..."

"Gambles," Tindale finished. "While his father's a sot. Billingsley's situation is not to be envied, but neither was it your problem to solve. You did the right thing by walking away, and God knows settlements prove difficult for many a titled family."

The solicitors had assured Anne that was so. Many couples, even couples who'd announced their engagements, quietly went their separate ways when nuptial finances proved too complicated to sort out. Anne would have rubbed along well enough with Billingsley himself, but his family would have run through her fortune in very short order.

And yet, there had been months of talk. In every whisper and aside, Anne had been the villain of the piece. *Airs above her station. Doesn't know her place. Too good for a peer's heir.*

"I paid off Billingsley's debts," Anne said. "I felt sorry for him. He's not a bad sort. He went on to marry some cit's daughter, and they had two little boys in quick succession." The gossips had stopped inflicting reports of Billingsley's marital bliss on her after that. He'd lost his wife last year to a lung fever, and Anne had sent the requisite note of condolence.

"You are generous in victory. A fine quality in any general."

Anne had felt more like a pawn than a general, but the solicitors were her late father's lawyers, and their loyalties were to her rather than to Aunt Daphne and Uncle Potter. She had resisted all of Uncle's demands to switch firms, and Uncle had eventually subsided into grumbling at Anne for being just like her mother.

"I wanted the whole business dealt with quietly. Generosity and understanding were a way to make that happen."

"I hope you will be similarly understanding with me when I tell you what I've done."

Tindale remained relaxed beside Anne, in so far as sitting right next to a man could communicate such a thing, but a subtle guardedness had crept into his tone.

"Did you spill punch on somebody's bodice, Your Grace?"

"Nothing so clumsy, I hope. Because Miss Carruthers has outwitted Lady Deschamps's attempt to take her out of the game in Mayfair, the numbers at the house party do not match."

If the seawater had risen up to envelop Anne, she could not have felt a more compelling sense of cold.

"Tindale, you didn't."

"I mentioned that I'd come across a young lady enjoying a seaside respite at the Siren's Retreat and hinted that you might be persuaded to attend a few events at Godmama's gathering."

"On what possible basis would I allow myself to be persuaded to take a front-row seat at the horse auction? I have no desire to watch a lot of pretty, wealthy young women step all over each other for the privilege of bothering you."

"Neither do I," Tindale said, taking her hand in a warm grip.

Anne had the sense he wasn't presuming with that gesture. He was ensuring she could not stalk off down the beach—and keep going all the way to Wales.

"So persuade me," Anne said, "and mind you make it sincere so when I laugh in your face, we can content ourselves that your best efforts were inadequate."

"I am sincerely, honestly asking you to accept my godmother's invitations, Anne Baxter, because I need you as I have never needed anybody and hope never to need anybody again."

Anne considered the waves chasing the seabirds along the waterline and considered Rose Cottage, so serene and sweet on its little promontory.

"I will grant you," she said, "the argument is original." Men had admitted to needing her money, though the admissions were grudging. They had offered assurances that they would relieve her of the burden of managing her funds, gracious clodpates that they were. "What precisely do you need me for?"

"Heiress repellent?"

"I am an heiress."

"Then I need you as my bodyguard and friend, Anne Baxter. My chaperone, my conspirator. In return, I offer you a decisive tool for establishing your independence from matchmakers, gossips, and even well-intended cousins."

He'd done some research, but then, a former solicitor would. "And how do you propose to effect that miracle?"

"Simple. The solution occurred to me as I hacked out this morning. I will court you for two weeks with the single-minded devotion of a man who doesn't know that's not how polite society goes on. I will be adoring and smitten and the despair of the matchmakers."

"And then you will toss me over?" A ducal rejection would certainly be a mark of... dubious distinction. No more talk of getting back on the horse, *ever*. Anne contemplated a life at Rose Cottage, or its inland equivalent, and the prospect was damnably alluring.

But to be rejected publicly *by Tindale*? That would be... hard. Different from the previous farces and disappointments.

"My dear Miss Baxter, I would never be so foolish as to reject your hand," Tindale said. "At the conclusion of the house party, when all are expecting an announcement, *you* will send *me* packing, and off I shall go. I will be devastated by your rejection, but bear up manfully nonetheless."

"Send *you* packing?" Anne did not know Tindale well, but she liked and respected him. Sending him packing did not follow from that foundation.

"Of course. I will be seen as the upstart duke who thought he could have the first young lady to catch his eye, the lofty peer who's taught a public and much-needed lesson in humility. You will be established as a woman who can have—or reject—any man she pleases."

The seabirds leaped into the air as a particularly vigorous wave slapped against the shore. Some flapped away to safety on the nearby rocks. An intrepid pair drifted back to the sand and resumed their seabird business.

From one perspective, Tindale's plan had all the elements of farce. From another... It could be like that wave. A decisive disruption of the pattern, one that allowed Anne to settle back to the business of her life however she pleased.

"Your strategy is different," Anne murmured. "Nobody will expect me to be so... so..."

"Self-possessed?" Tindale suggested. "Self-assured? More fool them. You'd get something else out of this arrangement."

"Freedom?" The word glimmered at the edge of Anne's ambitions, like a sliver of gilded sunset glimmered over an overcast horizon.

"Freedom and my eternal gratitude."

"Oh, that." And yet, Anne had the sense Tindale was not making this request lightly.

A silence stretched while she contemplated his scheme, and the tide came ever closer to their perch. An opportunity like this—to reject a duke—would not come along again. Helen would cease her carping, and Anne need not return to London in disgrace.

"I will give you my answer tomorrow," Anne said. "Thank you for another interesting conversation."

Tindale walked her to the door of Rose Cottage. When he should have bowed over her hand, he instead kissed her cheek and lingered near long enough to whisper, "Please, Anne."

She curtseyed. "Until tomorrow. Shall we say ten of the clock?"

He bowed and walked away. Anne watched his retreat until he was lost from sight.

CHAPTER THREE

"Tindale, have you taken leave of your senses?"

Augustus was tempted to tell his dear godmama that he had parted from his wits the day he'd learned that a title was to be slung about his neck.

"You aren't thinking strategically, my lady," Augustus replied, the elegant gilt chair creaking beneath him. He was in Godmama's private parlor, a blue and gold jewel box intended to show off Lady Deschamps's perfect coloring. "Miss Anne Baxter has gone to ground. Nobody knows where she is, and she is the talk of London. If she turns up at, of all places, *your* house party, then that gathering becomes the talk of London."

Lady Deschamps was referred to as a handsome widow. She was nearing fifty, but looked younger, at least by the time she emerged from her boudoir at midday. She had been more distant than doting as a godparent, but then, Mama had married down.

Her blond hair was styled in artful braids and loops. Her complexion was as perfect as subtle cosmetics could make it. Her afternoon dress was doubtless a Paris creation, and the gold locket about her neck hung just low enough to draw the eye to the swell of her breasts. She navigated the blue and gold tea service gracefully and occupied her tufted sofa with casual elegance.

She was what Anne Baxter should aspire to become—exquisitely fashionable—though Augustus hoped Anne could avoid that fate.

Continue to avoid it.

"Anne Baxter is out of the question, Tindale. You have no way of knowing this, but Miss Baxter let Lord Hume Billingsley slip through her fingers several years ago, and now Lord Corbett Hobbs has left her standing... Well, you were there."

Augustus, as best man, had been left to explain to Anne's uncle that Lord Corbett had run off with his doxy rather than marry the Baxter heiress. The uncle—to his everlasting disgrace—had reacted as if the insult, while predictable, had been done to him rather than to his niece.

"I know Lord Corbett Hobbs well, my lady, and I know the woman with whom he has eloped. Lord Corbett will be back in Town within a fortnight, tail between his legs, pockets even more to let. Marie will no more marry him than I'd marry Maybelline Carruthers."

A slight vertical line appeared between Lady Deschamps's perfectly plucked brows, suggesting the Carruthers Creature's defection had disturbed a deeper game than Augustus had perceived.

Bloody hell. Anne would have spotted Lady Deschamps's scheme from across the music room.

"Maybelline isn't silly, Augustus, and you were not raised in the same environment as your cousins. Maybelline could be counted on to make allowances accordingly, and she would know how to punish any who dared refuse your invitations. Her mother is among my dearest friends, and you could rely on me to keep your new duchess from putting a foot wrong—not that she would."

Maybelline Carruthers was calculating, in other words, and shallow enough to consider a refused invitation a declaration of social war. Moreover, Godmama saw Maybelline as a means of adding a duchess to the collection of women beholden to her matchmaking efforts.

"Maybelline isn't here, is she?" Augustus said, rising. "That doesn't speak well for her willingness to heed your guidance. Anne Baxter and her cousin, by contrast, are biding a mile down the coast at the Siren's Retreat. You could invite Miss Baxter to a few events, and I will publicly show her my favor, favor you were prepared to steer toward the fair and feckless Maybelline. The Carruthers Creature will rue the day she thought to turn up her nose at your consequence, my lady."

Lady Deschamps remained seated, her gaze appraising. "You were Lord Corbett's best man. Perhaps you feel some responsibility for his decision? Some pity for his jilt?"

Well, no. One emotion Augustus did not feel for Miss Baxter was pity. Respect, admiration, commiseration, liking, and a few other sentiments best left unacknowledged even in solitude, but not pity.

"I pity Lord Corbett. He has made a laughingstock of himself, and Miss Baxter had a narrow escape. If you declare it to be so, all of Society will agree with you, particularly when Miss Baxter turns around and catches the notice of an eligible duke."

Lady Deschamps rose on a soft rustle of blue silk. "I never cared for the Hobbs boy. Too frivolous. His parents alternately ignored him and indulged him. He's the caricature of the useless spare. I've always said that."

"While Miss Baxter remains an heiress, related to two earldoms, and quite comely."

The line reappeared between Godmama's brows. "'Quite comely' is doing it a bit brown, Tindale. Passably pretty, I grant you, though only passably."

When Anne Baxter closed her eyes as the surf lapped at her ankles and the sun kissed her cheeks, she was goddamned gorgeous. When she grew animated on the topic of women's contributions to the theater, she was riveting. When she fell into a pensive silence, she was breathtaking.

And in all of those moments, she was honestly *herself*, not some creation concocted by modistes, cosmetics, and deportment instructors. She wasn't an aging schoolgirl driven by a craving to revenge petty social slights, and she never would be.

"I shall be gracious," Lady Deschamps said. "I shall invite Miss Baxter and her cousin to tonight's card party. I have it on good authority that Helen Saunders is an excellent whist player, and she's sensible. Maybelline is overdue for a set-down, and allowing Anne Baxter to mince about on your arm a time or two will achieve that result."

Before the buffet was laid out, Godmama would have convinced herself and half of her guests that inviting Anne Baxter to make up the numbers had been her plan all along and that Miss Baxter was, after all, quite pretty.

Augustus bowed over her ladyship's hand and withdrew. He had achieved his objective and had to find his way back to his rooms without being accosted by any chaperones, matchmakers, diamonds, originals, or merry widows.

He had spoken honestly to Anne. He *needed* her. Needed her desperately, and the sooner she joined the house party, the safer Augustus's bachelorhood would be.

"They will say Tindale feels guilty," Helen murmured, running her hand over the soft, black leather of the coach seat. "They will say it was his responsibility as best man to get Lord Corbett to the church, and thus Tindale owes you the loan of his consequence."

The luxurious Tindale traveling coach had been sent to fetch Anne and Helen from the Siren's Retreat. With the windows open, the coachman, groom, and footmen—two on the boot—could overhear what was said inside.

About which, Anne did not care. "Tindale owes me nothing. Lord Corbett is not a toddler, to be kept on leading strings all the way to the church. Corbett changed his mind, and Lady Deschamps needs another female guest to make up her numbers."

"Lord Corbett lost his mind," Helen retorted. "But he's a man. He'll be considered dashing and romantic, bold, or amusingly eccentric. We cannot concern ourselves with him tonight. You will be meek, Anne. Do you hear me? Meek and sweet and a little dazed at such good fortune following swiftly on the heels of heartbreak. If you can muster a sniff or two into your handkerchief, a teary blink in the odd moment, that will invite pity. Pity is your best bet."

Helen went on lecturing as the coach rolled along a coastal highway with a magnificent view of the sea.

"You have my good offices to thank for this invitation," Helen said as the coach turned through towering white gateposts topped by stone lions sejant with pineapples crowning their heads. "Please promise me you won't bungle an opportunity I spent hours at the card table wrangling for you."

His Grace of Tindale had asked Anne to attend this function, had nearly begged her to come. What stopped Anne from disclosing that to Helen was primarily the need to avoid arguments. Helen meant well, she had Anne's best interests at heart, and as a widow with small children, she had better things to do than clean up Anne's wreckage.

Anne also kept her peace because the time spent with Tindale was personal and precious, a memory to revisit in the quiet nights of spinsterdom that Anne honestly longed for. She and Tindale had argued about the significance of women in breeches roles—did that device ridicule men or simply show off a lady's legs for the benefit of the males in the audience? Both?

She had held hands with him.

She had sat by his side and resisted the urge to lean into him for the sheer pleasure of bodily closeness with a fit, attentive male.

And those encounters were private, as was the gentlemanly kiss to her cheek that Anne treasured most of all.

This house party, by contrast, was not private. It was theater in the round, and Anne must not forget that she'd been recruited to play a role.

"If Tindale does show you any favor," Helen went on, "you will simper, Anne. Simper, do you hear me? Blush if you can manage it and try to look overwhelmed to have gained the notice of a duke. He might be a solicitor in duke's clothing, but his title is old and wealthy. Disdain his notice at your peril."

"I doubt he will do more than bow over my hand." He could start speculation with little more than that. Watching Anne from across a portrait gallery, bringing her a single glass of punch, or partnering her for a hand of cards would be sufficient to get the tabbies talking.

"Chin up," Helen whispered as the coach drew to a halt at the foot of an imposing cascade of marble steps. "Not up too high. Demure and dazed, but on your dignity—what's left of your dignity."

Anne's dignity was in very good repair, in part thanks to His Grace of Tindale. "You are kind to accompany me to an outing such as this, Helen. Expecting you to drop everything so I can make up the numbers was presuming of Lady Deschamps. I do appreciate your generosity."

Helen preened at Anne's thanks, and Anne had meant them. Widowhood was not for the faint of heart, and Helen never complained or caused talk, when doing both would have been easy.

The evening was informal, meaning the butler escorted Anne and Helen to a portrait gallery, where guests were mingling and chatting. Lady Deschamps greeted them with every appearance of good cheer, then introduced them to Lord Bertram and his adult son. Bertram was a widower, while the son, Lieutenant Charles Thurlow, had the bearing of a fellow intent on announcing his naval rank—all chest forward, shoulders back, his nose and chin forming the prow of a masculine ship of the line.

"Simper," Helen muttered just before Lord Bertram led her off on a tour of the paintings.

"Shall we admire the art?" Lieutenant Thurlow asked, "or admire the view from the back terrace? I must own that a view of the sea will always appeal to me more strongly than even the best works of the old masters."

"Then the back terrace it is." Anne could not muster a simper, but she could take Thurlow's arm. He was a fine specimen of an officer, with blond curls falling fashionably over his forehead, pale blue eyes, and a ruddy complexion indicative of years ruling the waves.

"I've heard of your recent disgrace," Thurlow said quietly. "I am not the judgmental sort, though, and when Lady Deschamps explained that you'd been treated ill by Lord Corbett Hobbs, I knew my sympathies would lie with the jilted bride."

He patted Anne's hand, and she sent up a silent prayer that Tindale would pop out from behind some old statue and pitch Thurlow into the ocean blue.

"Your sympathy is much appreciated," Anne replied, though Thurlow's blasted sympathy was also entirely unnecessary.

Nor did she crave sympathy when they stepped onto the back terrace and conversations paused as speculative looks were sent her way. When the talk resumed, the timbre had changed—softer and more intense.

From idle talk to gossip, in other words.

"The ducal lordlings," Thurlow went on, "are overindulged and underdisciplined, if you ask me." In the out of doors, his voice carried all too well. "Send them to sea at age eight, I say, then they'd know better than to leave a lady standing alone at the very altar."

Anne had actually been sitting in the front-row pew, Aunt Daphne on one side, Helen on the other, when Tindale had asked for a quiet word with Uncle Potter.

"Do you one day hope to make captain, Lieutenant?"

"One day? *One day*? My dear Miss Baxter, a captaincy is nearly a foregone conclusion, but the peace has bollixed up the works terribly. The senior officers are hanging on to their posts, and the admiralty is facing budgetary constraints. Pursuit of a captaincy, as with any worthy undertaking, will require ambition coupled with patience and persistence."

He sent Anne a look that involved one eyebrow lifted at an imperious angle, his head turned in three-quarter profile, and a knowing smile aimed at her... forecastle.

The Thurlow family must be nearly destitute if a disgraced heiress inspired the lieutenant to comport himself as a one-man press-gang. Next would come a little speech about how overwhelming it must be for a woman to endure the burden of an independent fortune.

"The view is spectacular," Anne said, disengaging her hand from Thurlow's arm and standing at the balustrade. "I quite agree with you that all the paintings in the world, as inspiring as they are, cannot compare with nature's splendor. The sea is proof to me of a Deity beyond our comprehension, if the seasons, forests, sky, and fields did not already make that case."

Thurlow took the place beside her—immediately beside her. He did this in full view of the other guests, who were sending Anne looks that oscillated between sneering, amused, and—from a few of the older women—sympathetic.

Anne drew her shawl closer about her shoulders and took half a step to the left. "How long will you be on leave, Lieutenant?"

"Until June. That much shore leave is akin to punishment for a naval man, Miss Baxter, or it would be, but for the pleasure of present company." He turned to perch a hip on the railing so the magnificent seascape served as a backdrop for his posturing. "I don't suppose it's easy for a young lady to be saddled with the burden of a fortune and have only solicitors and aging relatives to assist her with its management."

Nothing could be easier. Support the well-run charities. Don't support the other kind. Invest in the prudent ventures. Don't invest in the other kind. Live within your means on the interest and leave the principal to grow modestly over time. Anne's papa had explained it to her when she'd still been in the nursery.

"I manage." Anne was beginning to doubt that she'd be able to manage an entire evening of sly and sympathetic looks, much less

Thurlow's seventy-four gun wooing. "Might you introduce me to some of the other guests? I know a few of them, but others—that lady in the Bath chair, for instance—are strangers to me."

The woman sat alone near the balustrade in a corner of the terrace. She looked out to sea, and Anne realized the woman was not elderly. She was older than Helen, though far from doddering. No husband or adult child attended her, and she looked lonely.

"That's Mrs. Northrup. Carriage accident killed her husband, put her in that Bath chair. All quite sad, but years ago. Do you know the Misses Daley? Their papa is Viscount Easterly."

Anne knew them. They were not twins, but they'd been born within a year of each other and operated as a single, malevolent social entity.

"I'd rather make Mrs. Northrup's acquaintance."

"Nonsense," Thurlow retorted, placing Anne's hand on his arm and patting her knuckles. "The Daley daughters are all that is delightful. Come along."

Come along? The Daley daughters had handsome settlements, about which their mama reminded any bachelor within seven leagues.

"If you don't mind, Lieutenant, I will enjoy the view awhile longer."

Thurlow looked torn between issuing an order and delivering a lecture. In the back of her mind, Anne heard Helen's repeated admonitions to simper. Anne was constitutionally incapable of simpering, and her own cousin ought to know her at least that well.

"Miss Baxter." Tindale had sauntered up the steps from the formal garden. He bowed to Anne and smiled. "And Thurlow. A lovely evening to enjoy the view, and may I say, Miss Baxter, that the sea air agrees with you?"

"Thank you, Your Grace. A pleasure to see you."

"You two are acquainted?" Thurlow seemed none too pleased at the duke's arrival, while Anne wanted to throw her arms around His Grace's neck.

Tindale merely stared at Thurlow.

"Oh, right." Thurlow studied Anne's left shoulder. "At the church and all. I beg Your Grace's pardon. I was about to ask the Daley sisters if I might fetch them some punch. Miss Baxter, good evening. Enjoy the view." He came about and sailed off, apparently having realized that Tindale outgunned him.

"Thank you," Anne said. "He was growing presumptuous."

"I escaped the Daley Dragons not a quarter hour past. 'Tindale, fetch us some punch.' 'Tindale, my shawl is in the library.' I was to be their personal footman. Let's greet Mrs. Northrup, shall we?"

As Tindale escorted Anne to where Mrs. Northrup sat alone, the looks Anne received shifted, the sneering gazes became puzzled, the amused smiles faded to speculation.

"Tindale." Mrs. Northrup offered her hand. "You must be about ready to jump into the sea by now. I'd heard you were part of this gathering and concluded Mayfair was treating you very ill if you were willing to leap from frying pan to fire, as it were. Who is your young lady?"

"Mrs. Northrup, may I make known to you Miss Anne Baxter, whom I consider a dear friend. Miss Baxter, Mrs. Lily Northrup, another dear friend."

Anne curtseyed while Tindale pulled up a pair of wrought-iron chairs.

"Do sit," Mrs. Northrup said. "And don't mind me, Miss Baxter. I wanted to see who Camelia had assembled for her little party, but after this evening, I will likely keep to my rooms."

"You live here?"

A look passed between Tindale and Mrs. Northrup. "Thanks to Augustus, I own this property. He was my solicitor at the time of my husband's death. Or rather, he was the solicitor my daughter talked into taking my part when it became apparent my husband's family was intent on leaving us destitute. Lady Deschamps is my late husband's aunt-by-marriage, and the less said about her situation, the better. She is to be pitied. You are well rid of the Hobbs boy. A complete ninnyhammer."

Anne looked from Tindale to Mrs. Northrup, seeing only kindness and understanding. "He absolutely was. I thought I could manage him, but I'm glad to have been spared such a thankless task."

"Tindale, some punch," Mrs. Northrup said. "I am about to sing your praises to Miss Baxter, and that exercise will go more quickly in your absence."

She shooed him off with a wave of her gloved hand.

"You aren't interested in the punch," Anne said, watching Tindale cross the terrace. "And you need not sing His Grace's praises to me. I find him in every way to be an estimable man."

"And he considers you a dear friend," Mrs. Northrup said, "an announcement that both pleased and surprised you. Augustus is not one to dissemble, Miss Baxter, nor does he have many friends. I expect you know how that feels."

Anne considered Mrs. Northrup, a pretty woman whose features bore the stamp of pain and fortitude.

"I can always use another friend," Anne said, "and I suspect you could use the loan of my shawl."

As the evening wore on, Augustus realized how great a sacrifice he'd asked Anne Baxter to make. Amid a barrage of whispers and innuendo, she trod the line between witty banter and polite ignorance of what was being said behind her back. She lost graciously to Lieutenant Thurlow, though never very much at one time. She'd lent Lily Northrup her shawl and insisted that she and Lily partner each other at cards.

She endured Augustus's besotted glances, which were more sincere than Augustus had intended them to be, and when the card party broke up, he offered Anne a final turn on the terrace.

"Helen is deep in conversation with Lord Bertram," she said, slipping her hand about his arm. "Now would be a good moment to pretend some interest."

Augustus was not pretending, not with Anne. He wanted to tarry with her as he had at the beach, the conversation wandering in all directions, no audience to draw conclusions or overhear.

"Why did you lose to Thurlow?" he asked when they'd reached the relative quiet of the terrace.

"He's on leave mostly to escort his sister about the social Season," Anne replied, "but she lacks a dowry. As Mrs. Northrup explained it, the admiralty courts are dragging their feet settling some war prizes, which will considerably improve Thurlow's circumstances."

"Admiralty courts can take years to simply put pen to paper on a decision. For the duration of those years, the Navy invests the proceeds of its plundering. That still doesn't explain why you rewarded Thurlow's presumption with coin." The lieutenant had been all but physically pressing himself to Anne's side when Augustus had interrupted, and then Thurlow had raced away to impose himself on the Daley sisters instead.

"I suspect Thurlow was using me to inspire the notice of other women. He'd make either Daley sister a good husband, but they were too busy ordering you about. My fortune garners respect even while I merit only gossip."

The footmen had extinguished the torches in the formal garden, leaving only a pair of lit flambeaux on the terrace. The sound of the surf carried in the darkness, as peaceful as a lullaby.

"Let's sit, shall we?" Augustus suggested, leading Anne to the foot of the steps. A bench in half shadow afforded both privacy and a view of the moonlit sea. "You took pity on Thurlow."

"He has served his country loyally, and now he's supposed to use his leave to serve his sister loyally. Lady Deschamps clearly invited him simply to make up numbers, or that sister would be here along with Lord Bertram and Mr. Thurlow. The lieutenant wants for some temporary fortification, lest a pressing need to pay the trades see him matched to a harridan."

"You lost that much to him?"

"Between Mrs. Northrup and myself, by the end of the house party, the lieutenant won't be sailing so close to the wind."

Augustus rested his arm along the back of the bench. "I can help too."

"By sending a note to the admiralty? An excellent suggestion, Your Grace. Mention that you'd like your inquiries into Mr. Thurlow's prospects kept quiet, and his prizes will be awarded to him within a month."

"Because," Augustus said slowly, "the admiralty will think I am interested in Miss Thurlow's prospects."

Anne gathered her shawl more closely about her, a shawl Augustus had seen draped around Lily Northrup's shoulders for most of the evening.

"Who cares what the admiralty board thinks, Your Grace? They owe Mr. Thurlow money, and his sister has no prospects at all without coin."

"You are angry." Anne was also even more shrewd than Augustus had thought, and perhaps more bitter.

She glanced at him, and despite the shadows, he could see the battle light in her eyes. "They look at you as if some peacock has got loose amid the biddy hens. They don't know whether to capture you and turn you into a pie, marvel at your plumage, or try to steal your tail feathers for their own adornment."

"You are angry on *my* behalf?" As a solicitor, Augustus knew what it was to take up a client's cause. He'd done that for Lily Northrup, who had been shamefully treated by her husband's family. He did not know what it was to *be* somebody else's cause. "I am angry, too, now that you take the gloves off."

"And well you should be," Anne retorted. "Lady Deschamps needs a stern talking-to. Roberta Daley nearly sat in your lap, and her sister could not have been more closely draped about you if your valet had secreted her in your waistcoat."

"If I were to lecture Lady Deschamps on any topic, it would be her tendency to toss impecunious bachelors and widowers at you, or seat you at tables populated by the worst gossips." Augustus would deliver that lecture, and before noon tomorrow.

"Mrs. Northrup isn't a gossip," Anne said, sinking lower against the bench. "She knew my mother and had stories of Mama I'd never heard. You cannot know what that means to me, Tindale, especially now."

Augustus rested his arm around Anne's shoulders. "Tell me."

"I lost my parents too young, but in a sense, Mama was never really mine. She was besotted with my father and he with her, but Papa had more of a knack of talking with me. I was the only child, both son and daughter, and he made the effort to understand me. It's as if he knew I'd be orphaned, while my mother had no fear of the future. She once told me that every day she woke up beside my father, she was as joyous as a new bride."

"My parents were like that, but in a different way," Augustus said. "Mama was Papa's editor and copyist. She improved on his work, and he consulted her on every case and client. She knew the precedents better than the barristers did, and she often attended court to watch the trials."

"Did you become a solicitor solely to join that charmed circle, Tindale? I cannot imagine that a Society card party has anything to offer compared to a rousing debate about the legal status of women."

"Mama would have loved you." Between one wave crashing against the distant shore and the next, Augustus realized that *he* might very well love Anne Baxter. She was fierce and just and kind, and entirely her own woman.

She was also damnably pretty, particularly compared to the powdered and prissy Mayfair belles Lady Deschamps had assembled for her house party. They wielded their settlements and fortunes like lures dragged to train the hounds.

Anne used hers to keep another woman from ruin.

"I wanted what my parents had," she said. "I wanted a real marriage, one that brings joy, not slight smiles. One that makes both the future and the present moments more precious. I would never have had that with Lord Corbett Hobbs. I know that now, and perhaps he knew it too."

Augustus did not give a flying flambeau what Corbett Hobbs knew. "You want what our parents had," he said, "but you are an heiress. Polite society cannot see you because a great pile of money obscures you from view. They cannot see me because a title robs them of the plain sight of the man."

Anne nodded once. "I vowed I would hold out, but I've held out for years, and I find myself thinking, 'I could manage that one, and he *is* a ducal spare.' Another would be off to sea for years at a time—not a bad quality in a husband impressed with his own brilliance. A third at least has a sense of humor..."

"And soon," Augustus said, gathering her closer to his side, "your dreams and needs are pitched into the sea, and you've a Daley sister affixed to your person like a Brighton barnacle."

This was not why Augustus had asked Anne to join the house party. He'd honestly wanted to make a display of his regard for her, to keep the tiara hunters at bay. Also to give Anne the pleasure of rejecting a duke. He still meant for that to happen.

He owed her that.

"We should be going in," Anne said, though, if anything, she snuggled closer. "You have shown me enough marked favor for one night, Your Grace, and the hour grows late."

The hour wasn't that late. What Anne meant was that duty called to them both.

To hell with duty for once. "Your fortune is real and not going way," Augustus said, "and God knows I can't simply set aside a title as if it's a hat of the wrong color, but right now is real too, Anne. This moment, the glorious sight of the ocean beneath the moon, the pleasure of closeness to and honest conversation with a woman I esteem. That's all real and well worth treasuring."

She turned her face to his shoulder, then shifted to kiss him. Not on the cheek—Augustus had turned to face her too—but on the mouth.

Then she drew back, as if surprised at her own boldness.

A night of tedium and posturing washed away in a moment, and Augustus's whole being rejoiced.

"More," he said, grazing his nose along her cheek. "Please, Anne." He bussed the corner of her mouth and drew back. "Please."

The initiative had to be hers. Corbett, Billingsley, and even that long-ago ailing youth had all expected her to simply accommodate their whims. Augustus waited, lingering as near as he dared, but determined that the decision should remain hers.

Anne's next kiss was hesitant, the lack of confidence a surprise coming from a woman of decided opinions and keen understanding.

Augustus took her in his arms lest she remain unsure of her welcome, and the kiss became an adventure. Anne had the knack of nestling against him, fitting into his embrace in a manner as exciting and pleasurable as the soft press of mouth upon mouth.

She explored in gentle, thorough degrees, and Augustus followed her lead. Desire waxed increasingly insistent, until Anne was sitting across Augustus's lap, and he was contemplating far more than kisses.

"We must stop," she said, curling against his chest. "We must stop, or I won't be able to stop."

Augustus closed his eyes and inhaled a whiff of roses and the sea. "Well put. Do I need to apologize, Anne?"

"Whatever for?" She eased off his lap, and he let her go.

"For presuming on your person?"

"I rather presumed on yours first. It won't happen again."

He had *begged* her to presume. "Whyever not?"

That earned him a small smile, brittle around the edges. Exactly the kind of smile he deplored and she herself had spoken of disparagingly.

"We like each other, Your Grace, and we are allied for the nonce. I was simply... at low ebb. Now I am back on my mettle, and you will please see me to the coach. Helen will think I've subjected you to my theories regarding women and banking, and her lectures will never cease."

Anne sought a retreat from this lovely, stolen kiss, which was a backhanded form of encouragement. A lady did not need to retreat from meaningless encounters, did she?

Augustus rose and offered Anne his hand. She appeared physically none the worse for their mutual presuming—hair still tidy, no makeup to smudge, clothing quite in order—but he hoped that was not the case with her emotions.

He hoped, as false and tiresome as the entire evening had been, that their kiss had been real, for both of them.

CHAPTER FOUR

"You mustn't think anything of it," Helen said, stripping off her gloves as the coach pulled smoothly away from Lady Deschamps's steps. "Mr. Thurlow and the Daley girls are involved in some sort of game where each attempts to make the other jealous. You have the greater fortune, Tindale has a ducal title. Foolishness results."

"I don't think anything of it," Anne said, settling against the soft leather. In her mind's eye, she saw Tindale, his lean features illuminated by only the light of a distant torch. He was a careful kisser at first, until by subtle degrees, his caution turned to passion and then to...

Whatever jubilation of body and mind came after passion. Anne had been carried away in his arms, destitute of sense, awash in wonder. A kiss ought not to be able to *do* that. The whole stupid evening, with contrived losses to Mr. Thurlow, the contrived civility of Lady Deschamps, and Helen's incessant whispered orders...

It all fell into the sea, while Tindale's kiss warmed Anne's heart and a few other parts as well.

"I found the entire display between you, Thurlow, and the Daleys amusing," Helen said, "and that is progress, Anne. To be the butt of amusement rather than pity or malice is a step forward for you. The Daley girls have airs above their station, mark me on that. Tindale won't offer for either sister. I cannot fault his manners, but I suppose even a solicitor learns how to comport himself around his betters."

"Don't do that," Anne said, making no effort to keep her voice down. "Don't cast aspersions on a man who never sought the title and is doing his best to make a go of it. Did you know that Lady Deschamps doesn't even own that villa, but rather, is dependent on her niece's generosity for the use of it?"

Helen unclipped an earbob. "What are you going on about? Lady Deschamps is one of the premier hostesses of the spring Season."

"Mrs. Lily Northrup owns the venue where Lady Deschamps just entertained us. When Tindale was a solicitor, he saw the property settled on Mrs. Northrup by her late husband's family. Lady Deschamps married up, but she did not marry well."

Helen paused, one earbob still swinging from her earlobe to the rhythm of the swaying coach. "How on earth did you come by that information?"

"Mrs. Northrup told me when His Grace went to fetch us punch."

"Interesting. His Grace partnered you at whist, too, didn't he?"

"He opposed us for one round." A lively game.

"He smiled at you," Helen said, unclipping the second earbob. "I do recall that. Were you attempting to be witty, Anne?"

Anne had been attempting to lose money to Charles Thurlow, the fourth at the table. "Perish the thought that I'm capable of wit. I am relieved to have shown my face at a polite entertainment and very pleased to have made Mrs. Northrup's acquaintance."

"You will have another opportunity to show your face at a polite entertainment."

I'm not ready. Anne needed more time to hug the memory of Tindale's kiss close before she set it aside, a treasure to be admired again on some distant, less unsettled day.

"What have you done, Helen?"

"I have accepted Lady Deschamps's invitation for us to join her picnic outing the day after tomorrow. The tide will be low in the late morning, and the party can hunt for pretty shells on her beach, then enjoy a luncheon on the grounds. Lord Bertram told me he is looking particularly forward to searching the sand with me."

"He is pockets to let, Helen. Cannot dower his own daughter, cannot pay the trades. He's hoping his son's admiralty prizes bring the family right, but admiralty courts are fickle and ponderously slow."

These people are not who they seem to be. Anne wanted to shout that truth at her cousin, but the evidence ought to speak for itself. Helen had been presented at court, she was a mother twice over, a widow, and still, she believed the appearances over the substance.

Perhaps that was the trick of managing in polite society. Stop seeing the evidence, stop reasoning from facts. Play inane games at the punch bowl and lark off to Scotland with your mistress.

Though the evening had been a success from Anne's perspective. The punch-bowl games, the gossip, the sly looks, and Lady Deschamps's attempts to matchmake had all slid off Anne like surf draining away from a sheer rock face.

"I truly am relieved that Lord Corbett left me at the altar."

Helen unfastened a spray of dyed feathers from her hair. "You are daft. A ducal spare was a coup, Anne. With Billingsley, one could always hint that his contribution to the settlements wasn't adequate, but with Lord Corbett Hobbs... He rejected *you*, not only your settlements."

Blunt, even for Helen. "Corbett wasn't right for me. He had no conversation beyond *bon mots* and *on-dits*. His kisses were all fish-mouthed and fumbling, and he had no idea how to..." Anne waved a hand.

"Anne? You didn't really...?" Helen waved her hand too.

"We came close, but he was so inept, so bumbling, I was hard put not to laugh, and I certainly wasn't about to encourage him.

Billingsley wasn't any better." Though in Billingsley's defense, he'd been trying to manufacture desire in the absence of genuine passion. Not an easy feat for a basically honorable man.

"Hell hath no passion like a young gentleman who has secured a fiancée," Helen muttered. "At least you don't have that regret with Corbett, but I tell you this with your best interests at heart, Anne. If Corbett Hobbs should see the light of reason and come crawling back to you with hat in hand, you will accept him. You will put up with his fishy kisses and fumbling and be grateful."

"Because polite society assumes we did anticipate our vows?"

"Precisely. Used goods. Nobody said those words tonight, but they thought them. We must decide what you will wear to the picnic. Thank heavens it's informal, else we'd have to send to London for some dresses. We ought to send to London, in fact, and I think the blue sarcenet walking dress would do wonderfully."

Helen prattled on, about dresses and pelisses and heaven knew what, while Anne watched the vista of the moonlit sea beyond the coach's window.

Used goods. Anne *was* used goods—she'd anticipated vows with that young man who'd long since expired on a Greek island—but nobody referred to the presuming bridegroom as used goods. He might be a fashionable rake, a good catch, a man-about-Town.

While the lady was fast, ruined, *soiled.* Lord Corbett Hobbs had known exactly what Anne would face when he'd gone off to Scotland. He'd known her history with Billingsley, known how few friends and relatives she had to rehabilitate her reputation.

And to think she'd nearly married him.

Tindale's kiss might have been a passing indulgence on both of their parts, but for Anne, it had also been more than that. He'd shown her, with one kiss, how far wrong she'd nearly gone, accepting proposals from Billingsley and Hobbs. Anne wished them well, but she would never argue with them.

Never cuddle into their warmth and find a pleasure that hovered between comfort and daring.

Never long for more of their kisses.

If Lord Corbett Hobbs did come waltzing back to her, she'd refuse him out of hand, no matter what Helen said, no matter who was whispering slander on Anne's name behind a peacock-feather fan.

"I'm thinking of returning to Town," Augustus said, pacing the bounds of Lily Northrup's parlor. He hoped that a generous reading of his motives would be that he was taking time to reflect on his feelings for Anne Baxter.

An honest reading would not be half so flattering. He longed for more of her kisses, while she had said there need be no further lapses. She had also said she liked him—he more than liked her—and that she would have been unable to stop had they continued last night's intimacies.

Whatever was he to make of those conflicting messages?

He conferred with Lily behind a closed door, and bedamned to anybody who remarked his need for privacy. Her parlor was not a gilt and blue jewel box, but rather, a comfortable sitting room with a lovely view of the sea. No carpets, the better to accommodate Lily's Bath chair, though today she occupied a sofa, her chair at the ready next to her.

"You'd abandon the games just as they grow interesting?" she asked, knitting needles clicking away on soft blue yarn.

"I thought the Daleys were bad. Miss Honoraria Beecham came into my room last night after the card party. She pretended to be tipsy and lost."

"The tipsiness might well have been genuine. You intimidate these young women with your silences, Tindale, your sly humor, your size. The ladies here are like those big-game hunters who realize the tiger could be stalking them."

"I am not a wild animal, much less a predator, and besides, the tiger doesn't have a gun, so it's hardly a fair contest. The young ladies, by contrast, are definitely on the hunt." Unlike Anne, who sought only to be left in peace.

No, that wasn't accurate. Anne sought a loving marriage and a family of her own—or she had.

"Don't judge these women too harshly, Tindale. They all fear to end up as I nearly did—a poor relation dependent on the charity of others. That life is lonely and difficult for a woman raised to expect she'll someday rule over her own household."

"And Lady Deschamps isn't lonely? Her life is one of contentment and good works?"

Lily shifted the mass of knitting in her lap and started on a new row. "Stop being a lawyer."

"I studied long and hard to become a lawyer. I do not aspire to be some ambitious twit's prize duke. Miss Beecham was dressed for her slumbers when she stumbled into my room, and her ensemble left nothing—not one thing—to the imagination. It's a wonder she doesn't suffer a permanent lung fever, attired like that for bed."

When Augustus's panic had subsided, and he'd shooed the young lady into the corridor—and *not* escorted her back to her door—he'd been left with a sense of vast and tired pity.

Some of which was for himself.

"You cannot gallop back to Town just yet," Lily replied. "If Miss Baxter's companion is to attend the house-party events with her, then the numbers still don't match, do they? Lady Deschamps has hit upon a solution, and your leaving will upset her plans."

Tindale gazed past Lily's balcony to the serene silvery ocean in the distance. "I will hate this solution."

"Lord Hume Billingsley will join the guests this evening, and that, my dear Augustus, means you aren't going anywhere. I overheard Camelia cooing over Billingsley's acceptance earlier this morning. He's newly out of mourning, and a house party by the sea offers him a respite from grief and loneliness."

"Out of mourning?" Augustus did not like the sound of that one bit.

"He's a widower, and his wife's passing has left him well fixed with two young sons. You do know he has a past with Miss Baxter?"

A little boat with one triangular white sail came around the headland to the west. Augustus wished he and Anne were on it.

"I am aware of Billingsley's past with Miss Baxter." He was also aware that Anne had paid off Billingsley's debts. That was not the act of a woman indifferent to her erstwhile suitor.

"Then you won't be nipping back to London, will you? Our hostess is giving the young ladies another *eligible* to consider, and she's stirring the pot, of course."

The little boat made good progress sailing close to the wind. Who was enjoying the freedom of the waves in that small, intrepid vessel? Who had put out to sea the better to appreciate the lovely spring day?

"I am off to enjoy some solitude on the beach," Augustus said.

Lily's needles went still. "You will warn her, won't you, Augustus? Miss Baxter is softhearted, for all she seems so self-possessed. She deserves to be warned, lest that cousin of hers toss her at Lord Hume's head."

Nobody tossed Anne Baxter where she did not want to be tossed. Augustus would make sure of that much. "I will take a solitary walk on the beach before the big-game hunters stir from their rooms, and I might stop by Miss Baxter's cottage to exchange a civil greeting. May I escort you anywhere before I leave?"

Escort being a euphemism for pushing Lily's chair. She could stand unassisted for brief periods and even take a few cautious steps, but such exercises pained her needlessly.

"I am content on my sofa for the nonce," she said. "Fly to your damsel, Augustus, and recall that she's to rejoin the party for tomorrow's picnic."

"She might cry off."

"No, she will not. If any woman in all of polite society is incapable of crying off, it is she, more's the pity. Away with you."

Augustus tarried long enough to kiss Lily's cheek, then changed into his oldest pair of riding boots and struck out for the beach path. He was not running from the formal garden, precisely, but like that little sailboat, he made good time.

When he reached the beach, Anne was already there, her half boots and stockings piled on a rock, along with a floppy straw hat, parasol, and wicker hamper. She sat on the sand, building some sort of structure on the border between dry land and the tide line.

"The next high tide will wash that away," Augustus said, perching on the rock to remove his boots and stockings.

"That's half the pleasure of creating a sandcastle. The sea will reclaim my efforts, and I can start anew or pretend I would never waste my time with such foolishness." She shaded her eyes with a sandy hand to smile up at him. "Good day, Your Grace."

Her smile was genuine, though a little hesitant. Augustus dropped to his knees beside her. "I dreamed of you."

She was using a small glass to create mounded crenellations on her castle walls. "You need not flirt with me, sir. Build us a moat, why don't you, to hold back the tide?"

"You are supposed to say you dreamed of me too." Augustus considered the slope of the beach and the angle of the tide line. He used a stick of driftwood to mark out a wide half circle about six feet from the castle.

"You can cease playing the gallant, Tindale. I made it through last night's outing, and now I have a day to recover before tomorrow's picnic. That moat is rather distant to be any sort of fortification."

"The oldest castles had multiple mounded fortifications. I'm an old-fashioned sort of duke."

Augustus had no idea what sort of duke he was, but he was an honest man: He'd dreamed of Anne Baxter. It occurred to him, however, that she might have multiple fortifications, and for good reasons.

He set himself to scooping out a ditch on the sea side of his moat line and piling up the sand on the castle side. "Do you regret kissing me, Anne?"

"No." Another smile, bashful and genuine. "You are prodigiously inspired at kissing, Your Grace."

"I was prodigiously inspired to put my best foot forward—or my best lip." He was smiling, too, and tempted to steal another kiss, but no. The beach was in view of the cottage and parts of the inn. No stealing anything here. "I stopped by Lily's apartment this morning. I think you have an ally in her."

Anne considered her tower, which was squatty as towers went, but then, it was made of sand. "Mrs. Northrup is a dear, and she is your friend too, Tindale. I should have brought more cups and such. May I have your stick?"

Augustus passed over the requested item. "Lily gave me a warning that I think was meant for you."

Anne used the stick to drag a curving design into the outer wall of her tower. "I do not care if the Daleys call me names. I went through that whole mess once before with Billingsley. Eventually, the gossip moves on."

She had a sure, steady hand, and her tower was quickly acquiring what looked like vines of ivy.

"About Lord Hume. He'll be among the guests at the picnic tomorrow, and, Anne, he's through his period of mourning and possibly looking for a step-mother for his children. I thought you should know."

Augustus watched Anne closely for signs of ire, pleasure, anything. Instead, she set down her stick and gazed out across the water, her expression utterly composed.

"I wish I were on that vessel," she said, gesturing toward the little sailboat, which had crossed more than half the horizon, "with enough provisions to get me to France."

"I wish we were both on that vessel," Augustus said. "I will be remarkably attentive to you at the picnic, Anne, and you must promise not to let me out of your sight. To quote Lily, Lady

Deschamps is stirring the pot, adding another eligible to the mix. Billingsley apparently inherited means from his wife."

Anne resumed drawing with her stick. "He'll use that wealth wisely, though I'm sorry for his loss. Hume was never the problem in that family, and he loves his boys. I've seen him in the park with them, flying kites for them and playing tag. Build your moat, Your Grace, and I will share my hamper with you."

Augustus resumed scooping out sand with his hands. "Don't you ever get angry, Anne? Don't you ever want to rip up at the stupidity that passes for polite society?" Did she wish those boys playing catch had been hers?

"Yes, I lose my patience, but then I read a good play or novel, or I take Helen's children for an ice. I work at my embroidery and make something lovely and useful. I will get a dog, I think, when I return to Town. A nice, big, friendly hound who will woof at me in greeting."

The knees of Augustus's breeches were soaked, his hands were dirty, and he was... enjoying himself. "A dog is a good idea. I've always liked dogs. They are honest."

"Precisely. Horses are honest as well, while cats are too honest. I do believe you should have been a dyker, Your Grace. That moat qualifies as a seawall."

They argued about the Dutch practice of reclaiming land from the sea. They argued about breeds of dog. They shared Anne's sandwiches and her flask of tea, and by the time the sailboat had disappeared around the eastern headland, Augustus knew himself to be a man in love.

He had not kissed Anne since coming upon her on the beach, but he had delighted in every minute spent in her company. That mattered enormously, though he had no idea if his feelings were reciprocated.

He parted from her shortly after noon, knowing he'd be expected for the luncheon buffet at the house party. He carried Anne's effects to Rose Cottage, bowed over her hand in farewell, and made his way back down the beach past their sandcastle.

By the time they'd finished construction, the sandcastle had become fanciful, with bailey walls higher than the castle tower. Augustus made his way back to the western path, musing on the wisdom of giving Anne a puppy—she would probably want to pick out her own canine—when he noticed the sandy dirt at his feet.

His own boot prints were easy to recognize, because one heel had a nick along the outside edge. Two smaller pairs of prints were mixed in with his own tracks, though. Either diminutive men, or ladies. Two ladies who wore the same size boots.

Somebody had been spying on him and Anne.

When Augustus took up a plate in the buffet line an hour later, he noticed the Daley sisters across the terrace in earnest discussion with Lady Deschamps. They were looking at him and using their fans to hide their words.

They had intruded on the time he'd spent with Anne. That angered him to the point that he nearly hurled his plate of food at the nearest portrait. Instead, he asked the Daleys and Lieutenant Thurlow to share the meal with him, and all the while, he wished he and Anne were both on that boat headed for France.

"Miss Baxter." Lord Hume Billingsley bowed over Anne's hand *quite* correctly. "You are looking splendid."

Hume hadn't raised his voice, but he didn't need to. Anne curtseyed with equal correctness, knowing every gossip, tabby, and Daley sister was looking on.

"My lord, a pleasure to see you."

He squeezed her fingers gently and offered her the self-deprecating smile that had first gained Anne's notice. "Thank you. You are gracious as always. Shall we enjoy the garden?"

The picnic party was assembling in the out of doors and soon to make a slow progress down to the estate's private beach. Hume had apparently chosen this moment to ensure the whole assemblage could observe his reunion with a former intended.

Not exactly an ambush, but as displays of felicity went, disconcerting for its boldness. Anne took his arm and recalled that she'd truly liked Hume Billingsley. He wasn't proud, and he was quietly intelligent. He'd told Anne his financial particulars before the solicitors had even started wrangling.

"I heard your news," he said. "Please allow me to say that Corbett Hobbs hasn't a brain in his head, and now we know he hasn't an iota of honor in his heart either. Even for him, such behavior is beyond the pale. I considered calling him out."

"I hope you discarded the notion?" Anne offered a pleasantly vague nod in the direction of Lord Bertram and Lieutenant Thurlow.

"I did, reluctantly. You would not appreciate having your name become involved in a matter of honor, and I have cost you enough already."

"Old business, my lord. Old business that old friends need not remark."

They descended the steps as if making an entrance at a formal Mayfair ball. Heads turned, conversations paused. Anne should be accustomed to such rudeness, except... she wasn't. She increasingly had no patience for it whatsoever. Had Tindale not asked her to attend, she would be on the Rose Cottage beach right now, building another fanciful sandcastle.

"How are you, Anne?" Hume asked when they'd turned down a path bordered with silvery-green lavender. "You can be honest with me."

"I am managing. Lady Deschamps's gathering allows me to show my face without running the gauntlet of the whole carriage parade. Cousin Helen has been loyal."

Tindale had been more than loyal. Where was he, and had he made Lord Hume's acquaintance?

Anne's escort plucked a sprig of lavender, brushed it with his fingers, and held it to his nose. "I sought you out in part because it's good to see you, and I won't have anybody thinking we are less than cordial. I also sought you out to offer a warning. The news will be all over London soon enough, though I suspect I'm the only person aware of it here."

The lavender fragrance was bracing, a perfect complement to fresh sea air and a beautiful spring morning. Anne was abruptly certain that this was the last event she'd attend at Lady Deschamps's house party.

"Has something happened to Lord Corbett?" If so... Anne would feel some guilt, of all things. Had Corbett married her, she might have been able to curb the worst of his stupid wagers and excessive drinking.

"In a manner of speaking. Erskine Duddington nipped off to fetch his auntie to Town from Biggleswade—the auntie from whom he hopes to inherit. Whose coach should Duddy see heading south at a great rate while Duddy tooled north, but Lord Corbett Hobbs's? The crests were turned, but Lord Corbett drives a distinctive conveyance. Bright red wheels do stand out."

Anne settled onto the nearest bench. "Please sit with me, Hume."

He came down beside her, while on the terrace, somebody had inspired a ripple of laughter. The other guests could not know the news Hume brought, not yet, but within a few hours, by means of express letters and quiet talk, the whole gathering would know.

"Is there more?"

"Duddy asked around at the next change and learned that Lord Corbett's traveling companion had abandoned him in Peterborough. She disappeared with some German princeling of mature years."

Anne said the only thing she could think to say. "I appreciate the warning." But what did Hume expect her to *do* about Corbett's folly reaching its inevitable, Drury Lane conclusion? "Tindale predicted this."

Hume peered at her. "Tindale, as in His Grace of Tindale? Lady Deschamps didn't tell me he was here."

But she'd apparently told Hume that Anne was on hand. "Lady

Deschamps deserves a dunking in the Channel. She should not have recruited you in furtherance of her schemes."

Hume rose and extended his hand. "She said you were struggling under a weight of woe and mortification. I knew that could not be true, but I thought you could use a friend."

He winked at Anne, and she recalled something else about him. Hume could wield his charm with a subtlety that masked shrewd intent. When he'd told her of his straitened circumstances, he'd adopted the air of a martyr parting with reluctant confidences. In fact, he'd made the tactical choice to more or less throw himself on Anne's mercy, and his judgment had been vindicated by her subsequent generosity.

When he'd next gone courting, he'd been at least solvent and his family's situation much improved.

Anne accepted his hand and rose. "I am always happy to see my friends, but Lady Deschamps has taken advantage of your good nature to make up her numbers and cause talk. In the opinion of Cousin Helen, I am bearing up a little too well. I believe every bachelor on the premises would thank you if you showed marked attention to either Daley sister."

Hume grimaced. "Those two. My late wife did not have kind things to say about them."

Anne's opinion could not be rendered without resorting to profanity. "Tell me of your boys," she said as the group on the terrace began to move down the steps en masse. "They must be very lively."

His lordship waxed eloquent as only a doting papa could, and in this, Anne sensed that he was sincere. He and his late wife might not have been a love match, but they'd made a go of their marriage, and his children would want for nothing.

"Tindale is smart," Hume said as they wandered along in the wake of the greater crowd. "Witness, he's only now emerging from the house. If I were Lady Deschamps, seeing the new duke engaged at my house party would rank as the coup of a lifetime."

"His Grace is learning very quickly not to be deceived by the appearance of a gracious welcome. I doubt Lady Deschamps's ambitions will be realized."

"You know Tindale?" He posed the question with studied casualness.

"We are acquainted. His Grace has been nothing but kind to me, so don't think to add to the drama here. I will endure this shell-gathering outing and then return to the obscurity I hope to enjoy for the rest of my life."

Hume patted her hand. "You need time for the bruises to heal. I understand, believe me, Anne. I am here to help. I will be your loyal vassal and—"

Anne halted. "Pax. Having greeted me with all the cordiality of an old friend, you will now make your bow before Cousin Helen. I forgot my shawl, and the sea breezes can be fresh."

Anne had not forgotten her shawl. She'd left it on the terrace on purpose, in case she needed to extricate herself from any disobliging situation. That Hume's company fit that description was unsettling, but Anne had the distinct sense he was up to something.

"Very well, then," he said, bowing over her hand. "I will wish you a most pleasant outing and say again how lovely it is to see you. I mean that, Anne." He gazed into her eyes for the space of three heartbeats, then sauntered off, all blond good looks and excellent tailoring.

Anne was relieved to see him go, also resentful. Why *wouldn't* he be glad to see her? She'd saved his family from ruin and kept her mouth shut about the whole business.

The whole *old* business, as she'd said. She made her way back to the terrace as the guests began filing down the path that led from the park to the beach.

She needed time to think, to consider the significance, if any, of Corbett's failed attempt at an elopement. Corbett's bottomless pride would smart terribly, and if Anne was lucky, he'd pop over to Paris to lick his wounds.

When had she last been lucky?

"There you are." Tindale crossed the terrace from the doorway to the conservatory. "I waited on Lily's balcony until the enemy retreated. Lily hopes you will stop by before the day is over." He picked up Anne's shawl from the back of a wicker chair and draped it around her shoulders. "I am delighted to see you and would kiss you silly were we not in plain view of the house and grounds. Good morning, Miss Baxter."

He was smiling, mostly with his eyes.

The sight of him, the simple sight of him, brought Anne's day to rights. The house-party nonsense, Corbett's pride, Hume's hand-patting and winking... They all faded to nothing, washed out to sea by Tindale's slight, piratical smile.

"Good morning, Your Grace. As it happens, this shawl might be too light for chillier breezes on the beach. Perhaps you'd accompany me into the house while I fetch another?"

"Never let it be said that I allowed a lady to bring the wrong shawl to a picnic." He offered his arm and escorted Anne through the conservatory doors. The air inside was warm, still, and earthy, and the door had barely closed behind them before Anne was kissing him silly.

CHAPTER FIVE

Anne's kisses were sunshine on a peaceful ocean and fresh breezes on home shores. She advanced slowly into her kisses, like early spring gently waking the land. She gradually bundled closer and tightened her hold on Augustus's waist.

He tried for restraint, tried for delicacy, and only half succeeded. By the time he broke the kiss, he had Anne up against one of the conservatory's marble columns, and arousal was threatening to put common sense to rout.

Anne cuddled nearer on a sigh. "I am not by nature impulsive, though I am so very glad to see you, Tindale."

That Augustus could inspire her to yield to impulse was almost as gratifying as the resulting kisses had been.

"One hoped that was the case," he said, making the effort to step back. "I am only prone to rash behavior where you are concerned. Do you really need a different shawl?"

"No." Her expression held a ghost of her younger self, running barefoot half the summer, climbing trees, and galloping headlong over hill and dale.

"Then let's get ourselves down to the beach. As much as I want to lock that door and indulge in wild fantasies, we must confer."

Anne smoothed her fingers through his hair. "I contemplated sending my regrets this morning. Now I'm glad I showed up. Tell me of these wild fantasies, Your Grace."

The intensity of those fantasies shocked Augustus. Would they shock Anne? "First, assure me that Billingsley behaved like a gentleman. You are clearly able to handle him and any presumptions he might be entertaining, but I need to hear the words."

"Lord Hume was more than civil. I'll introduce you to him. About those fantasies?"

Augustus had seen Hume being *more than civil*. Billingsley had bent near to Anne whenever she'd spoken, sat right next to her on the garden bench, and patted her hand at least half a dozen times. Lily had counseled patience, while Augustus's instincts had advised pugilism.

"We will have no talk of wild fantasies," Augustus said, "when we must do the pretty before half the nitwits and ninnyhammers in polite society. Lily has spies in London, and they have sent news by express."

Anne fussed with her shawl. "Marie has thrown Corbett over for some German noble. Hume wanted to be the first to tell me."

Augustus led the way to the doors. "I knew she'd toss him over, but didn't think she'd manage it in such high style or quite so soon. Then again, a man who will abandon his bride at the altar deserves to be publicly abandoned in turn."

Anne remained near the marble column, brows knit. "You think Marie was intent on some sort of feminine justice?"

"I doubt she was intent on springtime in Berlin, and she had to know Corbett's parents would cut him off without a farthing if he went through with his latest blunder. Corbett got the least of what was coming to him, and I will ensure that my opinion on the matter is known to all."

Anne came along the fern-bordered path and kissed Augustus on the cheek, leaned against him for one sweet moment, then stepped out into the midday sunshine.

"You are so fierce, Tindale. I understand why Mrs. Northrup's daughter asked you to advocate on her mama's behalf. Dukes used to lead armies, and you apparently have an appetite for a fair fight."

"I like your other word better—justice. That Corbett behaves like a heedless toddler and suffers no consequences is unjust, to you, to his parents, even to Marie. I considered him a friend—note the past tense—but I knew not to turn my back on him."

"To a lesser degree, I feel the same way about Lord Hume. I can't put my finger on why, but I sense he saw some advantage in attending this house party. Lady Deschamps painted me as bowed down with humiliation, and even Hume knew that could not be the case."

"No," Augustus said, escorting Anne down into the garden, "that could never be the case with you. Was our castle obliterated by the high tides?"

"Alas, yes."

"Then we will have to build another, with better fortifications. Somebody spied on us when last we tarried on the beach, Anne. Two women, or two diminutive men. I suspect the Daleys." She needed to know this, though clearly the news did not surprise her.

"Spied on us as we played in the sand, debated the merits of Shakespeare's tragedies, and shared a snack? Hardly the stuff of scandal, Tindale. I hope the spies were sorely disappointed."

In the course of that prosaic afternoon, Tindale had fallen in love, or fallen more deeply in love, with his partner in play. The spies probably *had* been disappointed, while he most assuredly had not.

He and Anne caught up to the last of the stragglers making their way to the beach, and he shared her blanket when the picnic hampers were opened. They spent just enough time apart to appease convention, then paired up again for the walk back to the house.

"If looks could wound," Anne said quietly, "I would be lying in a bleeding heap at the feet of the Misses Daley."

"I don't gather Billingsley is best pleased with me either," Augustus said, though the fellow had been entirely polite when Anne had seen to the introductions. "I suspect he intends to offer for you."

Anne nearly stumbled, but Augustus caught her.

"Offer for me? He tried that. It did not go well." She seemed genuinely horrified by the notion of becoming Billingsley's wife.

"You were willing to marry him once upon a time." For which Augustus tried not to resent the handsome, smiling widower.

"Once upon a time, when I had far less grasp of what a Society marriage entails." She stared in the direction of the manor house as if all the evils of the underworld lurked within its wall. "If being a mere heiress has subjected me to endless judgment and gossip, then can you imagine what being married to a marquess's heir would entail? Hume has landed on his feet, as the saying goes. As his wife, I would be expected to entertain, to support the correct charities rather than the meaningful charities, to circulate at the infernal house parties—I hate house parties, Tindale, in case there was any doubt of that. I hate all of it, which is why I could be persuaded to entertain the suit of a duke's fribbling younger son."

Anne's pace had picked up, though she kept her voice down. "Corbett would never have troubled me much to do the pretty, but Lord Hume, as a marquess's heir... That would mean court functions and political dinners, *state* dinners. At the rate the present marquess is drinking, he's not long for this world, and I am far less gullible than I was several years ago. Hume must be daft."

For Anne, this amounted to a tirade, and yet, she was absolutely correct. A Society marriage, a Society *life,* was one of little privacy and less depth. Augustus had spent the past six months absorbing that lesson until it made him bilious.

He took Anne's hand, lest she fly off back to her little cottage and never be seen again. "Billingsley is proud, Anne. You rescued him. Now he wants to rescue you, to be the knight in shining armor."

Her steps slowed. "That makes a kind of simple masculine sense, but I don't need or want rescuing. I will disabuse Hume of his gallant notions, except as you say, he's not being gallant. He's polishing his halo before polite society, finding a mother for his boys, a hostess, and proving to my aunt and uncle—and the whole world—that they were wrong about him. The scorned suitor saves the day in every proper farce, doesn't he?"

"But you *were* right about him. He was not worthy of consideration for the honor of your hand, his financial situation aside, because he had failed to win your heart."

Anne shifted her grip to Augustus's arm, the posture of a proper lady with a proper escort. "I did not want anybody winning my heart. Perhaps Hume's pride took a few blows on that score as well. Let's look in on Mrs. Northrup, shall we? Then I can quit this infernal gathering and go back to building sandcastles on the beach."

Fortunately for Augustus, Lily asked Anne to be her partner at the following night's card party, and he was thus spared having to beg Anne not to abandon him to the tender mercies of spies and schemers.

Or beg her to marry him. As he handed Anne up into his coach and endured the fluttering farewells of her widowed cousin, Augustus managed to impersonate a cordial peer, though the day had left him distinctly unhappy.

If Anne now dreaded the prospect of marrying a future marquess, what on earth could induce her to marry a duke?

"We owe this to Tindale," Charlotte Daley said, capping the ink bottle and sprinkling sand over the missive. "Solicitors are accustomed to consorting with criminals, and now here's His Grace, bumbling about among the cream of Society. The duke can't possibly know what association with that creature will do to his reputation."

"To his children's reputations," Roberta replied, pacing before the sitting room hearth. "Why the Duchess of Tindale doesn't take him in hand, I vow I do not know."

Charlotte had almost forgotten there was a widowed Duchess of Tindale. Jennifer or Janine—Eugenia? "She's a mousy creature. Her people were in beer, or coal, or something dreadfully plebeian. Besides, as all of society knows, she failed..."

Roberta joined in, "To provide her husband an heir. Poor thing."

Charlotte shook the sand from the page. "We really are awful, Bobbie, but in the nicest possible way."

"In the prettiest possible way. I do think Lieutenant Thurlow fancies you, Charl. He's not bad looking, if you don't mind that weathered-sea-captain complexion."

He also had that magnificent military posture and was ever so quick to fetch a lady's fan. "He hasn't a feather to fly with, alas, though he does seem to be lucky at cards. If you wear my green sarcenet, he's sure to ask you to partner him."

Roberta peered out the window, which overlooked the front drive. "I'm saving your green sarcenet for flying kites."

"But any decent breeze will lift the skirts halfway to your knees if you wear that dress, it's too... You devilish creature. You want to show off your ankles."

"She's finally leaving." Roberta twitched the lacy curtain aside. "Taking Tindale's coach to go precisely one mile down the beach to that poky little inn."

Charlotte joined her sister at the window. "Is she taking her poky cousin with her? I would not put it past Helen Saunders to set her cap for Lord Hume. Both are bereaved, both have children. She hasn't let her figure go, we must give her that."

"Must we? She looks a bit droopy, to me, and skinny. Child-bearing destroys a figure."

Charlotte watched as Miss Anne Baxter was handed into the coach by no less personage than His Grace of Tindale.

"He fancies her," Charlotte said, a forlorn note creeping into her words. Something about the way Tindale bowed over Miss Baxter's hand and leaned closer to her while offering his farewells stirred a longing Charlotte would not admit to even her sister.

"He fancies her money," Roberta retorted. "The last Duke of Tindale was very likely as land-poor as the rest of us, and now the present duke, who has little enough in the way of private means, must somehow bring it all to rights."

"I don't think that's it, Bobbie." Tindale had been a successful solicitor, and they generally did all right for themselves. The previous Duke of Tindale had been a prudent sort, save for his choice of duchess.

Roberta flounced away from the window. "Then Tindale can set the Baxter Bride up as his mistress, if our plans for her fail—though they won't. Your idea is brilliant, Charl."

Roberta's gift for nicknames was brilliant, if a trifle nasty. "I think you fancy Lord Hume, don't you, Bobbie?"

Roberta examined her reflection in the cheval mirror for the twentieth time that day. "Lord Hume's first wife was brunette. I am brunette. His first wife was demure and sweet. I am demure and sweet, at least when the gentlemen are within earshot. She was a fine dancer—one must be honest about that—and I am an excellent dancer. I do believe Lord Hume and I would suit."

"You'd leave Tindale to me?"

Roberta sent a particular look over her shoulder. In public, Bobbie was vague about which of the Daley sisters was the elder, but in private, she occasionally resorted to the status of older and wiser sibling.

"Tindale is a duke, so of course I could never castigate any woman for securing his suit, least of all my own sister. But, Charlotte, you will have your work cut out for you. He's from a cadet branch of the family, a solicitor is not a gentleman in the received sense, and he's... His proportions bring to mind plows and forges rather than quadrilles and card parties."

Charlotte liked his proportions. One could not say that. "He's not stupid."

Roberta went back to the window as Tindale's matched grays moved off to circle the fountain before the house.

"You have that much right, Charl. His Grace's show of attention to the Baxter Bride is shrewd. He's seen as taking pity on a fellow outsider, which makes him look gallant and above it all. But we saw them on the beach, playing in the sand when they might have been trysting in that little cottage. A man—a duke—does not while away an afternoon in the most idle of pursuits when he's private with a woman who interests him."

Charlotte had tried to reassure herself with that very point. "But if Helen Saunders was doing her bit as chaperone, then the cottage would not be available for Miss Baxter's ruination."

"Simpering Saunders spends her afternoons playing whist with the other widows. She's all but tossing her cousin under the wheels of scandal while pretending to be a conscientious relative. Not everybody is as loyal to family as we are, Charl."

The coach rolled away, and Tindale remained on the steps, watching its departure. Not until the conveyance turned at the gateposts did he disappear inside the house.

I want a man who watches my departing coach like that. I want a man who will idle away an afternoon on the beach with me. I want a man who is genuinely gallant and above it all.

"Speaking of loyal family, do you think Papa really means that this will be our last London Season?"

Roberta's perpetually assured air faltered. "Mama will bring him 'round. She scored a coup securing this invitation for us, and Papa has to be sensible of the challenge we face. How is a gentleman to choose between us?"

Bobbie offered that perennial jest with a hint of desperation.

"I don't need a duke, Bobbie. If Thurlow offered for me, I'd accept him."

"Nonsense, dearest. You are to have Tindale if it's Tindale you want. I will have Lord Hume, and Papa will see that every bill from the milliners or glovemakers was paid to good effect. Let's seal up your letter and find a footman to send it up to Town for us. An express should be there by morning, and Lord Corbett might well join the party by supper tomorrow."

"We are to attend the final ball," Helen said, fingering a cream stock invitation. "Yesterday's little outing to look for shells must have convinced Lady Deschamps that Tindale is interested in you."

How Anne hated—hated—the speculation in Helen's tone. The maid had already come by to clear up the breakfast dishes, and if the sunshine pouring down on Rose Cottage's terrace was any indication, the day would be even more glorious than yesterday.

Why couldn't this respite by the sea truly *be* a respite? "I would rather not attend any balls, Helen."

"You want to waltz with Tindale. I know you do."

Anne wanted to do much more than waltz with His Grace. "And you want to dance with Lord Bertram?"

Helen set the invitation aside. "He's comely. He's an excellent conversationalist and every inch a gentleman." She sat up a little straighter. "I suspect he's lonely. He loves his children, Anne, but to be a Papa unable to dower one's daughter is a terrible thing."

The morning light revealed what candlelight kindly did not. Helen would not see thirty again, and yet, the life of a widow—providing chaperonage, making up numbers, raising half-orphaned children—had not been in her plans.

Helen was lonely, too, and prepared to do something about it.

"I like Lord Bertram," Anne said, "and if you are asking me to dower his daughter, should you and he marry, I would be more than happy to. We can make those arrangements in your settlement agreements, or I can simply gift the girl with the money anonymously. I have reason to hope, though, that Lieutenant Thurlow's situation will soon improve."

Helen's countenance brightened. "He intends to offer for you?"

"I certainly hope not," Anne replied, rising, "but why must everything, every single, blasted thing, revolve around who is marrying whom? I would not accept Thurlow's suit if he were titled, wealthy, a decorated war hero, and the last bachelor standing."

This week by the sea had taught Anne that much. Tindale had said it indirectly: Anne had been foolish to think a practical match would suit her, despite practical matches being the preferred choice in polite society. She could be content with that sort of arrangement, but she could not be *happy*.

"That is sour grapes talking," Helen said, tucking the invitation into her reticule. "You have not been widowed, Anne. You've never faced years of nights made lonelier because you know what comfort a wife can derive from a husband's friendly companionship—or his affection. Your innocence spares you awareness of what you're missing. In another five years, you might see the whole situation differently."

In another five years, Anne would very likely be living the life of a confirmed spinster, dwelling in a pretty cottage in the Midlands, and reading Shakespeare to her pets. She knew, though, the pleasure and affection a woman could find in the arms of a husband.

Or, more accurately, a lover.

"Why not set your cap for Tindale?" Helen asked, getting to her feet. "He isn't a bad sort, despite the talk. They're all just men when the candles are out."

Anne watched the sea shining painfully bright under the morning sun. Down at the beach, gulls wheeled over whitecaps, and the roar and retreat of the surf lured the senses. That reasoning—*they're all just men*—had been part of the foolishness that had led her to accept Lord Corbett's suit.

They were individual people, with dreams, unique humor, strengths, and failings.

"Tindale will have to establish himself in Society," Anne said. "He must vote his seat, host the right entertainments, attend the right gatherings, bow over the right hands in the carriage parade, and never put a foot wrong. Even with all that effort, years from now, he will still be the upstart duke, the presuming mushroom. Received everywhere, but included nowhere. His duchess will face a constant battle. To be what he needs, she must be nothing less than a paragon, which I do not aspire to be."

For once, Anne wished Helen would point out the weaknesses of Anne's logic. Instead, Helen pulled on a pair of blue gloves.

"None of that would matter if he was the man you loved, Anne, not that dukes typically make love matches. I'm off to Brighton's better shops for a spot of shopping. I've sent to London for some dresses suitable for the final ball—don't bother to thank me—but I'm in want of the right fripperies to set off my finery. Tindale's coach will be at the inn in a quarter hour, and I thought to perhaps see a little of the countryside too. Shall you come with me?"

Thank God for Helen's love of shopping. "You asked for the loan of the duke's coach?"

"I did, and Lord Bertram will accompany me." That announcement was made a shade too casually, and Anne was abruptly ashamed of herself. Lady Deschamps's house party was not exactly a romp across the village green for Helen either.

"Enjoy your day out, Cousin. Heaven knows you've earned it. Tryst with Lord Bertram halfway to Land's End and back, dazzle him with your wit, and know that if he's your choice, I will do all in my power to support the match as you have always supported me. You deserve to be happy, and so does his lordship."

Helen became absorbed with organizing the strings of her reticule. "It's merely a day of shopping, and maybe a picnic on some scenic bluff."

"If that's all it is, Lord Bertram is a slow top indeed." Anne hugged her cousin, feeling an odd sense of roles reversing. "No need to hurry back. I'll have a tray sent down from the inn for supper. Do send a note if a carriage accident necessitates spending the night in some quaint hostelry ten miles down the coast."

Helen hugged her tight. "You are wicked, Anne Baxter. Wicked, wicked, wicked. Also my favorite cousin."

"Away with you. Choosing the right fripperies takes time and thought."

"Too true, too true." Helen all but scampered into the cottage, and five minutes later, Anne heard the front door close.

Tallyho, Cousin Helen. Perhaps Anne should have been jealous, but she instead wished Helen and his lordship a lovely day of stolen pleasure, or affectionate friendship, or courting. Whatever the two of them wanted to make of an unforeseen opportunity.

Anne resumed her place at the table, knowing she ought to fetch a hat. The tide was out, meaning the morning would be an opportunity to hunt for shells, build sandcastles, and simply watch the waves.

While she planned her excursion, a lone figure emerged from the path at the western end of the beach. Tall, dark-haired, bareheaded, striding along the packed sand near the water's edge. Anne already knew Tindale from his walk, and when he shaded his eyes to peer up at the cottage, she waved.

He waved back and motioned her to come down to the water.

She ought not. She ought to leave him to enjoy the beach in solitude. Instead, she blew Tindale a kiss and hurried to fetch her hat.

CHAPTER SIX

The pleasure Augustus took at Anne's greeting was ridiculous. He'd come down to the beach, hoping to find her, and seen only the empty expanse of sand. Then a flutter of pale blue on the promontory had caught his eye, and his heart had leaped up.

He met her on the path, took the hat from her hand, and put it on her head. "You did not go shopping."

"By now, news of my disgrace—my latest disgrace—is all over Brighton," Anne said. "Why on earth would I give that crowd a chance to gawk at me when I can instead be here?"

With you. She did not need to add those words, because her bashful smile said them clearly.

"Then you weren't staying here merely to give Lord Bertram a chance to woo the fair Helen?" Augustus asked.

"The fair Helen has designs of her own on his lordship. Lady Deschamps's gathering has resulted in at least one happy pairing."

Not two? "Shall we wander by the water, Anne?"

She glanced back at the cottage. "Would you be shocked if I proposed another destination?"

A wave crashed against the shore, its force suggesting an incoming tide. "That depends on the destination."

Anne took Augustus by the hand and led him up the path. All manner of emotions accompanied Augustus as he and Anne approached the little stone cottage. Hope, because she intended to be private with him. Dismay, because he hadn't yet established an understanding with her, and joy, because this was Anne, and he was happy simply to spend time with her.

They reached the front steps, and she kept right on going, towing him inside her temporary abode. The cottage itself was shielded from view on the inn side by a stand of majestic elms. The beach had been deserted, and thus the risk of discovery was minimal.

And yet, Augustus hesitated just inside the door. "Are we courting, Anne?" He wanted to court her, but did she want to become his duchess?

"We are enjoying a day of unlooked-for privacy." She took off her hat and tossed it onto the sofa. "If you are willing?"

Augustus took the hat from the sofa and hung it over a peg by the door. He called upon his solicitor's training, sorting options, risks, and strategies. To reject Anne's invitation would hurt her. To press her for some sort of commitment at this point—given her tirade about the horrors of Society marriage—would fail.

Where was the harm in indulging their passion, if it brought them closer to sharing their lives?

Augustus examined that question from all sides while Anne stood by the window, gazing out at the sea.

"If there's a child," he said, "we will marry, Anne. Promise me that."

"The time is wrong for me to conceive."

She would take the steps necessary to educate herself in that regard, regardless of how desperately society tried to keep young ladies in ignorance.

"And if we cause a scandal?" Augustus did not dare move close enough to take her in his arms, or this necessary cross-examination would descend into kissing. "We were spied on once before."

"Then I will be ruined, which will honestly be a relief."

Augustus's mentors as he'd read law had pounded one notion in particular into his head as he'd memorized cases and statutes: If your opponent at the bargaining table appears to have blundered, to have made an offer too good to be true without realizing it, assume his blunder is not a mistake, but a brilliant ploy. Assume that taking advantage of his apparent mistake will expose you to grievous harm. Puzzle out what the harm might be before making the next move.

He could hear his old mentors railing at him now.

"Do you *seek* to be ruined, Anne? If that's the case, you need not bed me to see that accomplished. We can play a few games of chess, a hand or two of cribbage. Anything that keeps us private for more than five minutes will do, provided that privacy has witnesses."

Though Augustus most assuredly did not like this plan of hers, if a plan it was.

She turned from the window to glower at him. "In the first place, do you find it so difficult to imagine that I could seek to share some pleasure with you, Tindale? If the notion surprises, then you have a sad lack of appreciation for your own keen mind, nimble wit, fine form, and impressive kisses. In the second place, if I sought ruin at your hands, that would—albeit temporarily—redound to your discredit, and you are the last man I would ask to take on such a burden. In the third place..."

She turned back to the window.

"In the third place...?"

"I forget what's in the third place, because seeing you here, under this roof, knowing nobody will disturb us for the whole day parts me from my wits. My bedroom is through that door," she said, gesturing across the room. "Do we stand here arguing like barristers, or start tearing each other's clothes off?"

She was so dear when she was bungling a seduction. "Neither,"

Augustus said, prowling closer. "I prefer a leisurely prelude to my pleasures, as best I can recall. What about you?"

Anne patted his lapel when he'd come within embracing distance. "We're to discuss our lovemaking?"

He caught her hand and kissed her fingers. "I delight in our conversations, and it seems to me, lovemaking will be more enjoyable for a little parleying. Do you prefer to be on top or on the bottom, for example? A pillow beneath your hips? Your back to the wall? With you, Anne Baxter, my imagination runs riot."

She bundled close, not fast enough to hide her blush. "I have no established preferences, Tindale. I simply want to be close to you. I want to share this day with you. Intimately."

Her honesty obliterated Augustus's store of seductive banter. He stroked her hair and realized that trysting with Anne would not be a mere romp stolen along the way to enticing her to the altar. This intimacy she craved would be on her terms, a closeness of body, mind, *and* heart, rather than a maneuver in service to some strategic objective.

He could not be the duke with her, and he could not be the solicitor either. She demanded that he come to her purely as her lover. A terrifying prospect, which left Augustus questioning his own protestations that the title was merely a pesky nuisance.

"I want to be close to you too," he said. "Intimately close."

Anne eased away and led him into a tidy, unassuming bedroom. Two chairs were arranged by the window, and a vase of daffodils stood on a table between the chairs. The bed lacked a canopy, and the quilt—doves and roses—was worn soft. Braided rugs covered most of the flagstone floor, and the far wall included a door that might have led to a dressing closet. A chest, likely cedar lined, sat at the foot of the bed.

"Not quite spartan," Augustus observed. "I like it, though in winter the lack of a fireplace might make it chilly."

"I suspect the hearth in the next room is enough to heat the whole cottage," Anne said, unclasping a locket from her neck and putting it on the bedside table.

The gesture was simple and graceful and should not have been arousing. It wasn't, truly, but something inside Augustus shifted at the sight. He sat on the chest and pulled off his boots.

"Do you suppose Lord Bertram has aspirations in your cousin's direction?" he asked.

Anne sat on the other end of the chest and raised her skirts enough to untie her garters. "I hope he does. Helen likes to manage, and her children will soon require less of her in that regard. She misses having a husband, though Bertram's finances do not recommend him as a spouse."

She toed off her slippers and peeled out of her stockings, starting a pile of clothing between them on the chest.

"If she's comfortably well-off, his finances need not come into it."

"She seems well situated, but I have never asked her for particulars. Would you mind undoing my hooks?" Anne turned and swept her hair off her nape.

That something shifting inside Augustus lurched again. He tended to her hooks—not too many, thank heavens, because this was a day dress—and then untied her laces.

"You have a freckle," he said, touching a finger to her nape. "Pale, but I suspect in want of kissing." So he kissed that freckle, and Anne shivered.

She rose and slanted a smile at him over her shoulder. "The washstand is in the dressing closet. Feel free to borrow my toothbrush, though I will go first if you don't mind." She disappeared into the dressing closet, while Augustus was left to ponder his reactions.

He was in a state of pleasant sexual anticipation, not roaringly aroused, and feelings other than mere desire were afoot in this modest bedroom. He liked the quiet chatting. He liked the unassuming business of assisting Anne with her hooks and stays. He liked knowing she had a lone freckle on the back of her neck. He liked... *her*. Desired her, had fallen in love with her, and liked *her*.

He was still musing on that development when Anne emerged from the dressing closet, wearing a brown velvet dressing gown.

"Your turn, Tindale."

He'd shed his cravat, coat, waistcoat, boots, and stockings. "Might you call me Augustus?"

She picked up his coat from the pile on the chest and draped it over the back of one of the chairs. "Augustus. That suits you. Shall I await you in bed?"

She draped his waistcoat over the coat, then laid his cravat over that waistcoat. All orderly and neat. Wifely, one might say.

"You shall do as you please." Augustus rose and stretched. "You can watch me wash, climb beneath the covers, or kiss me this very moment. You might be surprised to learn that my sexual adventures have been few and tame, Anne. I had no time for entanglements as a solicitor, and men of the law are prone to gossip and scandalmongering when they aren't supporting the pillars of justice."

She tucked up against him. "Were you lonely?"

Not a question Augustus would have even understood as he was trying to establish his practice. "Terribly."

"And hard work helped," Anne said, patting his bum and easing away. "Tend to your ablutions, Augustus. I'm for bed."

That sweet little pat to his backside, her use of his name, that tone of gentle command... The last of Augustus's hesitation about this encounter wafted away on the shore breeze. Anne would take a prodigious amount of wooing. Her trust had been abused, her dreams trampled, but Augustus had developed a reputation as a solicitor of last resort.

He had worked harder, prepared longer, and persisted in the face of more obstacles than his colleagues had thought wise. The result had been success in some very challenging cases and a reputation to be proud of in the legal community.

As he shed more clothing, scrubbed himself, and brushed his teeth, he realized that much of his hard work had been—exactly as Anne had surmised—an attempt to combat loneliness.

If Anne Baxter was not the next Duchess of Tindale, mere loneliness would be the least of Augustus's heartaches.

Bond Street did not create fine clothing so much as it created heroic costumes. A fellow with narrow shoulders was given the padding he needed to cut a more imposing figure. A portly man could be equipped with a corset before stepping into breeches sewn to fit his artificially trimmer waist. The subterfuges were endless and skillful, and thus Anne was prepared for Tindale to be slightly less imposing in the flesh, as she doubtless was.

More fool her.

He emerged from the dressing closet, his hair damp-combed, his shirt off. He wore only his breeches, unbuttoned at the knee, one flap of his falls half undone, and the result was... To say Anne's breath was stolen was an understatement.

Here was the strutting male beast in his prime. Muscle rippled and flexed when Tindale bent to step out of his breeches, and every proportion begged Anne to measure it with touch and taste.

"I ride," he said, draping his breeches over the chest at the foot of the bed. "I fence. I like to go for long walks when I'm ruminating on a problem. The result is..."

"Good health," Anne said, glad she was sitting on the bed. "Grand good health."

He was also aroused, and that was a grand occasion as well, though Tindale didn't seem to take notice of his own rampant erection.

He was darker above the waist than below, suggesting he occasionally labored in the sun with his shirt off. Something only a wife, lover, or close friend would know about him. He took the place beside Anne on the bed and looped an arm around her waist.

"No second thoughts, Anne?"

"Barely any thoughts at all, you make such a powerful impression."

He kissed her temple. "You are thinking of your first love, the one with consumption. Sad thoughts."

How did he know that? "Yes and no. Sad thoughts, because he should not have died so young, but fierce thoughts too. At least he and I knew some pleasure before he surrendered to illness, at least we tried for some happiness. He had lovely memories to savor on that distant island."

Another kiss, this one to her cheek. "You think like a duchess."

"You're on close terms with many duchesses?" He smelled good, of Anne's rose-scented soap and something spicier—cedar, perhaps. Rosemary?

"My late cousin's wife, Eugenia, is quite the duchess. You'd like her, and I can assure you on the strength of my acquaintance with her and her friends that duchesses are very fierce. Also sweet and pragmatic. Let's get beneath the covers, shall we?"

"Yes." Anne had kept her robe and chemise on. She draped the robe over Tindale's discarded breeches and scooted beneath the quilts. When she'd imagined trysting with Tindale—which she had, at length—she'd never seen them being intimate in daylight.

Sunshine put a different complexion on the whole undertaking and left a lady wishing for candlelight—on her side of the bed.

Tindale made the mattress rock as he joined her beneath the covers, and Anne was again reminded of how different he was from her first love. Christian had been slender, pale, and sweet, while Tindale was... also sweet, but there the similarity ended.

"Cuddle up," he said, threading an arm beneath Anne's neck. "I understand you've been invited to the Friday-night ball and tomorrow night's card party. You will save your supper waltz for me, please."

He was warm, all-over warm. Anne snuggled close, her head pillowed on the hollow of his shoulder. "I'd rather not attend any balls, but Helen would disown me for such cowardice. I will save my supper waltz for you."

She wanted to tell him that she'd save him more than that, that this need not be their only tryst, except that at the end of this week, Tindale would go back to Town, and Anne would... not. She'd finish out her fortnight at the Siren's Retreat and then maybe go hillwalking in the Lakes and, this time, actually enjoy the scenery.

Or in Bavaria, now that Europe was at peace.

"My dancing is merely adequate," Tindale said. "Ladies have shorter legs, while I... I hope my lovemaking recommends me to you if my waltzing cannot."

Had a window banged open on a fresh breeze, Anne could not have been more surprised. "Don't be nervous, Tindale. We are above all else friends, and I desire you madly."

"Do you really? Perhaps you might consider bestowing a few kisses on the fellow you profess to desire?"

Anne shifted to straddle him, her own boldness shocking her, but feeling right with Tindale. "Prepare to be kissed."

She was aware of his arousal, snug against her intimate parts, and aware of his smile, more buccaneering than its previous incarnations.

"Do your damnedest, Miss Baxter, and I shall give no quarter."

She began gently, suspecting that Tindale, for all his robust health, had known little of tenderness or sweetness. She pressed her lips to his brow, his cheek, the corner of his mouth and felt him gradually relaxing beneath her.

"More," he whispered. "Please, Anne."

He trailed his fingers over her arms, then along her jaw, and back to the chignon at her nape. After a few slight tugs, Anne's braid slipped down over her shoulder.

"I want you undone," he said, frothing her chemise up around her thighs. "Utterly cast away with pleasure."

He bowed up, and the kissing took on an intensity as Anne realized that through the material of her chemise, Tindale was stroking her breasts.

"That is... That is *sumptuous.*"

He knew what to do with his hands, knew how to provoke magic and fire and an urgency that obliterated reason.

"I'm wearing white," Anne said. The thought came from nowhere and made little sense. Her wedding dress had been white, as if she'd been a virgin sacrifice in some old pagan ritual. "I don't want to wear white with you."

Tindale undid the bow of the décolletage and gathered up the fabric. "Then don't." He eased the chemise over Anne's head, leaving her naked and straddling her lover. She crossed her arms over her chest, smitten by self-consciousness. No man, not even her first, long-ago lover, had seen her thus.

If she and Tindale ever made love again, which was unlikely, they'd do so after dark.

He pulled the covers up over her shoulders and wrapped his arms around her. "You have no need for shyness. You were a bold and fearless girl, to hear you tell it. Racketing about barefoot wherever you pleased, exploring wherever your curiosity led. Recall that fierce, well-loved younger Anne and introduce her to the woman who just kissed me witless."

His words reminded her of much that had been lost when she'd been orphaned and also inspired her to move on her lover, to be again curious and bold and *confident.*

Tindale sank back against the pillows. "Fiend, beautiful, lovely... Take me inside you, Anne, or I will make a very unimpressive showing as your lover."

Anne took him in hand, though he needed little enough guidance. While she crouched above him, he began slowly, each thrust a slight advance over the previous one.

"Don't rush," she said, curling onto his chest. "Don't hurry. I need..."

"What do you need, Anne?"

To make this last, to understand, to hoard up the beauty and longing and pleasure... "I need you, Augustus."

Quiet enveloped them, bracketed by the distant roar of the surf and the soft rustle of bedclothes. Tindale granted Anne's wish, keeping the tempo slow, even as her desire mounted to a frantic pitch.

He'd wanted her undone, and Anne obliged him, shuddering in his arms as sensation coalesced into unspeakably intense satisfaction. She clung and shook, and when the pleasure rebounded and crested yet higher, she held to him more tightly still.

"Undone," she whispered, subsiding against him. "Utterly, absolutely."

His response was to visit upon her a series of revelations about the depths of bodily joy a lady might plumb with a skilled and generous lover. Augustus was as relentless as the tides, until Anne was tossed from one pleasure to the next, drifting sweetly one moment and thrashing through another fierce tumult minutes later.

When she was replete beyond her wildest imaginings, Augustus withdrew and stroked himself to a swift completion. He lay on his back in decadent repose, eyes closed, chest heaving.

"I should get up," he said. "Fetch you a flannel, open the window."

Anne extricated herself from him and from the bedclothes. "You have earned your rest." She tottered to the dressing closet, intent on finding a damp cloth, and caught sight of herself in the mirror over the washstand.

Hair half undone, cheeks rosy, gaze *sparkling*. The gleam in her eyes delighted her as hard gallops and midnight moonrises once had. This interlude with Augustus had given her back a precious part of herself that she must never be parted from again.

Her soul, perhaps. Her wits, her *self*.

She wrung out a cloth and brought it to the bed. When Augustus made no move to take it from her, she tidied him up and hung the cloth over the bedpost. Silly man, to think she'd hesitate to handle him intimately now.

Anne cracked a window and climbed back beneath the covers,

snuggling up to Augustus as if they'd spent years of afternoons in such wanton intimacy.

"Sleep," he said, wrapping an arm around her shoulders. "I will be here when you waken."

Anne allowed herself the exquisite pleasure of sinking into slumber in her lover's arms. She was owed that much, and so was Augustus.

CHAPTER SEVEN

Augustus awoke feeling as stuporous as if he'd overimbibed, though in place of all the nasty effects of intemperance, his languor was suffused with sweetness. Every part of him—body, mind, heart—was saturated with peaceful joy all tied up in a lacy bow of quiet sexual awareness.

He was curled around Anne, and without knowing how, he could tell that she, too, was awake.

"Love me again, Augustus. This time, I want to be on my back."

"Any way you please, Anne." The angle of the sun slanting in the windows told him they'd slept only briefly, so he took his time. Intimacy with Anne Baxter was to be savored, and in her slow caresses and sinuous undulations, she cherished him as well.

The joining became a homecoming, and the pleasure threatened Augustus's control. This was not a wild ride or a delicious nightcap. This was profound, courageous intimacy with the woman he loved.

He tried to draw out the climb to satisfaction, to explore the side paths—Anne was ticklish below her ribs, and she knew precisely how hard to dig her nails into Augustus's backside—but she was not to be denied, and soon Augustus's arms were full of a sighing, well-pleasured lady.

He eased away and spent on her belly, longing for the day when that precaution wouldn't be needed. He hung over her, replete and ready to contemplate another nap. He levered up, intent on tidying up.

Unease crept through his lassitude as he beheld his beloved. "Anne Baxter, look at me."

She used the sheet to wipe at her cheeks, then offered him a smile. "Your turn to fetch the flannel, Your Grace. *Noblesse oblige* for the party on top."

He wrapped his arms around her. "Tears, Anne? At least tell me why."

She stroked his hair, and he could feel her choosing words. "I have been lonely too, Augustus. You assuage that loneliness and allow me to admit how difficult the past years have been."

That was an honest answer, also a prevarication. August held her for a while longer, hoping she'd say more. The distant tide surged and retreated, and Anne's fingers drifted through his hair, but she gave him no more words.

Noblesse oblige. Nobility obliges—or obligates. Augustus left the bed, returned with a flannel, and tended to his lover.

"Shall we nap again?"

Anne elbow-walked closer to the window side of the bed. "A cuddle, to restore my equilibrium. The idea of popping back into my clothes, raiding the larder, and nipping down to the beach... That is beyond me now."

"Good, because popping, raiding, and nipping are beyond me as well. Cuddling is well within my powers." He banked the pillows so he could half recline, his arm around Anne as she snuggled up to his side.

"Now will you tell me why you were moved to tears, Anne?"

She fussed with the covers, hitched her leg across his thighs, and then toyed with the hair on his chest.

"I felt sad. After being so close to a lover, some sadness afterward is to be expected."

The witness was avoiding the question. "You were not crying afterward, Anne. You cried while I was yet inside you."

The duke in Augustus told him to desist, to stop pestering the lady for what might not lend itself to words. The solicitor in him agreed, because a badgered witness could give untrustworthy testimony, but the lover in him had to know what troubled her.

"Our scheme," Anne said, "your scheme, in which I have been complicit, is not working, Augustus."

He had to exert mental effort to parse her meaning. "The scheme where you reject my advances? I see no reason to abandon that little diversion now. Toss me over at the ball, and all and sundry will say I got what I deserved. I will become the object of talk rather than you. After a suitable period of manly brooding, I will renew my addresses to you and—"

She put her fingers to his lips. "No, Augustus. I want no part of farces, diversions, or subterfuges. That would make you look foolish, which I am unwilling to do. Your kind attentions to me have kept the gossips in check, and we must content ourselves with that much."

He grasped her fingers gently. "I am more than willing to look foolish before a lot of buffoons and imbeciles who mean nothing to me."

Anne's removed her leg from his thighs. "Those buffoons and imbeciles will decide if any of the bills you introduce in Parliament have a prayer of becoming law. They will decide if your daughters *take*, or have no suitors. Their children will either befriend your sons or make their public-school years hell. The buffoons matter, Augustus, more than you know."

Despite Anne's naked warmth pressed to Augustus's side, a chill gripped him. "You *are* rejecting me." He had no daughters, he'd as yet introduced no bills, and he had no sons. That left... only him. The lover, the duke, *and* the solicitor.

"I am thanking you for all you've done for me just in the past week. I am profoundly grateful for the time spent with you, and I hope we can be friends, but, Augustus... those people will make your life a misery if you give them the slightest opening. They already gossip about you, and when Lord Corbett comes back to Town, as he inevitably will, he will expect you to console him for his foolishness, not make sheep's eyes at me."

"Lord Corbett can"—bugger himself—"take a flying leap into the Thames."

"Lord Corbett can make your life very difficult, and my life difficult, too, lest you forget."

Every instinct Augustus possessed, honed over years of wrestling complex legalities, wanted to argue with Anne, but she'd cited an irrefutable truth. Lord Corbett Hobbs could speak ill of Augustus in the clubs, disparage him before his friends, cut him in the carriage parade.

None of that mattered, nor did it compare to what his lordship might do *to Anne* if he took a notion to indulge in the wrong sort of tantrum.

"They were already whispering about me," Anne said, pushing herself upright to sit beside Augustus. "I'm used goods. I cannot buy a husband even with all my wealth. I must have a love child somewhere if Lord Corbett set me aside in that humiliating fashion. All of those whispers have been silenced by your marked courtesy to me."

Augustus brought her hand to his lips and kissed her knuckles. "*Marked courtesy*? I have never regarded glorious lovemaking as a marked courtesy, Anne."

She eased from his grip. "Hume Billingsley would not have been half so gallant to me had you not already set the bar at least that high. Lord Bertram would not be making overtures to Helen if this house party had turned me into an object of scorn. I'm an object of whispers and, perhaps, pity, and that is as good an outcome as I could have hoped for."

She sounded so cool, so logical, and yet, she had cried in his arms.

"Please assure me you will not marry Billingsley, Anne. He does not deserve you and never has."

She smoothed her palm over the worn quilt. "I might have, before today. I'm fortified against such weakness now."

That remark perplexed Augustus. When he would have asked Anne to explain, she kissed his shoulder, then rose and shrugged into her dressing gown.

"My hair is a fright. Perhaps you'd help me put it to rights, Your Grace?"

Your Grace. Proper address should have no place between lovers when private, but Anne was making a point. Augustus brushed out her hair, and they assisted each other to dress, but some boundary, some properly defended border, had been reestablished.

"You won't accept Thurlow as a spouse?" Augustus asked as he and Anne made their way down to the beach.

"Gracious days, of course not. I'll lose more to him at tomorrow night's card party, but that's the limit of my charity where he's concerned. Shall we build another sandcastle, Tindale?"

How could she do this? How could she pretend that the past two hours hadn't happened? But then, Augustus knew how. Of necessity, Anne had grown adept at pretending, at ignoring slights, at not overhearing what had been said loudly enough to wound her.

"You won't marry Thurlow, you won't marry Billingsley, and you won't marry me," Augustus said. "Do I have that right?"

Anne faced the sea, her hat brim riffling in the breeze. "My best option, Tindale, is to slip into genteel spinsterhood, donating generously to charities, and having the curate and his sweetheart to dine on Sundays."

"You aren't telling me the whole of it." Her reasoning was sound. The tabbies and schoolgirls had sheathed their claws. The men were keeping any ribald remarks about Anne to themselves. Augustus's attentions had protected Anne's prospects to that limited extent.

Anne was far better acquainted with these people than Augustus was, and he knew she had a point: If she humiliated him publicly, her consequence might rise—and it might not—but his would surely fall.

Where had that keen insight on her part been a week ago?

And even if Anne's determination to quietly go her own way was the best possible ending to this house-party tribulation, why did her pragmatic, selfless decision leave her in tears and Augustus wanting to demolish this entire pretty little cottage by the sea?

"I've changed my mind," Anne said. "You will have to attend the card party without me."

Helen, who had been notably quiet since returning last night from her shopping expedition, poured herself a second cup of tea.

"Will you claim a megrim, Anne, or a case of cold feet? Matters are progressing nicely, if you ask me. Lord Hume has shown you nothing but cordial good manners, the Daleys have retreated behind their fans, and according to Bertie—Lord Bertram, rather—Lieutenant Thurlow has become your champion in the men's retiring room. Lose a few more hands of cards to him, and he'll be singing your praises at the punch bowl."

The morning was brilliant and the air mild, a harbinger of warmer weather and a reminder that Anne could not tarry by the sea much longer. Rose Cottage was in demand, as well it should be.

As for Lieutenant Thurlow... "The lieutenant took a young lady strolling by the sea last night. Miss Charlotte Daley, if the lady's taste in evening gowns was any indication." Charlotte still wore the pale colors of the recent schoolgirl, while Roberta preferred patterned muslins. Both sisters wore the same elaborate flounces.

"We must not hold that gallantry against the lieutenant," Helen said. "Charlotte is to be pitied, after all. Until her older sister finds a husband, Charlotte is more or less doomed to idle flirtations."

The notion that Anne should pity a woman who'd spied on her... Though, in fact, Anne did feel some pity. A smidgeon of pity.

"Go to the card party without me, Helen. I have shown the flag and weathered even Lord Hume's gracious pity."

Helen sipped her tea, studying Anne over the rim of her cup. "This has to do with Tindale, doesn't it?"

Most of Anne's waking and dreaming thoughts had to do with Tindale, and probably would for some time.

"His Grace has been an ally, and he has my gratitude, but he's done what he can. Anything more than gentlemanly regard could only redound to his discredit."

Helen put down her cup. "He's a *duke*. In case you've forgotten, a duke can live openly with his wife *and* his mistress, the resulting miscellany populating his nursery, and nobody dares say a word about it."

"*To him*," Anne said, rising. "Nobody dares say a word to the duke. Old Devonshire has been gone for more than five years, and people still talk about his household in scandalized tones. I'll not..."

Helen remained seated. "You are protecting Tindale from the gossips?"

"They are waiting to pounce, Helen. Augustus came across plenty of aristocratic dirty linen in the course of his legal practice. His peers will take any opportunity to remind him that solicitors are not gentlemen, even when they luck into a ducal title." Lily Northrup had passed along a few general details regarding the cases Augustus had handled.

Gambling debts so enormous they necessitated confining the irresponsible *noble scion* to a sanitorium until he could be declared legally incompetent and thus not liable for his wagers.

A fine lady's bastard child quietly entrusted to a rural vicar.

Genuine madness. Marital violence. Shocking meanness toward impecunious siblings and offspring. Augustus had seen much and heard more. Society would ensure that he kept his mouth shut about the whole of it.

Though Society was utterly blockheaded. Augustus would never divulge a confidence entrusted to him in either a personal or a professional capacity.

"You'll let them win, then? The Daleys and their ilk? You'll give Lady Deschamps the pleasure of telling all of Debrett's that you rudely rejected her efforts to rehabilitate your reputation?"

"My reputation needs no rehabilitation." *Yet.* "Lady Deschamps can take a flying leap into the Thames."

Helen took another sip of tea. "That is something you would have said as a schoolgirl. You are a hoyden at heart, Anne, but you have managed to overcome your wild impulses. You are so close to victory that I cannot imagine why you'd quit the field now."

Defeat had arrived in the person of one dear, tenderhearted, ferocious duke. "I haven't overcome my wild impulses, Helen. Not entirely. I never did. I am certain in my bones, though, that Tindale, Billingsley, and whoever else Lady Deschamps means to toss at me are not such as I would marry. I have no wish to move in Society, and I cannot see that changing. I should have retired to the countryside years ago."

"Now you talk like a widow, exhausted by the social affray, but you aren't a widow."

Anne was not a hoyden and not a widow, but she was no stranger to grief either. "Tindale knows not to expect me."

"I haven't sent your regrets to Lady Deschamps, Anne. You cannot think to simply—"

A maid came through the garden gate, a folded piece of paper in her hands. "Beggin' yer pardon, ladies. I have a note for Miss Baxter. Came from that fancy house party, and there's a crest pressed into the wax."

Anne took the message and examined the seal. She knew the coat of arms, because it adorned Tindale's coach.

"You may be excused," Helen said, "and might you please take the breakfast dishes with you?"

Anne waited until the maid had gathered up a tray full of cups and dishes, then slit the seal.

. . .

Miss Baxter,

Lord Corbett Hobbs has joined Lady Deschamps's gathering. The perishing imbecile is impersonating a tragic hero from some Greek drama, lurking in corners and staring pensively at nothing. I have not yet acknowledged him, nor do I intend to. I thought you deserved notice of this most farcical development.

I remain, yours respectfully,

Tindale

Oh, Augustus. If he cut Corbett Hobbs, Hobbs could provoke a scene, or even issue a challenge. The talk would be nothing compared to the repercussions if either man were injured—or worse.

Anne passed the note over to Helen.

"I see the pretty hands of the Daley sisters in this development," Helen said, wrinkling her nose. "And Lady Deschamps will be delighted to host the drama of the Season."

The vile, reeking Thames was too good for Lady Deschamps. "Can a duke's son challenge a duke?" Anne asked.

"Technically, no, but in terms of family standing, both fellows would be equal. As my late husband used to say, when drunken men get to feeling slighted, nonsense can ensue."

"Deadly nonsense. I will attend that card party after all, Helen, and I must send a note to His Grace."

Helen folded up the missive. "What will you tell him?"

"I will beg him to please be civil at all times. To recall his standing and his dignity, and to see no insult where only stupidity is on display."

"Some men call that stupidity honor."

Anne took one last look at the placid majesty of the sea. "Corbett Hobbs hasn't the first notion of honor. Perhaps the sight of me will help him recall his passing acquaintance with discretion."

Tindale watched the drive from Lily's sitting room. "The coach approaches."

"Then perhaps you will cease pacing a hole in my carpets, Augustus."

"I half expected Anne to leave me..."

Lily looked up from her knitting. "At the altar? Has she accepted your proposal, then?"

For a woman who spent much of her day in her apartment, Lily knew nearly everything that transpired under her roof.

"Anne doesn't want me to propose," Augustus said. "The original plan was for her to throw me over, to show polite society that she can have—or reject—any man she pleases. She has since forbidden me to do the bended-knee bit."

The sound of a coach clattering up to the front door nearly had Augustus bolting from the parlor.

"Because you would be proposing in earnest."

Lily's needles clicked away, the soft blue wool cascading over her knees.

"Maybe I wouldn't be in earnest this time," Augustus said, "but yes, I would like to marry Anne. She has all but sent me away with a flea in my ear." After crying in his arms. What was he to make of that? "I suspect she's trying to protect me."

"I more than suspect it. Your duchess must be as far above reproach as the Dover cliffs rise above the sea."

Voices drifted up from the foyer. "Because I am a jumped-up solicitor?"

"Your grandchildren will have that thrown in their faces, Augustus. Anne is absolutely right to be concerned for your acceptance in society. Times have changed, and propriety has a hold on society it will not easily give up. The middling classes might not have the vote, but they run the newspapers, the print shops, the schools, and the churches. They have had enough of a wastrel monarch and his greedy, licentious peerage."

"How odd," Augustus said. "Here I thought a solicitor was from the middling classes, and all I seek is to offer a lifetime of marital devotion to the woman I esteem greatly."

Lily gestured with her chin toward the door. "Go sprinkle duke dust on Camelia's card party. Do not call out Lord Corbett, or I shall be quite severe with you."

"I can't call him out." *More's the pity.*

"Because he lacks a title?"

"Because Anne forbade me to and because I do not make sport of dumb animals. Besides, an affair of honor would implicate Anne's good name, and that is a risk I would never take." Duke dust, as if this gathering were some sort of fairy tale.

"Lord Corbett can still issue a challenge, Tindale. He's that much of a dunderpate. Go carefully."

Augustus bowed on that excellent advice, assembled the dignity Anne had admonished him to keep on hand, and made a slow descent of the main staircase to greet the new arrivals.

"Mrs. Saunders." He bowed over Helen's hand. "Miss Baxter, a pleasure as always. Shall I find you ladies some punch?"

A dozen guests, including both Daleys, apparently found it necessary to tarry in the foyer, all eyes on Anne.

Who appeared as serene as the sea on a sunny summer day. "Punch would be appreciated, Your Grace." Anne replied.

Augustus offered an arm to each lady, though Helen was soon waylaid—happily, it seemed—by Lord Bertram.

"Lord Corbett has kept his distance," Augustus said. "Shall we greet him now? The punch bowl is on the terrace, and he's keeping company with a potted palm along the balustrade."

"You will be civil?"

"I would rather shove his head into the nearest horse trough." The Daleys apparently felt a pressing need for some fresh air, for they trailed Augustus and Anne by three not-very-discreet yards.

"I would rather have stayed in my nice, cozy cottage," Anne said, "watching the light change over the sea as the sun set while I revisited some lovely memories."

Augustus stopped a few steps onto the terrace. By the light of the waning sun, Anne's composure took on a brittle appearance.

"You've been crying." *Again.*

"The salt air and the bright sun must have irritated my eyes. I spent the afternoon building another sandcastle."

"I spent the afternoon on correspondence, lest I accidently pitch Hobbs over some obliging balcony."

Anne leaned infinitesimally closer. "Please, Augustus. No drama."

"Oh, very well. Let's get this over with." He did not exactly tow Anne across the terrace to the balcony, but neither did Anne march along smartly at his side. A crowd formed in the main doorway to the terrace, with a smaller cluster of spectators on the steps to the conservatory entrance.

Corbett tried to look past Augustus's shoulder, then tried to gaze at the sea, but Augustus had made his living sorting through necessary confrontations, and this moment could go a long way toward restoring Anne's peace of mind.

"Hobbs," Augustus said. "Shrewd of you to choose this venue. Polite society is on hand, but not in overwhelming numbers."

The compliment apparently confused his lordship. "Tindale, Miss Baxter." Hobbs bowed over Anne's hand, probably out of habit more than manners. "Miss Baxter, you are looking... well." He had the sense to offer that compliment cautiously.

"I am well, thank you, my lord. And you?"

"In the very pink," Hobbs said, and at that moment, his complexion was pink enough to suggest he'd fortified himself with a quantity of Lady Deschamps's excellent rum punch. "I say, Miss Baxter, you seem to have weathered—"

Augustus cleared his throat.

Anne cocked her head. "I came to the seaside to recover my spirits, my lord, after most upsetting developments in Town which were in no way the result of my own actions. Lady Deschamps has been good enough to include me in some of her events. What brings you here?"

Bravo, Anne.

"I wanted... That is to say, I don't suppose..." Hobbs looked from Anne to Augustus, and Augustus had the sinking impression that Hobbs meant to renew his proposal of marriage.

"Did your parents threaten to cut you off unless you talked Anne around?" Augustus asked.

Hobbs resumed studying the sea. "Her Grace might have implied that it's not too late... and there's nothing to say that Miss Baxter and I won't suit, except nobody knew where Miss Baxter had got off to, and why am I discussing this with you, Tindale?"

"Because," Anne said, "Tindale was left to clean up your mess, my lord. If you have an apology to make, I'm happy to hear it, but please don't think I'll entertain another proposal from you."

Hobbs risked a glance in Anne's direction. "Is that how the wind blows? You're throwing me over for a duke?"

Anne's grip on Augustus's arm tightened. "You threw me over for *your mistress*, Corbett, and a man who will toss aside his intended should anticipate being tossed aside himself. If your problem is excessive indebtedness incurred as a result of your expectations in my direction, you should have thought of that before you decamped for Scotland. Roberta Daley has a sizable dowry, and she's ready to settle down."

"They wrote to me," Hobbs said. "The Daley sisters. I've known Bobbie forever, but... all those flounces give a man pause." Hobbs's pale blue eyes had acquired a speculative gleam.

"Before you trot off to begin your wooing," Augustus said, "you owe Miss Baxter an apology, and make it convincing, Hobbs, lest Miss Baxter think ill of you."

Hobbs blinked, he frowned, he looked as if he were preparing for his first Speech Day effort, then he put his hands behind his back.

"I am sorry," he said. "Badly done of me. I was an idiot. Mama says so too. She says so frequently. Don't know what came over me." He tried for a smile that Anne did not return. "I do apologize."

Anne held Hobbs's gaze long enough that even Augustus felt an inclination to fidget.

"That will suffice, my lord," Anne said at length. "Apology accepted. I wish you a pleasant evening."

Hobbs looked from Anne to Augustus, then seemed to realize he'd done all that was required of him. He remembered to bow before haring off straight for Miss Roberta Daley.

"They deserve each other," Augustus said. "That was brilliantly done. We never did get that glass of punch."

Anne remained by the balustrade, her fingers curled around his arm. "I was an idiot to think I could have made him an adequate wife, but one does grow tired. After a few years, the line between pretending and reality blurs to a dangerous extent."

"Pretending?"

"I wanted to slap him, Augustus. I forbade you to call him out, but I wanted to kick him hard, to do violence to his person... but he's the same overindulged lordling I was engaged to. I cannot expect him to ever be otherwise, despite a towering need to backhand him before a large audience."

"Right now," Augustus said as the crowd began to file back inside, "I want to take you in my arms and hold you until you are free of all the violence, and tears, and pretending. I want to tell that tittering lot of scandalmongers calling themselves polite society to choke on their damned gossip."

Anne blinked, and a tear splashed on the coat of Augustus's sleeve. "You are so very dear, Tindale. Perhaps you'd fetch me a glass of punch?"

Bedamned to the punch. "So you can compose yourself enough to face an evening of cards with people you loathe."

Lord Bertram and Helen remained on the terrace, reminding Augustus that Helen was technically Anne's chaperone.

Anne rubbed her forehead as footmen began lighting torches in the formal garden. "I don't loathe them." Said with weary bitterness.

Augustus shifted so he could lean his hips against the railing and see Anne's face. "I was curious to know if you'd take pity on Hobbs. I did not think you'd have him, not if you won't have Billingsley, and you won't have me."

"Augustus, please, not now."

She wiped another tear from her cheek, and Augustus realized that the woman he loved had hit the limit of her vast stores of composure. She had hit the limit of her patience, her courage, her self-restraint... Her dignity teetered on the brink of collapse, and yet, she intended to soldier on, smiling politely and losing with good grace to an impecunious naval lieutenant.

Why? Why suffer like that, why reject a duke, why *protect* a duke? Why reject the lover who would give his life for her? He thought back over years of quietly solving such problems as found their way to a lawyer's office, to family secrets and private humiliations.

"Anne," he asked, taking her hand, "was there a love child?"

CHAPTER EIGHT

I never wanted you to know. She would rather have been left at the altar a thousand times over, while all of Mayfair laughed at her, than have Augustus quietly guess at a secret she'd gone to such lengths to keep hidden.

She took a final swipe at her cheeks. "Don't be ridiculous, Tindale. Any woman would find it taxing to confront the man who jilted her. If we tarry out here much longer, our absence from the card tables will be remarked."

Tindale considered her, though Anne could barely meet his gaze. "The consumptive lad, the one who went off to Greece. Did he know he left you with child?"

Oh, God. The vast ocean was not deep enough to hold the pain Tindale's questions caused.

"This does not bear discussion, Your Grace."

"Your tears are more important to me than any card game, scandal, farce, or drama happening anywhere on this entire sceptered isle, Anne Baxter."

Tindale led her by the hand to where Helen and Lord Bertram hovered by the punch bowl.

"Tindale, you must not... I only need a moment... What are you doing?"

"Miss Baxter is feeling unwell," Augustus said. "I am seeing her home. Tell Lady Deschamps and her harpies and imps to go to hell."

"A megrim," Helen said. "Understandable in the circumstances."

"Can come on quite suddenly," Lord Bertram added. "And don't worry. We'll partner Hobbs and the Daley creature and ensure their conversation is all that it should be. Thurlow has designs on the other sister, and it would not do for scandal to interfere with the boy's plans just as his ship is coming in, so to speak."

"Lord Hume and Mrs. Northrup will take over for us when the tables switch," Helen said. "Hobbs will comport himself like a gentleman if we have to nanny him all the way back to London. Anne, take His Grace's kind offer of an escort. Camelia's pot-stirring is over and done with."

"Helen, no... If I leave..."

Helen hugged Anne tight, not a cousinly hug, more of a motherly hug. "Go with His Grace, for God's sake, Anne. What you just did... You were magnificent. Leave this pack of jackals to gape in awe at your self-possession."

"I will never feel self-possessed again."

Tindale slipped an arm around her waist. "We'll walk back to the cottage. The sea air might restore your spirits." He bowed to Helen, nodded to Bertram, and Anne found herself crossing the park and holding hands with His Grace of Tindale.

He could have gone to fetch her a glass of punch, could have allowed her to slip back to the cottage with a quiet word to her hostess. But here he was, holding her hand, walking her home, and telling polite society to go to blazes.

I will never find another like him, and I must find the strength to be honest with him. The sentiment settled over Anne's heart as peacefully as moonlight illuminates a seascape. Tindale had divined the scandal in Anne's past without Anne saying so much as a word, and his reaction had been to take her hand.

To take her part.

"There was a child," she said as they gained the trail that led down to the sea. "A girl. She lived to be four. My solicitors arranged everything. Measles took her." A handful of simple sentences to describe enough joy and sorrow for a lifetime.

"Tell me about her."

Anne had to stop on the path and lean into Tindale to withstand the caring in that simple request. Words that had reverberated silently inside Anne's heart—*my daughter, precious, darling, beautiful, perfect*—found their way into the night air, slowly at first. More tears came as well, along with remembered joy and abiding love.

Anne was still talking—jabbering—by the time she and Tindale were climbing the path that led to the cottage. She'd taken off her slippers and stockings to cross the beach and had to go carefully on the trail in the dark.

"Christina was so bright," Anne said, "so inquisitive. She had my curiosity and her father's quiet nature and his fair coloring. Her parents adored her."

"Her foster parents," Tindale said. "You were her mother. Did her father know?"

Anne shook her head. "Christian had sailed before I realized I was carrying. To summon him back would have been to cut short his life. He would have returned, too, to marry me, and then he would have been trapped. He believed consumption was contagious, and ours would have been a marriage in name only. He did not deserve that, and I had the means to deal with the situation."

Augustus escorted her up the steps to the cottage's front porch. "Those means allowed you to know your daughter."

"I spent the first three months of her life with her. After that, I was her godmother, as far as she knew. An old friend of her mother's. I had hoped that someday Christina might learn the truth, but that day never came."

"What of your family? Your aunt and uncle?"

"They knew I had cared for Christian. When I announced a plan to take an extended tour of the Lakes, they did not interfere. I hired a discreet companion and a year later sent her on her way with enough coin to ensure her silence. My solicitors are not my uncle's solicitors, and thus I have avoided scandal."

"So far," Tindale said.

Anne was tired to her bones, from crying, from pretending, from revisiting a time in her life that had nearly broken her.

"When I came back south, my aunt and uncle were determined that I take my proper place in Society, and, Augustus, they would not let up. They threw bachelors and widowers, officers and heirs at me like an infantry square fires at the oncoming enemy. I realized I would have to choose a husband or leave England altogether."

Leaving England had begun to look appallingly attractive, which brought another lump to Anne's throat. "Thank you for seeing me home, Tindale."

He stood at the front door to the cottage, his features obscured by the moon shadows. "You are sending me on my way?"

"If you don't return promptly..." She would never be able to let him go. Anne watched the waves on the beach, and told herself not to start crying again.

"I do not give that,"—fingers snapped crisply in the darkness —"for what that crowd of lackwits thinks of me, Anne, but if you care what they think of you, then I will march off to play bedamned whist and swill tepid punch while making inane small talk."

"You are angry," Anne said, both longing to slip into the peace and quiet of the cottage and loath to part from Augustus when he was in a temper. "I am sorry, Tindale. The habit of guarding my privacy is ingrained, and I never meant to offend you."

He paced away and took a piece of Anne's heart with him. "You thought to marry Lord Hume Billingsley because he was too destitute to inquire closely into your situation. Thank heavens the solicitors intervened. Then you thought to marry Corbett because he's too stupid to even wonder about your past. Divine providence alone spared you from that purgatory."

Augustus strode toward Anne, stopping three feet away. "I understand that you sought to placate your family and appease convention—or some such rot—by marrying, but why in the hell won't you marry me?"

"Your duchess, of all duchesses, must be above approach, Tindale."

"My duchess won't organize her life around the opinions of a lot of petty gossips, and neither will her duke. Tell me the truth. Did I bungle the lovemaking? Is a former solicitor too lowly? Tell me what I must do, who I must be... Please, Anne, tell me the truth."

She put her hand over his mouth. "You must be yourself. I must be myself, and those two people cannot succeed if they are married to one another. Someday, somebody will whisper in your ear that your duchess is not all that she should be. You will shrug that off, but then another somebody will whisper that the mother of your children has a past. That she mis-stepped, and then it will be too late, Augustus. You'll be s-stuck with me, and I could not bear..."

He pulled her hand away and enveloped it in both of his. "My dearest, darling Anne, you seek to protect *yourself*, because nobody has ever done a proper job of assisting you in that regard. You think I will turn from you because your past at some point could become known."

Now that Anne could not see his features clearly, she wished for light.

"My family would have turned from me," she went on. "Helen might suspect—few young ladies prefer an extended tour of the Lakes to making their come out. My aunt and uncle would be scandalized. Lily reminded me that solicitors know all the secrets, and if you did not hear my story from some gossip, you might eventually hear it from a former legal associate. My family will leave me in peace after this, but the gossips never go quiet for long."

Tindale tugged on Anne's hand, drawing her into his arms. "I probably have heard your story, though without enough details to identify the parties involved. A young woman, anticipating vows, cheated of marriage by death or misfortune, scurrying away before polite society has a chance to form any impression of her... It happens more often than you think, Anne."

She let herself rest against him, let herself feel the warmth of his embrace. "But this happened to *me*, and I would rather have one stolen moment with you by the sea than see your regard for me slowly erode, year by year, as the comments at the club and the veiled allusions at Angelo's chip away at your esteem. Sooner or later, there will be talk, Tindale."

His arms settled around Anne more securely. "Oh, probably, and we will ignore the talk, or we will order a magnificent headstone for the child's grave, and everybody will assume she was my by-blow."

The words were simple, but the emotions they evoked—bewilderment, wonder, gratitude, *hope*—were not. "You would acknowledge my daughter as your offspring?"

"Anne Baxter, if we are to be duke and duchess, then we need not acknowledge, explain, or make excuses for anything. Your past and my past are nobody's business. You are absolutely right that we will be in the public eye to some unavoidable extent, but we will be there together. When you thought Corbett Hobbs might tempt me to stupidity, you rushed to my side. When you need me, I will rush to your side as well. That's what the vows are about."

"I think I'm about to cry again." Tindale would mean his vows. He'd take that cherishing part very seriously.

So would Anne.

He passed her a handkerchief. "I suspect you have held back an ocean of tears. This cottage has a lovely little terrace, out of the wind, with a fine view of the sea. When you have finished with your next bout of the weeps, we can watch the stars come out together."

Together. Not a word Anne had much experience with. She contemplated that word while snuggled in Tindale's lap as the stars winked into view, and the rhythm of the surf lulled her to sleep.

She awoke to bright sunlight streaming in her bedroom window. Some considerate fellow had removed her slippers and stockings, undone her hooks, and loosened her stays, but she was in her bed alone, and no sweet little note graced her night table.

"I sent a note with yesterday's flowers," Augustus said. "Anne did not reply." He paced Lily's sitting room, trying to will the sun to set.

Lily wheeled herself to the open French doors that led to her balcony. "What did you send, Tindale?"

Augustus wanted to stare down the drive until his coach appeared. Instead, he guided Lily's Bath chair over the threshold and onto the balcony. "Purple gladiolus. Purple is the dominant color on the Tindale crest."

"Gladiolus, for remembrance, faithfulness, and sincerity. Interesting choice. And today's flowers?"

"Which Anne has also not acknowledged." Nor had she responded to Augustus's note informing her that his carriage would pick her up at half past the hour. "Today, I sent red roses and lavender."

"And you are wearing that combination in your boutonniere—passionate love and devotion. You will cause quite a stir. Thurlow has asked the younger Daley sister for permission to pay his addresses. Some communication from the admiralty courts has put the lieutenant in fine spirits."

"So he'll be wearing red roses too?" Not that Augustus cared.

"And the older Daley sister was seen emerging from Lord Corbett's bedchamber last evening by no less than Camelia's lady's maid, who felt compelled to report that scandalous development to her employer."

Where was Anne? Would she attend the ball, and if she did not, was Augustus to conclude that she meant to enjoy her hard-earned freedom for the rest of her life? Was he to give her time to find her bearings? Court her publicly?

"Roberta and Corbett will manage splendidly," Augustus said, "if the opening maneuvers are any indication. What about you? Will you swear off allowing Camelia to hold her house parties here?"

"Might I have my shawl, Tindale?"

Augustus took the shawl from the back of the Bath chair, a pretty blue silk that went well with Lily's fair coloring. "What aren't you telling me, Lily?"

"I partnered Lord Hume at the last cards night."

"And he was your dinner companion at last night's buffet." A very attentive dinner companion.

"He is eight years my junior."

"And a decent enough fellow, though I won't envy you your in-laws."

"I've already told him that his mother is not to visit, and my daughter will think I'm daft."

"Your daughter is one-and-twenty, Lily, and newly married." Augustus had handled the settlements. "She has always been an authority on everything, and now you need no longer worry about her. Marry Lord Hume, and she might worry a bit less about you."

Lily took his hand and squeezed it. "The legal profession lost a fine counselor when you went for a duke, Tindale. I am lonely, and this house longs for children to fill it with noise and activity. Lord Hume is settled, solvent, and a fine... conversationalist."

"Lily Northrup, I'm shocked." Also pleased. So very, very pleased.

"You will attend the wedding?"

"I will give away the bride, if you choose to so honor me, though I am done with being anybody's best man."

Lord Hume was coming up the steps on the terrace below the balcony. He waved to Lily, who waved back.

"Shoo, Tindale. Miss Baxter will be here soon—Mrs. Saunders asked for the loan of a pair of my ruby earbobs, because only rubies would do for Miss Baxter's ensemble. Your place is to wait patiently at the foot of the ballroom stairs."

"My place is at Anne Baxter's side." *If she'll have me.*

"Away with you. Hume is due to pay a call, and for that, I need no chaperone."

Augustus kissed Lily's cheek and took himself off. He passed Billingsley on the landing and paused long enough to spear his lordship with a look.

"If you make Lily unhappy, if you disappoint her, if you give her any reason to regret trusting you with her future..."

Billingsley smiled. "If you make Anne unhappy, if you disappoint her, if you give her any reason to regret trusting you with her future..."

"We understand each other." Augustus would have tarried on the landing, practicing his ducal glower, but the sound of heavy carriage wheels on the front drive had him instead trotting down the steps.

He considered lurking in the foyer and discarded the notion. Anne deserved to make an entrance, and besides, there was Lord Bertram, looking quite splendid—and nervous—in his evening regalia.

Augustus instead took himself to the ballroom, where guests were milling about as the string quartet tuned up. The scent of beeswax tapers blended with the fragrance of lavender and the perfumes and pomades of scores of guests. The house-party assemblage had been joined by local gentry, a few luminaries from the Brighton crowd, and some of the more distinguished guests from the inn.

Ten feet from the men's punch bowl—a location only slight less visible than the top of the steps—Roberta Daley was plastered to Corbett Hobbs's side, while Hobbs wore the dazed expression of a man who found a lady's bosom pressed to his arm and wasn't sure what to do about it.

Thurlow and Charlotte Daley were being more decorous, but only just.

The herald announced some squire or other, a dowager viscountess, and then... Mrs. Helen Saunders and the Right Honorable Lord

Bertram. Helen and her escort came down the steps at a dignified pace, which meant Augustus had a long moment to behold his beloved.

From the top of the steps, Anne gazed out over the ballroom with an air of gracious detachment, then waved off the waiting footman and began her descent alone.

Augustus waited at the foot of the steps, resisting the urge to go to her. The ballroom quieted, for she made an absolutely stunning picture against the steps' red carpet.

When she reached the third step from the bottom, Augustus held out his hand. "Miss Baxter, you wore my colors."

Her dress was a deep, shimmering purple velvet—the same purple adorning Augustus's waistcoat—and her corsage was a cluster of roses and lavender.

"Your Grace." She took his hand and kept right on coming before kissing his cheek in front of the whole, sighing ballroom. "Helen found the fabric in Brighton, and we've been sewing madly for three days. Shall we promenade?"

Augustus placed her hand over his arm. "I don't care to perishing promenade."

Anne's smile was serenity itself. "What would you rather do?"

"Propose." He waited for Anne's response, for a smile, a scold, anything.

"You needn't, Tindale. I hope you know that."

"I must. I hope you know that." He led Anne to the center of the room, kept hold of her hand, and dropped to one knee.

"Anne Baxter," Tindale said. "Will you marry me?"

The ballroom had gone silent on a final squeak of a violin, and in the ensuing quiet, Tindale's voice carried to every corner of the room. "Will you do me the very great honor of becoming my wife? Will you allow me to cherish you for the rest of our days and build a future with you, come what may? Will you build a life with me on a foundation of love, trust, and joy and take my heart into your keeping?"

Anne could muster only one thought: *They are all looking at me.* The bachelors and chaperones and gossips were all looking at her, gawking, watching, her worst fear come to life.

Except, Charlotte Daley appeared to be on the verge of tears, while Roberta was plainly envious. Lady Deschamps looked wistful, and Lord Hume Billingsley had taken Lily Northrup's hand.

The words *Arise, Sir Knight* came to mind, but this was not a farce or a melodrama or theater of any kind. This was Augustus, asking Anne for her trust and her future. The same Augustus who had heard all of her regrets and fears, who had walked barefoot with her on the shore, who had seen the truth of her loneliness.

"I will marry you," Anne said, drawing him to his feet. "On one condition."

"Name it."

"We will always make time to build sandcastles, Your Grace. We will wander hand in hand on the shore, watch the moonglow dance over the waves. Polite society can think of us what it will, but we will not care, as long as we have each other."

He swept the ballroom with his gaze, then smiled down at Anne. "We will not care *in the least* for the opinions of the small-minded few, and you will *always* have my devotion."

He kissed her, not exactly chastely, but Anne could taste restraint in his overture too. Applause rose around them, and the quartet swung into a lively promenade.

"I want a special license," Anne said as Augustus tucked her hand over his arm.

"We will cry the banns, and for at least three weeks, I will court you within an inch of your... corset."

"A long courtship might be a tribulation for all concerned, Your Grace." Anne kept her voice down, as Lily, her Bath chair pushed by Lord Hume, approached them.

"We will do this properly, Anne," Tindale said, nearly whispering in her ear.

"We will do this speedily," Anne replied. "Else we shall not do it at all." She knew full well that Tindale would fly off to London and procure a special license, did she truly ask it of him, but the negotiation was invigorating, and really, one ought to begin as one intended to go on.

"A fortnight, then," Tindale said. "And I promise you my devoted attention for the duration. I know these idiots have daunted your courage. They daunt mine as well, truth be told. But I have promised you summers building sandcastles, evenings with good books, and nights of shared joy. You must allow me a fortnight to be the doting swain."

"And if a fortnight is too long to wait?"

Lily came to a halt before them.

"If you refuse me this request," Tindale said, "I will become a spinster duke and spend all my time brooding by the sea, because the woman I love, the woman I need and adore, has refused to allow me two weeks to cherish her publicly."

"You'd best concede, Anne," Lily said. "You cannot have a spinster duke on your conscience."

Tindale kissed Anne's hand, batted his lashes, and looked like he was preparing to do the bended-knee bit again.

"I concede," Anne said, barely restraining her laughter. "Two weeks, meaning two weeks from this very day, I will become your duchess. But they will be a long two weeks, Tindale."

Her intended kept hold of her hand as every guest in the ballroom came up to wish them well. When the dancing began, Tindale ignored protocol and danced only with his intended, and not a soul—not a gossip, not a tattler, not a matchmaker, nor a footman—remarked the duke and his prospective duchess's choice.

Two weeks later, Augustus, Duke of Tindale, married Miss Anne Baxter in a chapel overlooking the sea. All present agreed that the bride and groom were clearly a love match, and those guests were absolutely, eternally right!

Made in the USA
Coppell, TX
06 January 2023